THE
DRAGON
COLLECTOR

Book One of The Dragon Stalker Bloodlines Saga

D.K. Drake

Dream Doers Publishing, LLC
North Carolina

FOR MY PARENTS, HARRY AND JANICE

You believed in me, loved me, and led me to Christ.
You taught me how to dream, how to love, and how to live for God.
You gave me the freedom and encouragement I needed to make my own path
in life, even if it didn't always make much sense. Thank you for being great parents!

NOVELS BY D.K. DRAKE

The Dragon Stalker Bloodlines Saga

BOOK 1: **The Dragon Collector**
BOOK 2: **The Dragon Hunter**
BOOK 3: **The Dragon Protector**
BOOK 4: **The Dragon Destroyer** *(coming soon)*

Get Exclusive Access to More {FREE} Stories Today!

When you become one of my email buddies, you get FREE access to the D.K. Drake starter library that includes the short story "Cops, Robbers...and Dragons?" (This is the story that sparked the idea for the entire Saga!)

You'll also get notified about new books and deals, have a chance to join the Advanced Reader Team, and keep up with my real-life adventures as an author, a runner, and a foster parent.

All you have to do is visit **www.AuthorDKDrake.com** and sign up to the Insiders mailing list for FREE today.

YOU ARE NOW ENTERING THE LAND OF ZANDADOR...

PROLOGUE I

Rescue the Newborn

The 13th Day of the Earth Month July
in the Zandadorian Year of 3185

Kenton steered Skylark toward the highest window in the castle tower for the eleventh night in a row. This time he saw what he had been hoping to see for over a week: a white cloth hanging from the wooden shutter. "Finally." He tapped the dragon's neck, and she coasted to a hovering stop outside the open window.

"I won't be gone long." Kenton stood, found his balance on the slippery scales and brushed past Ravier. "Keep her here and keep her invisible. Omri has eyes everywhere. If we're spotted, that child we're about to rescue has no hope."

Ravier turned and glared at Kenton. "I still think I should be the one to get the baby."

"Why? So you can harass Esmeralda about what happened to your son? You'd both end up in the dungeon, and the baby would become the king's property. That's what we're trying to avoid."

"I can be calm."

"I'm not going to chance it. Stay put."

Kenton ignored Ravier's grumbling and spoke to his dragon. "Now, Skylark."

The dragon wrapped the tip of her long tail around Kenton's waist, picked him up and lowered him onto the ledge of the window the midwife had left open for him. He stepped onto the windowseat and patted the cool grey scales of the dragon's tail. Skylark let go, and Kenton quietly approached the woman on the bed in the small, dimly lit room.

Esmeralda's sweet young face glistened with a combination of sweat, joy, exhaustion and distress. She cuddled a tiny swaddled figure with a full head of midnight black hair that matched her own and hummed to muffle his cries.

Darla, the midwife, did her part to help. She stood by the door imitating Esmeralda's screams. That kept the soldiers stationed on the other side firmly planted in their posts. Kenton had to get out of there before they realized the baby had been born.

"Esmeralda." He held out his hands and spoke in a whisper. "We must move quickly."

She scrunched her face, held the baby tighter, and shook her head. Tears flooded her cheeks as she kissed the baby's forehead. "I need more time with him."

Her barely audible words melted Kenton's heart, but he had a job to do. "I will get him to Earth and keep him safe. I will teach him everything I know about you and his father and collecting—"

"No." She snatched Kenton's shirt and jerked. He lurched forward, and she spoke again when his face was inches from hers. "You will take him to Earth, and you will make sure he stays safe, but you will NOT tell him anything about his family, his heritage or dragons."

"He needs to know who he is in order to prepare for the Battle of the Throne." Kenton leaned over a bit further in an attempt to get a good look at the baby's face. "What color are his eyes? He could be the answer to the prophecy."

"He isn't. Dartez is."

"Dartez is gone."

"He has only been banished."

"Yeah. To the Land of No Return." Kenton hated to be so blunt, but he had to help her understand reality. "People don't come back from the Land of No Return. That's why they call it—"

"His dragon will find him. They will find me. And together we will find our son...after Dartez wins the throne. In the meantime, my child must know nothing of this dimension. I have written him a note that explains only the things I want him to know."

"What if Dartez isn't back to challenge the King during the next Battle year? Your son needs to be ready to take on that challenge himself."

"He will only be fifteen. No child that age could ever be ready for such a challenge, and I will not put him in that impossible situation."

A pounding on the door shook the room. "Open this door," a male voice ordered. "I want to know what's going on in there."

"There have been some complications." Darla leaned her back against the door and motioned for them to hurry up. "I'm not sure I'm going to be able to save the baby."

Esmeralda groaned loudly, then put the baby in Kenton's arms. "Please." She locked eyes with Kenton. "Promise me you'll do as I ask."

Against his better judgment, he nodded. "I promise."

"Thank you." She kissed the baby, stuffed the note in the folds of his swaddling blanket, and shoved Kenton. "Go."

He made it as far as the window before turning around. "What's his name?"

"Javan. His name is Javan."

"Nice." At least the child was named after the first and greatest Dragon Collector who ever lived. Kenton stepped on the windowseat. "Javan, meet Skylark."

At the sound of her name, the dragon uncloaked herself. The massive grey creature hovered in front of them and flapped her wings as if to say hello. A second later, she vanished.

Trusting she was still there, Kenton leapt.

PROLOGUE II

Javan's Seventh Birthday
The 13th Day of the Earth Month July
in the Zandadorian Year of 3192

Javan clomped into the barn wearing his brand new boots over his old jeans, stopped in the center, closed his strange eyes and inhaled. Ahh. Hay. Horse sweat. Leather. Manure. Wood. Sawdust. That wonderful mixture of smells is exactly what he slipped away from his own birthday party to enjoy.

The neigh of the horse in the corner stall brought a smile to his face. "Don't worry, boy. I'm coming to say hello." He walked over to Storm and rubbed his long nose. "I asked Mama Sandra if you could come to my party, but she said it was only for people."

The black horse snorted.

"I know. Silly, right? I didn't even have any people to invite. You're the only real friend I have. Well, you and the dog." He didn't mention that the dog got to come. He didn't want to hurt Storm's feelings. "You didn't miss much. The two foster kids Mama Sandra and Papa Tim took in last month came, but that was it. Just the four of us. They didn't even notice when I left."

The horse nudged Javan's shoulder.

"Yeah, I know. You would have noticed."

Javan had noticed Storm at a horse auction two years ago. The horse had a wild streak that scared adults but drew Javan to him. He somehow knew how to talk to Storm and seemed to sense what the horse was thinking.

When he convinced Storm to let him jump on his back from the top of the fence, the adult folks had freaked out. Storm didn't, though. He stayed calm for the first time ever and let the five-year-old ride him. Storm had belonged to Javan ever since.

He grabbed Storm's brush, climbed over the stall door and began brushing the parts of the horse he could reach. "I read my mom's note again today. I wish she would come and get me already. I feel forgotten."

The note told him she loved him and missed him and would come for him as soon as she could. That was it. No name. No explanation. No nothing that would tell him who he was or where he came from. How could she just leave him with strangers on a ranch in the middle of Montana?

Why did she leave him?

When would she be back?

"What if..." Javan bit his lip. Should he think this thought out loud? "What if we went to find her?"

Storm neighed and stomped.

"Why not? Where's your sense of adventure? Don't you ever get tired of being stuck here day after day with nothing new to do?"

Storm stomped again, flicked his head back and forth and swished his tail. The other three horses in the barn also began twitching and neighing and acting nervous.

He put his hand on Storm's side. "You're scared. Why are you scared?"

"You horses need to calm down." A female voice coming from somewhere outside the barn made him freeze. "I'm not here to hurt you."

Keeping the brush in front of him like a weapon, Javan exited the stall and tiptoed toward the barn door. He eased it open and stuck his head out. "Who's there?"

Nothing except grass and the old dirt road filled the space between the barn and the back porch of the house, but he had a hunch someone or something was watching him. "I know I heard something." Javan mumbled to himself and looked to his left. Nothing.

"I hoped I would find you here."

Javan snapped his head to the right. An old guy with white hair, whiskers and a cowboy hat appeared beside him. "Whoa. Who are you?"

"Name's not important. I just came to give you a birthday present." He handed him a small square box.

"Umm...I'm not supposed to talk to strangers." And he was pretty sure he wasn't supposed to take gifts from strangers, either.

"I get that. But I'm not really a stranger. We've met before."

"We have?"

"You were a wee little thing, so I don't expect you remember." The man winked and placed the box in Javan's free hand. "Open it."

Javan studied the brush in his left hand and the box in his right. If he was smart, he would throw the brush at the man's face, drop the box and run. Only he was too curious to be smart. He had to know what was in the box.

5

He dropped the brush and took the top off the box. "Mister," he said, disappointed. "It's just a rock in the shape of a triangle."

"It's much more than that, and it's quite valuable where we come from. You might want to hang on to it."

He looked down at the rock. "How could this be valuable?" When the man didn't answer, Javan looked up and found himself all alone.

The stranger had vanished.

PROLOGUE III

Esmeralda's Turn

The 13ᵗʰ Day of the Earth Month July
in the Zandadorian Year of 4200

Fifteen years. She had been sitting on this same stone window seat and staring out this same window for the last fifteen years. Waiting. Waiting for her Dartez to come for her. Waiting to defeat the Dark King. Waiting to see her son again.

"Happy birthday, my boy." She whispered into the night, wondering if Javan could see the same stars she saw despite living in different dimensions.

The creak of the door handle followed by the scraping of the wooden door on the stone floor snapped her out of her wistful stupor. She dashed to the bed to retrieve the knife hidden under her pillow, but she wasn't fast enough. An icy hand smothered her mouth, and the intruder's other arm latched onto her wrist before she could touch the handle.

"If you want your freedom," the man whispered in her ear, "don't fight me."

Freedom?

Esmeralda froze, and not just because the obnoxiously strong bearded man had her pinned in place on her bed. As a slave in the palace of the Dark King, freedom was not a general topic of discussion. Any mention of the word got one whipped, as attributed by the scars on her back.

The man spoke again. "Can I trust you to stay quiet?"

Esmeralda studied his hazel eyes. At least she imagined them to be hazel. It was difficult to tell in the dimly lit room in the middle of the night. Regardless of their color and despite the lack of light, she could see a sense of urgency in the man's eyes. That, she trusted. Under the pressure of his hand on her face, she nodded yes.

"Good," he whispered. "In a second, I'm going to move my hand, pick you up and carry you out of here. All you have to do is stay quiet. Deal?"

She nodded again. He slowly moved his hand away from her mouth.

She wanted to ask for some clothes and shoes. Being hoisted around while wearing only her white nightgown was not her ideal escape outfit, but the idea of freedom was more enticing than her fashion choices. Besides, her only option was the same drab brown dress every other woman in Zandador was forced to wear day in and day out. So she remained silent.

With seemingly no effort, he picked her up and tossed her tiny frame over his right shoulder. Her long, silky black hair swept the floor as he carried her out of the room and down the long hallway to the windy staircase.

She was expecting to travel up the stairs; they went down instead.

"We're going down?" She started beating his back with her fists. "Why are we going down? The dungeon is not exactly my idea of freedom."

"Quiet!" he hissed. "We're not headed to the dungeon."

"There's nothing else down here." She tried to wiggle off his shoulder, but his grip on her legs was too tight.

Down the stairs they went.

She was beginning to think she had been captured by some lunatic who liked to carry women around the castle in the middle of the night for fun when they at last exited the dizzying staircase, traveled down a creepy hallway and entered a huge oval room.

The sudden burst of light forced her to cover her pale blue eyes.

As the stranger set her on her feet, she began the painful process of blinking to let her eyes adjust to the glowing room. When she could finally see, her eyes were drawn to the brilliant multi-colored circle on the floor in the middle of the room. It was surrounded by a similar rainbow colored three-foot high wall with all kinds of fancy buttons on top of it.

"Where are we?" Esmeralda asked, wandering toward the wall. She stopped halfway there, turning her attention to the stranger instead. "And who are you? Why did you bring me here? What is going on?"

"I don't have time for long explanations. Guards will be here any minute. I can explain my presence here, but not yours. I need you to stop asking questions and listen."

Esmeralda crossed her arms, cocked her head and stared at the stranger. Turns out she was right. He did have hazel eyes. Just like her Dartez.

Actually, a lot about this man reminded her of Dartez. His hazel eyes. His bushy hair. His wide, solid shoulders. His tan skin. His deep voice. Only this man was much older.

"You're Vince," she said, summoning every ounce of hatred she'd built up over the last fifteen years. "You're the family traitor. You're the reason I was brought here. And you're the reason Dartez was banished."

She charged at Vince and pounded the chest of her husband's grandfather. The tears cascaded down her cheeks as she landed blow after blow.

"Enough!" He grabbed her wrists and pushed her away. She kept trying to hit him anyway. She wasn't successful. "I did what I had to do back then, just like I'm doing now. This time my loyalty lies with family, not the king. You have to bring Javan home and enter him in the Battle for the Throne."

Esmeralda went limp at the mention of her son's name. No one was supposed to know his name. "I can't. He died the night he was born."

Vince dropped her wrists and squeezed her shoulders instead. "Don't lie to me. I was there that night. I saw my son carry that very live baby away on the back of my grandfather's dragon."

He saw Ravier fly away with Kenton on Skylark? How was that possible? And why hadn't he informed the king? If Vince really knew about Javan, he wouldn't have let her get away with feigning his death all those years ago.

"You're mistaken." Esmeralda had been protecting this secret too long to divulge the truth now. Besides, it wasn't time. At fifteen, Javan was still too young. "My son is dead."

"Your son is the only hope the people—and dragons—of Zandador have. I work for the king. I've seen his plans. If no one challenges him, and he is allowed to rule for another hundred years, he will wipe out the dragons and their territories and enslave the people in ways you can't even begin to imagine."

"Only a handful of dragons remain, and he already controls every aspect of every person's life throughout the Great Rift. There's nothing to fear other than more of the same."

"That's where you're wrong. At least now you can think for yourself. Soon that won't be an option."

"What do you mean?"

"I don't have time to explain." He picked her up, carried her to the yellow circle, plopped her down and backed away. "You have to get to Javan. You have to enter him in the Battle. And he has to win. He's the one of whom the prophecy speaks."

"He's not. He can't be. He's too young."

"I knew he was alive." Vince smiled and started pressing buttons on top of the wall. "I'm sending you to Ravier. He knows you are coming and will take you to wherever he is hiding Javan. You have just under six months to find him, train him and help him collect all four Dragon Stalkers while uniting the Bloodlines. If he fails, we all face a fate worse than death."

"Wait!"

Instead of waiting, he pressed one final button, transporting Esmeralda out of the castle.

CHAPTER 1

Second String

(Three weeks after the escape of Esmeralda)

Javan paced the sideline of the football field behind the coach, decked out in full practice gear and holding the helmet he hadn't yet needed. Practice would be over any minute, and Coach Benton still hadn't given him a chance to play.

The short, stocky coach with the buzzed hair and tight shorts blew his loud whistle. "That's it, boys. We're done for the day. I don't want to see your ugly faces back here until Monday morning."

"One more play, coach," Javan said, darting in front of the man. "Put me in at quarterback. Let me show you what I can do."

"Maybe next time."

Javan grit his teeth and watched the coach walk away. How was he supposed to prove himself if he never got the chance?

"Why do you even bother?" Gavin, the starting quarterback, snatched Javan's helmet. "You sat the bench all last year because I'm too good to ever come out of the game, and you have no hope of playing this year, either."

"If you're so good, why are you still playing JV?" Javan knew that would irritate the bully. Gavin hadn't been allowed to tryout for varsity because he missed too many conditioning practices in June and July.

"I'm needed here because you're too pathetic. Look at you. You've been lifting weights all summer, and you're still skinnier than a skeleton."

"My leanness makes me agile." He feigned confidence even though he didn't much like his lanky frame or the lousy skin that came with it. His pale skin always burned, never tanned, and his face seemed to stay in a state of perpetual acne breakout. The only cool feature about him was his ragged jet black hair that dangled just above his intentionally boring brown eyes, covered the tips of his ears and brushed the back of his neck.

"You'll never be able to replace me."

"I can outthink, outrun and outthrow you any day, any place, any time."

"Doubtful, but I wasn't just referring to football. I know you have a crush on my girlfriend."

Javan's face flushed at the mention of Julianne. He had been trying to impress her since sixth grade. She liked athletes. She was the reason he needed to be good at football. All the other sports he had attempted to master had ended in epic failures.

"This is your warning to stay away from her. She deserves a star like me, not an invisible second stringer like you."

The words stung, mostly because Javan knew they were true. If he revealed the true color of his eyes, though, he certainly wouldn't be invisible any longer. *No*, he thought, shaking the idea out of his head. He'd rather be a background geek than a front and center freak any day.

"Give me my helmet." He reclaimed his football helmet, traded it for his bike helmet, and pedaled the five back road miles home as fast as he could go.

CHAPTER 2

The Unexpected Guests

The August heat in Montana wasn't brutal, but it was hot enough to have him drenched in sweat by the time he rode under the iron arches of the Rickman Family Ranch. This was the place he called home, but even here he was a second place kid.

One thing. That's all he wanted. One thing he was great at. One thing he was better at than everyone else. One thing that made him stand out. One thing that made him important. One thing that made him *someone*.

Sighing at the futility of such a dream, he bypassed the main house and rode straight to the barn. He propped his bike against the building when the same eerie feeling he had on his seventh birthday washed over him. He looked around, certain he was being watched by something he couldn't see.

"Nonsense." He shook the feeling away and entered the barn. The sight of the black stallion eased the frustration that had been building up all morning. "Good to see you, buddy. I hope you're ready for a long ride. We've got a lot to talk about."

He reached for the latch on the stall door but was stopped by the sound of a text message: *Need you at the house.*

"That's Mama Sandra." He rubbed his horse's neck. "Better not ignore her. We'll ride later."

Storm snorted his displeasure.

"I'm not thrilled either, but it does give us a chance to show off our newest trick." He unlatched the door and led Storm to the front of the barn. "Stay here until I get inside, then wait for me by the back porch. Don't move until you hear me whistle. You remember what to do, right?"

Storm shot Javan that wicked horse's smile only Javan would recognize, neighed and batted his head up and down.

"Good boy." Javan laughed and began the short trek to the house, still convinced he was being watched.

◊   ◊   ◊

"Mama Sandra?" Javan found her in the kitchen chopping tomatoes for a big bowl of salad. She was sniffling, and her plump cheeks were stained with tears. "Are you okay?"

"Oh, Javan!" A new flood of waterworks gushed from her eyes. She dropped the knife and shuffled over to hug him. "Don't mind me," she said, squeezing him. "These are happy sad tears."

"You only cry happy sad tears when you have to say goodbye to one of the foster kids." And that didn't happen unless a judge ordered it. He didn't recall any recent family court cases. Had he been so consumed with football that he lost track of the house happenings? "Who has to go home, Norman or Ahala?"

"These are my happiest saddest tears of all." She placed her warm hands on his cheeks. "These tears are for you."

His knees buckled, and he grabbed onto Mama Sandra's arms to keep from falling. "You mean..."

"Yes, dear. She's here. Your mother is here. You want to meet her?"

"No. I mean yes. I mean...I don't know. What if she doesn't like me?"

"You're her son. She loves you."

"But she tossed me aside for fifteen years." A touch of anger helped him regain his ability to stand on his own.

"Maybe you should go find out why."

"Yeah." He nodded. "I guess I should."

With her arm around his shoulders, Mama Sandra led him into the living room and introduced him to a woman sitting on the couch. "Javan, this is Esmeralda, your mother. Esmeralda, this is Javan."

Esmeralda wore a yellow sundress and stood as they approached. She was a touch shorter than his 5'6" height and had the same black hair as him. Only hers was braided, slung over her shoulder and hung just past her waist. With her perfectly tan skin and angelic complexion, she didn't appear to be a day over twenty, making her entirely too young to be his mother. But something about her penetrating blue eyes made him believe she was much older than she looked.

"Hi. Nice to meet you." He lifted his hand and offered a wimpy wave.

"I'm going to let you all get acquainted." Mama Sandra wiped her eyes and left the room. Silence followed her exit as Esmeralda and Javan stared at one another.

14

Why wasn't she saying anything?

Why couldn't he remember any of the ten trillion questions he wanted to ask her?

How did he know this was actually his mother?

After what seemed like an eternity, a vaguely familiar voice ended the staredown. "Just say hello and tell the kid why we're here. We need to get on our way. Moments matter."

Javan turned to find an old man in a button-downed beige shirt, brown pants and leather boots standing beside him. He was a good six inches taller than Javan and hid a wild batch of white hair under a black cowboy hat.

"Hey." Javan snapped his fingers. "I know you. You once gave me a triangle rock for my birthday."

"Don't say that around Skylark. She will be extremely offended if you refer to one of her scales as a rock."

"Who is Skylark? And who are you?"

"Skylark is my dragon. A Noon Stalker to be exact."

"Right." He took a step back. "Your dragon."

His mother shoved the old man and spoke for the first time. "I told you not to mention anything to him about our dimension."

"I didn't. He didn't know it was a dragon scale until just now."

"True story," Javan said, supporting the old man, "but I still don't know who you are."

"The name's Kenton. I'm your great-great-great-grandfather."

Okay. These people were officially delusional. He needed to get away. Fast. "I'm...ummm...I'm gonna go see if the salad is ready."

"Wait." His mother grabbed his wrist. "When I said goodbye to you the night you were born, you had the most beautiful emerald eyes. You're hiding them now, though. How?"

Javan's mouth went dry. If she knew about his eyes, she really was his mother.

"You can tell her all about the wonders of contacts later," Kenton said. "Right now we need to get going. You, young man, are the last of the Collector Bloodline and the only hope the people and dragons of Zandador have left."

"Collector bloodline? Dragons? Zanda what?" He put his fingers in his mouth and whistled, hoping it was loud enough for Storm to hear. "You're not making any sense, so I think it's time for me and my horse to go."

He was about to whistle again when the back door flung open and Storm charged in. Javan used the couch as a springboard and jumped onto the rearing horse. Rather than have him show off his trick and open the front door as well, Javan turned Storm around, trampled past a yelling Mama Sandra and rode bareback toward the hills.

CHAPTER 3

Lightning and Smoke

"Unbelievable!" Pushing the horse as fast as he could get him to go along the river that ran through the ranch nestled near the foothills of the Columbia Mountains, Javan shouted his frustration to his best friend. "I hope I haven't waited my whole life for those crazies.

"That man put one too many 'greats' in front of grandfather to sound sane, and if anything, that girl is my sister, not my mom. There's no way she's old enough to have a fifteen-year-old son!"

She knew about his eyes, though. He'd hated his eyes since he was three and the kids in his preschool class wouldn't play with him because of his "scary eyes." So he wore Papa Tim's dark sunglasses everywhere he went.

That had lasted about a week. The only way Mama Sandra could convince him to take off the shades was to get him colored contact lenses. His eyes had been a boring brown ever since.

Maybe Esmeralda had been one of the preschoolers in his class. Maybe that's how she knew about his eyes. Still, that didn't explain why she showed up today claiming to be his mother.

"Storm, if they were my family, I'm better off not knowing where I came from and would rather run away with you. Let's ride!"

He prodded the horse with his heels, encouraging Storm to quicken his already fast pace. Soon they would be off the ranch property and into the mountains. He knew the area well. He could easily hide over the weekend.

He would return on Monday and hope the visitors were gone. Or he could just stay lost. Start over somewhere else. New high school. New football team. New girls. The no money thing could prove to be a problem when he and his horse got hungry and needed a place to stay, though.

"We'll figure something out, Storm. Just keep rid—whoa. What...is...that?"

Storm didn't care to stick around to find out. He stopped in his tracks and reared back, throwing Javan onto the bank of the river at the sight of the giant grey scaly creature with pointy wings and a spike on the top of his massive head lurking in the water ahead of them.

By the time Javan stopped himself from rolling into the cold river water, Storm was gone.

The creature remained. Javan's initial inclination was to describe it as a dragon, but he wasn't insane. Dragons didn't exist.

Whatever this creature was called, it spanned nearly half the width of the fifty-foot wide river and stood with the top of his body showing in the twelve-foot deep water. Its long neck swiveled its head in Javan's direction. Its nose was the size of Javan's head and was almost close enough for Javan to touch. He didn't.

He also wasn't sure if he should stay flat on his stomach and wait the creature out or jump to his feet and take his chances with an all-out sprint towards home.

The creature lifted his head and snorted a lightning bolt into the blue afternoon sky.

"Staying put," Javan decided. If he was going to die by a bolt of electricity from the mouth of a monster, it wasn't going to be while running. Running was the one activity he hated most in life; he certainly didn't want that miserable feeling of forcing one foot in front of the other at an unnaturally fast pace to be his last memory.

Silverspike, stop scaring the kid. The ground rumbled as a similar creature landed a few yards away from Javan. Only this one was smaller, spikeless and sported round wings on its grey, scaly body.

I don't trust him. Silverspike splashed the water with his long, pointy tail. *Something's wrong with his eyes.*

"Really?" Javan smacked the ground. "Even these bizarre creatures know about my eyes. Why do I even bother with these color contacts anymore?"

No way. The land-based creature crouched to Javan's level. *You can hear us?*

"Of course." Javan cocked his head toward the creature, half-expecting it to open its mouth and bite his head off. "I mean, I can usually sense what animals are thinking. Can't everybody?"

No.

"Oh." Javan gulped. "Well, it is a little weird that I can understand you so clearly. That's definitely new."

"You can understand the dragons?" The human voice of Kenton—who arrived on the back of Izzie, one of the ranch horses—joined the conversation. "You can hear their thoughts?"

Javan winced. Like his bright green eyes, his way of communicating with animals made him a freak. So he preferred to keep his peculiar communication skills between him and the animals. "It's no big deal." At least it wasn't until Kenton's description of the creatures sunk in. "Hold on."

Javan rolled over and slowly stood. "These things are dragons?"

"Dragon Stalkers. Yes."

"Dragon Stalkers? Are they stalking me? Do they want to eat me?"

"Relax, kid. This here is Skylark, a Noon Stalker," Kenton said, pointing to the smaller dragon. "And that is Silverspike, a Midnight Stalker. Skylark only eats around noon, and Silverspike only eats around midnight. It's just past four o'clock, so you're good."

"That makes absolutely no sense to me."

Skylark chuckled and puffed a cloud of smoke in Javan's face. *Sorry*, she said. *I tend to smoke when I laugh.*

"It will make more sense once we get you to Zandador."

"To where?"

"The Land of Zandador. Where you're from. We had to hide you on earth to protect you. Now that you're old enough to fight for the throne, you're needed."

"The throne? You want me to be king or something?"

"Exactly."

"I was joking."

"I'm not." Kenton, still sitting on the horse, crossed his arms. "The current king needs to be overthrown. The only way to overthrow him is for a Collector such as you to collect all four Dragon Stalkers by the end of the year."

"Dude, stop talking. The more you say, the crazier you sound."

"It only sounds crazy until you step through that portal and experience life in the dragon dimension for yourself."

"Portal? Dragon dimension? You need to be institutionalized." For the first time in his life, Javan actually wanted to run. But with Kenton in front of him, the dragons beside and behind him and Esmeralda approaching on horseback, he was stuck.

"Thanks for taking off without me, Kenton," she said as she trotted up...on a calm Storm. "So glad we're in this together."

"You're riding Storm?" Javan couldn't believe his eyes. Storm was letting someone else ride him, and he wasn't even fidgeting at the sight of *two* dragons. "I'm the only one he ever lets ride him."

"Now we have something in common." Esmeralda gracefully slid off the back of the horse and walked up to Javan. "I assume Kenton has told you by now why we need you back in Zandador."

"He mentioned something about overthrowing a rotten king by collecting dragons. As fun as that sounds, I think I'll pass."

"The people need you, Javan. The dragons need you." She put her hand on his shoulder. "I need you."

In that moment, he almost wanted her to be his mother. But she wasn't. They had the wrong kid. "Look," he said, pulling her hand away from him, "you've made a mistake. I'm not the guy you need. I'm only fifteen. I can't even make the starting lineup on my JV high school football team. There's no way I can take on an evil king and win. You people just need to go back to wherever you came from and leave me alone."

Javan hopped on Storm's back, but Esmeralda grabbed Javan's ankle before he could ride away. "Three days," she said. "Come with us for three days. See the land. Meet the people. Then make your decision. If you choose to return, I'll bring you back myself and promise to never contact you again."

"Three days?"

"Three days."

Javan took a deep breath in and slowly exhaled. Having a tale of adventure to share at the start of school sure would help increase his cool factor. And he needed all the help he could get in that department. "You promise to bring me back if I don't want to stay?"

"Promise."

"Okay, then," Javan said. "I guess we're going to the Land of Zandador."

CHAPTER 4

Feeding Time

Saying goodbye to Storm proved to be the most difficult part of Javan's departure. Sure, he would miss Mama Sandra and Papa Tim, but they were so busy keeping up with the ranch, their kids and grandkids and all the foster kids that constantly came and went, that they never really had much time for him anyway.

Although he had guys from school and church he talked to, none were his buddies that he hung out with. He even doubted any of his football teammates would realize he wasn't there if he missed a practice or two.

Storm was his only constant companion, his only true friend. He was the only one who would miss him and the only one he didn't want to leave. Javan had tried to convince his mom and Kenton to let Storm come along, but they said they had no way to transport him.

With a tearful goodbye, he locked Storm in his stall, made Mama Sandra promise to take special care of Storm and plopped in the back of the red rental car his family had arrived in.

Javan didn't realize it was a rental until they returned it to the rental company in town and left on foot.

"Uh, is this Zandador place close?" Javan asked as he followed Kenton and Esmeralda down the quiet street. He was carrying a backpack stuffed with two changes of clothes, his iPad, phone and other miscellaneous goodies like contacts and a toothbrush, but he noticed they weren't carrying any suitcases. Esmeralda had a purse and Kenton had a leather bag draped over his shoulder, but that was it. What had he gotten himself into?

"No," said Kenton.

"Then why did we just give up our wheels? I'm not a big fan of walking long distances."

"We won't be walking far."

"But you just said Zandador isn't close."

"It's not."

"Do you have another car stashed somewhere?"

"No."

"Truck? Train? Plane? What's the deal?" Javan stopped walking. "I can still turn around and walk the ten miles back to the ranch if I need to." It was an empty threat. He wasn't about to walk that far, but he could pick up the phone and call Mama Sandra for a ride.

Kenton sighed and retraced his steps back to Javan. Under his breath, he said, "Have you already forgotten the winged creatures you met an hour ago?" He grabbed Javan's elbow, led him up the street to the big grassy field beside the tiny city hall building and pointed. "We travel by dragon."

"I remember the dragons," Javan whispered, "but you're pointing to grass. The dragons aren't there."

"Skylark," Kenton said, "show yourself."

The grey dragon appeared for an instant, then disappeared just as quickly.

"Whoa," Javan said. "She can do invisible." Maybe the "dragons" weren't just oversized lizards from a science experiment gone bad.

"Neat, huh?" Esmeralda smiled. "She can cloak herself and anything she touches. Once you touch her, you'll be able to see her but will become invisible to everything around you. And when we fly, she'll keep her tail intertwined with Silverspike's. He doesn't much like it, but it keeps us all from being seen."

"Enough gawking," Kenton said. "We need to get to the Everglades before Silverspike is ready to eat."

"The Everglades? We're going to Florida?" Javan hadn't packed for a tropical trip. He needed swim shorts, sunglasses and some heavy-duty sunscreen. His fair skin would burn badly in the summer southern sun.

"That's where the portal is," Kenton said.

"Right." Javan nodded. "The portal. To the Land of Zandador." Despite the invisible dragon standing somewhere in front of him, Javan was still convinced that the "Land of Zandador" was some backwoods town in the middle of nowhere built to let these eccentric folks believe they lived in a different dimension.

"Exactly," said Kenton. "Now let's ride." Kenton marched forward and disappeared into thin air within five steps.

"Our turn," Esmeralda said. She linked her arm with Javan's and led him to the place where Kenton had just vanished. "Put your hand out."

Javan slowly lifted his right arm up and out. The second the tips of his fingers connected with a rough, scaly surface, he could see both dragons. He could also see Kenton perched at the base of Silverspike's neck. When Javan pulled his hand back, they all disappeared. He repeated the process several times. "Weird."

"Stop playing and climb up," the cloaked Kenton said.

"You're no fun," Javan mumbled.

He can be a bit of a drag when he's on a mission, Skylark said. *But he's right. We need to get going. We don't want to be in the air when Silverspike gets hungry. He gets mean. I'd be tempted to uncloak him and let the humans discover him.*

Javan chuckled and touched Skylark's thick leg again. Her grey body appeared, and he kept in contact with her as she leaned her head down. *Simply grab onto my lovely scales and pull yourself onto my neck. Then slide down to the spot between my wings. I think you'll find that a fabulous seat for our cross-country flight.*

"Yes, ma'am." He grabbed onto one triangle-shaped scale after another and hoisted himself up. Before sliding down Skylark's long neck to her wide back, he helped Esmeralda up.

As soon as they came to a sliding stop, Skylark flapped her round wings, and they began their invisible flight toward Florida.

◊ ◊ ◊

Flying across the country at twice the speed of an airplane on the back of an invisible dragon attached to another dragon carrying his triple great grandfather while listening to the telepathic banter of the dragons and making sure his long-lost sleeping mother didn't fall seemed surreal. But Javan knew he was very much awake and actually experiencing this bizarre scenario.

He also knew he couldn't tell anyone, or he would find himself locked up in the nearest insane asylum. When he returned to the ranch in three days, though, he would at least have a story about a trip to Florida to share. That story was sure to require some major editing, but for once he was glad to be in the role of storyteller rather than the unnoticed background listener.

It was just past nine when they landed on a deserted road in the middle of the marshy Everglades. Esmeralda woke up; Skylark promptly zonked out. Apparently flying for several hours while invoking her invisibility (a feature, Javan had learned, that was unique to the Noon Stalkers), carrying several humans and keeping her tail attached to a dragon larger than her was exhausting.

"So," Javan said, sliding off the sleeping dragon, "where's this portal?"

"Close," Kenton said. "First, we let Skylark rest and Silverspike eat."

I am getting hungry. Silverspike stretched his legs and spread his wings.

"Hold on," Javan said. He walked around Silverspike, certain his eyes were playing tricks on him. "I know it's getting dark out, but are your scales turning black?"

Silverspike huffed. *Yes. They do every night when I start to get hungry. If any more turn black before I get a snack, you're going to start looking tasty. So if you don't mind, I'm going hunting.*

"Hunt away."

Thanks.

Javan noted a hint of sarcasm in the dragon's response and watched him fly away. "What does he eat?" he asked Kenton.

"Anything from grass to plants to animals. Here, he's probably hunting alligators."

Javan nodded toward Skylark. "Why aren't her scales turning black?"

"Because she's a Noon Stalker. Her scales turn a golden color when she gets hungry, which will be in about twelve hours."

"So you know dragons are hungry when their scales change colors? That's cool."

"You have to make sure they eat as soon as their scales start to change," Esmeralda said. "If they don't get fed before all their scales change, they become crazy, food obsessed creatures. They'll binge for three days before their appetite is satisfied and they return to their normal eating cycle."

"During these binges," Kenton added, "humans are especially appetizing."

Javan gulped. "Good to know." He hoped Silverspike was a good alligator hunter and wasn't planning on returning until his scales were grey again.

"You also need to know about Dawn Stalkers and Dusk Stalkers," Kenton said.

"What are those?"

"The other two types of dragons that aren't part of Kenton's collection," Esmeralda said. "They're smaller, have white scales and no wings. When they get hungry around dawn and dusk, their scales turn rainbow colors."

"That I'd like to see."

"You will. Once we get to Zandador."

Javan rolled his eyes. She really believed this Zandador place existed. But it sounded more and more outlandish. Wingless, rainbow-colored dragons? Really?

Time to go, Skylark. Silverspike swooshed in and hovered just above Skylark. *Some humans in a boat spotted me and are headed in this direction.*

A groggy Skylark opened her eyes. *I'm too tired to cloak us.*

Then pick up your humans and fly. Meet you at the portal. Silverspike snatched Kenton with his front claw and flew into the dark sky above.

He's so dramatic, Skylark said. *Humans driving a boat in the dark aren't going to be able to find us.*

"What's going on?" Esmeralda asked.

"Some people saw Silverspike, and he thinks they're chasing him." The sound of an approaching engine drowned out the last few words of Javan's response.

Then again, maybe Silverspike's hunch was right. Without warning, Skylark wrapped one of her claws around Javan and the other around Esmeralda and lifted them all into the air.

Javan hoped that so-called portal wasn't too far away. He was finding it difficult to breathe with a dragon's claw clutching his chest.

CHAPTER 5

Through the Portal

The lack of oxygen during the abrupt night flight left Javan feeling woozy when Skylark dumped him on a sandy shore beside Esmeralda. He coughed, rubbed his chest and looked around. He couldn't see Kenton and Silverspike, but thanks to the low tide and bright moon, he could make out a fossil reef interspersed with mangrove trees spread out before him. He also noticed the lights of a city skyline in the distance.

"Where...are...we?" he finally spit out. "Is this Zandador?"

"Of course not," Kenton said, approaching from behind him. "We're in Bear Cut Nature Preserve in Key Biscayne. That city across the bay is Miami."

"We have to go through the portal to get to the Land of Zandador," Esmeralda said.

"Right." Javan nodded, playing along. "The portal."

You'll believe soon enough, Skylark said.

How absurd. Silverspike spit a lightning bolt into the sand. *Flying with dragons and reading their minds apparently isn't enough evidence to convince the fake-eyed kid that our home is real.*

Ignore him. He's grumpy because he's still hungry. Skylark lowered her head so that it was even with Javan's. *I look forward to someday meeting the dragons you collect. Good luck to you.*

She lifted her wings, but Javan stopped her from taking flight. "Wait! Aren't you coming with us?"

Not this time. We're wanted creatures in Zandador. It's too dangerous for us there until you win the throne. Right now I need to help Silverspike hunt or his mood is going to become unbearable. If that happens, I'm never going to get any sleep. Skylark bowed her head as she wrapped her tail around Silverspike's tail. *Farewell, young Collector.* With that, both dragons vanished.

Once the breeze from their departure subsided, Kenton spoke. "Come. Let's get you two through the portal."

"You're not coming either?"

"I'm an outlaw in Zandador. Keeping my dragons a secret from the Earthlings can be tricky, but living here is ultimately safer for the three of us. Once you win the throne, we will return."

"How am I supposed to win the throne if you don't teach me how to do the whole dragon-collecting thing?"

"Ravier—my grandson, your grandfather—will teach you."

"My grandfather?" Javan froze at the thought of meeting yet another blood relative. This sudden influx of relatives after a lifetime of loneliness was difficult to process. At least the prospect of meeting a grandfather was believable; Javan still didn't understand why Kenton claimed to be his grandfather's grandfather.

"Yes," Esmeralda said. "He's been expecting us, and we're wasting time here. Let's go."

They made their way across the tide pools of the bumpy fossil reef to a lone mangrove tree. Three paces from the left of the tree, Kenton pushed a chunk of fossil about five feet long and four feet wide to the side to reveal a dark hole in the ground. "Down we go."

"Down there? Into the dark, scary hole?"

"That's where the portal is."

"No way." Javan wasn't about to jump to his death. Or into a trap. For all he knew, Kenton and Esmeralda were human traffickers who wanted him stuck in this cave until they found a willing buyer for a teenage boy. Or they could be using him as a guinea pig for psycho experiments no company or government would ever approve funding for. "You go first."

"Jump," Kenton ordered. "It's not that far down."

Javan crossed his arms and sat down. "No."

"Javan, if you don't--"

"Boys, now is not the time to act like...well...boys." Esmeralda pushed past Kenton and lowered her legs into the hole. Looking directly into Javan's eyes, she said, "I expect you to follow me."

"Yes, ma'am."

With a curt nod of her head, Esmeralda jumped into the darkness.

Javan heard a thump. Great. That meant it was his turn. "I'd prefer to see what I'm jumping into." Javan retrieved his phone from his pocket and turned its flashlight on. Once he could see the ground below, he eased himself into the hole and let go.

◇   ◇   ◇

"Where are we?" Javan found himself in a cave about twice the size of Storm's stall. Only this space had stone floors and walls with an ominous-looking tunnel at the end of the room to Javan's left.

"This way," Kenton said, pointing to the tunnel that Esmeralda was already walking toward.

"Great," Javan mumbled. He never understood why idiots in movies walked unprepared into strange, foreboding places. Now he was doing exactly that, and he was with two people who had yet to gain his trust. He hung his head as he walked toward the tunnel, chastising himself for becoming one of the idiots on the screen he yelled at.

With Esmeralda leading the way and Kenton keeping Javan stuck in the middle, they descended a steep flight of narrow stairs much farther below ground than Javan was comfortable with. He was starting to feel too claustrophobic to breathe when the stairs dead-ended into a room the size of his twin bed.

"We're here," Esmeralda said.

"We're where?"

"The portal room."

Javan wanted to point out that they were surrounded by rocks at the end of a cramped staircase with no portal in sight. Instead, he focused on something just as obvious. "If this is the portal room, how do the dragons use the portal? They could never fit through that hole we jumped through or navigate these stairs."

"There's a larger entrance to the room from the other side," Kenton said, "but you have to do a bit of swimming to reach it."

"The other side? There is no other side! There aren't any doors or windows or ways for any fresh air to circulate to keep us all alive! So let's be real. Meeting you was interesting and riding the dragon was fun, but there's no portal here."

"You don't see the portal because it's shielded," said Esmeralda.

"Shielded?"

Esmeralda reached in her purse, grabbed a handful of dust and threw it in the air. The stone wall in front of her vaporized, revealing a much larger cavern filled with light behind the doorway she just created. She walked through and urged Javan to follow. "Quickly. The shield will repair itself in less than a minute."

Javan couldn't make himself move. "What just happened?"

"She threw stalker dust on the invisibility shield to create an opening for us. Move." Just as Kenton guided Javan through the entrance, the shield reformed.

"Now this is a cool room." The space was easily the size of his high school gym but much more impressive with its ragged rock walls and smooth stone floors. But the central focus of the room—a colorful octagon glowing on the wall straight ahead—left Javan too awestruck to remember to turn his flashlight app off. He simply stood as silent as a statue shining his light at the octagon that dominated the twenty-foot high wall.

"If you think this is impressive," Esmeralda said, "just wait until you see it activated."

"How do you activate it?"

"By inserting the four types of dragon stalker scales on the dial in the right order using precise timing, turning the dial right three clicks, then left seven clicks, then...how about you just watch?"

"Good idea."

Javan felt like a midget as he approached the glowing wall. Once he was in arm's reach, he could see that the massive octagon was actually a mosaic of dragon scale pieces of varying shapes and colors.

On the wall to the left of the octagon was a much smaller circle that looked to Javan like a pie plate with four triangle-shaped slots. That's the circle that captivated the attention of Esmeralda and Kenton.

"Kenton," she said, "the scales."

Kenton reached in his bag and retrieved four scales, two white ones and two grey ones. Esmeralda took the white ones first and inserted them simultaneously in the right and left slots. She waited for ten seconds, then inserted the grey ones in the top and bottom slots. After ten more seconds, she turned the dial to the right. It clicked three times. She paused for five seconds and turned it to the left until it clicked seven times.

Three seconds after the final click, she pushed the dial in. A low hum followed by flickering scales within the octagon caused Javan to take a few steps back. He wasn't sure if this thing was about to explode or suck him in.

"Can you read the pattern?" Kenton asked.

"Shh," Esmeralda whispered. "I'm concentrating."

Javan watched Esmeralda watch the flickering lights on the octagon. He bit his lip to keep himself from asking what she was doing. Whatever it was had her complete attention.

After several minutes, she finally spoke. "Got it."

"You're sure?" Kenton asked. "It's been a while since you've deciphered the code. If you don't get it right..."

"I'm well aware of the consequences, Kenton. Just trust me."

"What code?" Javan asked. "What consequences? What's going on?"

"The portal to Zandador is set up in a triangle network," Esmeralda explained. "I believe you here on earth call it the Bermuda Triangle. The network is always on and will take us to North Zandador which correlates with your Bermuda or South Zandador which correlates with your Puerto Rico.

"But it's not activated until I dial the numerical address of the other end of the portal in Zandador. I have to dial the right number the same way you dial a number when you use your phone. The number is always changing, however, to prevent unrestricted interdimensional travel. Only Dragon Protectors like myself know how to operate the portal by deciphering the code that contains the current correct number. I have three tries to get it right."

"And if you still get it wrong after the third try?"

"We'll drown in an acid shower."

Javan gulped. "That's not good."

"So it's a good thing I know what I'm doing." Esmeralda turned her attention back to the dial. She tapped a grey scale twice, a white scale once, the other grey scale nine times, the other white scale six times and the first grey scale three times.

The giant circle blinked off and on and off and on. Then the lights of the scales began flickering again. "Oops."

"Oops?" Javan and Kenton asked together.

"I know where I messed up. I'll get it right this time."

She tapped the scales in the same pattern but started with a white scale. When she finished, the giant octagon blinked off and on and off and on.

And off.

The three of them stood in silent darkness for several seconds. Until the lights of the scales surged on, ten times brighter than before. The lighted scales began whirling around like a pinwheel. The whirling slowed and the scales seemed to melt together, creating a watery rainbow in the wall. Esmeralda smiled and hooked her arm around Javan's. "Ready to go home?"

"We're walking through there?"

"It'll feel like you're walking through a vat of Jello in the middle of a windstorm in the dead of winter," Kenton said, "but it's a quick trip. Just keep moving until you get to the other side."

Javan swallowed. "I'm not so sure about this."

"You'll be fine." Kenton slapped Javan on the shoulder. "Send for me when you've collected your final dragon. Good luck."

"This is too bizarre." Javan unhooked his arm from Esmeralda. "I want to go back to the ranch."

"You promised me three days," Esmeralda said, "so three days is what you're going to give me."

She reclaimed Javan's arm and tugged him with her into the watery wall.

CHAPTER 6

The Land of Zandador

Sticky darkness. Cold wind. Uncontrollable laughter. Javan experienced all these sensations as he was transported through the portal with his mother by his side.

He had no idea what was so funny. He certainly didn't enjoy blindly moving forward in the overwhelming darkness while a brisk, chilling wind pushed at him from behind. But he couldn't stop laughing, and he noticed Esmeralda couldn't stop sneezing.

He kept laughing and Esmeralda kept sneezing even after they exited the portal onto the shore of a river moments later. Javan turned around and watched as the shimmering rock wall they had just stepped through returned to a solid colorful glowing octagon like the one on earth.

They both stood on the sand in the dead of night laughing and sneezing and shivering for a good five minutes.

When Javan's laughter downgraded to giggling and he could once again feel his toes, he spoke between giggles. "Why...am...I...laughing?"

Esmeralda sneezed. "It's a side effect of interdimensional travel." She sneezed again. "There. I think I'm done. I sneeze. Some twitch. Some laugh. Some cry. Some get mad. Some get sad. You never know until you step through the portal. You are obviously a laugher."

Javan took a deep breath and found himself in control of his emotions once again. "Better than crying, I guess." He walked around, observing his surroundings. From the light of the normal-looking moon and stars, he could see a wide river in front of him and a forest behind him. "Are we really in another dimension? This looks just like earth."

"The landscapes of Earth and Zandador look similar; the same God created them both. Although we have our unique quirks, this dimension mimics your pre-flood earth. God created this dimension to preserve the animals that couldn't survive in the post-flood earth's atmosphere. Here, the oxygen is much higher and purer, allowing everything—plants, people, animals—to live about ten times longer than the average lifespan of things on earth."

"So how old are you?"

"I'm only 147."

"Only? That's old!"

"Not here, not when you consider that most people live to be between 800-1000 years old."

"People live to be 1000?" Wide-eyed, Javan realized Kenton really could be his great-great-great grandfather. "Then how old is Kenton?"

"He's 699."

"Whoa."

Esmeralda chuckled. "You'll get used to it. Just don't tell anyone you're fifteen. Fifteen-year-olds here are considered incompetent, ignorant children." She sized him up. "Let's add a zero to the end of your age. You could probably pass for 150."

"You mean I look older than you, my own mother? That's too weird to even think about."

"You've had a long day and been bombarded with a lot of new information. Let's get to the village. You could probably use a good night's rest."

"Yes, I could." Javan followed Esmeralda along the moonlit path through the woods, but he wasn't going to be able to sleep tonight. Too many questions and not enough answers were keeping his mind too stimulated to rest.

◊   ◊   ◊

Javan kept expecting himself to wake up. Walking through increasingly dense woods after midnight in another dimension with his mother seemed too far-fetched to be real. Yet riding a dragon, traveling through a portal and walking in another dimension seemed more plausible than connecting with his family.

Could Esmeralda really be his mother? Could she really be leading him to a place where he belonged? Could he really be an important person with an important role to play? These were things he wanted more than anything, but he wasn't used to getting what he wanted.

He was used to feeling like an unwanted, insignificant outcast. That was his painful yet comfortable reality. If this walk through the woods wasn't a dream, he was going to have to rethink what was real and reshape everything he believed about himself.

Only he wasn't ready to change his entire identity. He'd rather remain an unpopular, invisible, girlfriendless high school student athlete who rode the bench during football games.

"Esmeralda," Javan said, halting in his tracks, "I'm turning around. I want to go back home."

She paused and pointed straight ahead. "Home is this way."

"No." He crossed his arms. "Home is in Montana. I'm going back with or without you."

Esmeralda ignored his empty threat and kept walking forward.

Javan tapped his foot and waited for her to come back. As he waited, he began to notice the eerie sounds of the woods and imagined the eyes of murderous animals watching him, coordinating their attack and preparing to strike.

Perhaps he should follow Esmeralda now and wait until daylight to make his way back to the portal. "All right. I'm coming."

He sprinted to catch up with Esmeralda. When he reached her, he made her stop and asked, "Were you really going to leave me by myself?"

She tilted her head. "Were you really going to try to activate the portal without the keys or knowing how to decipher the code?"

"Oh. Guess not."

"If you still want to leave in three days, I'll take you back like I promised. Until then, I expect your cooperation like you promised."

"Okay." Javan nodded, took a deep breath and proceeded. He only made it three steps before ramming into an invisible wall. He faltered backwards and would have fallen if Esmeralda hadn't caught him. "What was that?"

"You found the invisibility shield that protects Gri, our village."

He worked to regain his balance, then asked, "Why do you need a shield to protect your village?"

"Let's just say we don't agree with the way the king runs his kingdom."

"Does that mean you're a bunch of rebels?" Javan wasn't sure if that was a good thing or a bad thing.

"Something like that. Our choices are hide, enslavement, imprisonment, banishment or death."

"I can see why you went with hiding."

"Glad you approve." She reached into her purse and tossed stalker dust in the air. When it landed on the shield, it created an opening. "After you."

Javan bit his lip and walked through the makeshift door. He found himself on top of a wooded hill that overlooked a village in the valley below. With the aide of the moonlight, he could see that three large buildings formed the hub of the village, and dozens of streets spanned out from the hub like spokes on a wheel. Small, flat-roofed homes lined each of the streets. He could also make out several farms and ranches on the outskirts of the village.

"Which one's your house?"

Esmeralda stepped beside Javan and pointed to one of the ranches on the far left end of the village. "That's us. Ready to go home?"

Javan nodded. "Ready."

They walked side-by-side down the hill. No lights were on and no people were milling about as they entered the quiet streets. With the size and shape of the stone houses and the quaint layout of the village, Javan felt like he had stepped back in time to medieval England.

He was starting to relax and enjoy the experience when three men ambushed them at the village edge. One tore Esmeralda away from him. One grabbed him from behind by the throat. And one stood in front of him holding a sword to his forehead.

The sword-holding villain was the only one to speak. "Don't move," he ordered.

With the tip of the sword pressing into his skin and causing a trickle of blood to run down his nose, Javan felt inclined to obey the order.

CHAPTER 7

Ravier and Red Rain

"Ravier!" The intensity of Esmeralda's shriek surprised Javan. She knew this man? "Put your sword down this instant."

"Esmeralda?" Ravier lowered his sword a few inches so that it was hovering just above Javan's right eye. He was a bear of a man with slicked-back, shoulder-length brown hair, intimidating green eyes and a wild beard that covered half his face.

"Yes." She shook off her captor and lunged for Ravier's arm, forcing his sword to the ground. "Are you trying to poke your grandson's eye out?"

"You found him?" Ravier looked Javan up and down. "He's scrawny. The first dragon he meets will snap him like a twig."

"Hey!" Javan yelled in his own defense. "I've already met two dragons, and neither one of them did any snapping of this *lean* and *trim* body."

"He's tough," Esmeralda said. "Now let him go."

Ravier nodded to the man holding Javan. The man released Javan and stepped back. While Javan coughed to recover from the stranglehold, Esmeralda introduced the men. "Javan, this is your grandfather Ravier. Ravier, Javan."

Ravier grunted at Javan.

Javan glared at Ravier. Some grandfather. First he threatened Javan's life. Then he insulted him. Now he couldn't even say a proper hello.

"Great. We all know each other," Esmeralda said. "Ravier, please be a good host and take us home."

"Fine," he said and started walking toward the farm.

This wasn't exactly the warm and fuzzy greeting Javan had hoped for, but it would have to do. He was tired and wanted sleep.

◊   ◊   ◊

Tap, tap, tap. Tap, tap, tap. Tap, tap, tap.

Javan covered his head with his pillow, annoyed by the unusual sound of his alarm. It normally made an obnoxious beeping noise, not an irritating tapping one.

Why was his alarm going off anyway? It was Saturday, his day to sleep in. After the dream he'd had last night that left him feeling physically exhausted, he needed a little extra sleep.

Tap, tap, tap. Tap, tap, tap. Tap, tap, tap.

"Enough!" Javan sat up and threw his pillow at the night stand to silence the alarm.

Tap, tap, tap. Tap, tap, tap. Tap, tap, tap.

"Aaaahhhh!" He rolled over to smack the alarm, but the only thing he found to smack was thin air. His nightstand wasn't where it was supposed to be. As he looked around, he realized *he* wasn't where he was supposed to be.

Instead of lying in his bed in his carpeted room and poster-covered walls, he was lying on a cot in a tiny room with a wood floor, bare yet textured stone walls and a ceiling also made with planks of wood. Either he was still dreaming, or that entire experience last night was real.

He hoped he was still dreaming.

Tap, tap, tap. Tap, tap, tap. Tap, tap, tap.

Javan slapped the bed and stood. "What is that noise?"

He looked under the bed. Nothing.

The room had no closet, so it couldn't be coming from there.

The window. Something had to be tapping on the window. Javan walked across the empty room, opened the wooden shutters and looked outside to get his first glimpse of Zandador in the daylight.

He stood a good three stories up and could see miles of rolling hills with gorgeous green grass interspersed with extravagant patches of flowers and spots of blue where lakes and creeks broke up the land. Beyond the hills stood a vast mountain range that he had a sudden itching to explore.

Only he had no Storm to ride.

Javan dropped his head and closed his eyes. He sure did miss his favorite friend.

Tap, tap, tap.

Javan jerked his head up and found himself in a staring contest with what looked like an overgrown dragonfly three times the size of an eagle. It had six skinny little legs underneath its sleek, beautiful black body, and it hovered in the air by way of its luminous blue wings—all eight of them, four on each side with one shorter pair stacked atop a longer, thicker pair.

Its face, however, was not as pleasant to behold. The creature's face was disturbingly ugly with bulging brown eyes the size of basketballs, a tiny white nose the size of a baseball and a mouthful of toothpick-sized teeth. Two long antennae that curved over its eyes were tapping the glass of the window.

"Now I know I'm dreaming." Javan closed the shutters and jumped back in bed. "Wake up, wake up, wake up," he muttered over and over as he squeezed his eyes shut and curled into a ball.

After a few minutes, he peeked out of his left eye to see the same barren room he had just tried to escape from. "Great. I'm stuck in Zandador."

A soft knock on the door confirmed his new reality. "Javan," Esmeralda said, "if you're awake, I'd like to take you to lunch."

Javan checked his watch, then wondered if time worked the same way in this dimension. His body didn't care. According to his time zone, it was nearly noon. And his stomach was rumbling. "Yeah, I'm awake. I'll be out in a minute."

He was going to lunch with his mom. That was something worth getting up for.

◊   ◊   ◊

Javan dressed himself in a fresh t-shirt and shorts, popped in a clean pair of non-prescription lenses to cover his freaky eyes and met Esmeralda downstairs.

He couldn't see anything when he walked through the dark place last night, but now that the sun was streaming through the windows, he liked what he saw. All the walls in the spacious first floor room were made of varying shapes, sizes and colors of stone ranging from bold colors such as jade, indigo and amber to the more subtle white, gray and black. The wood floors and ceilings added to the rustic look.

The winding staircase in the back left corner of the room wound over top of the bathroom and stood opposite the fireplace that dominated the front right corner. Cabinets lined the walls of the back right corner.

The only furniture in the room was a long table with benches for seats in the front left corner opposite the cabinets. Esmeralda was sitting at one of the benches drumming her fingers on the table.

"I'm ready," he said.

"Great." She hopped up, looking more unnerved than a dog who just discovered a bee's nest. "Let's...ummm...go to town. Your grandmother will want to meet you. She runs the restaurant."

Javan didn't question the fidgety Esmeralda as they walked the mile into town on the dusty pathway. He did notice her seeming inability to speak, as well as the constant darting of her eyes in every direction.

What had her so on edge?

Once they made it to the village streets, Esmeralda picked up her pace. He nearly had to sprint to keep up, not giving him any time to drink in the sights and sounds of the village or observe the people watching them from their yards and windows.

They went straight to the first building in the middle of the village with a sign over the door that read, "Eat Here."

Esmeralda stopped at the door and froze.

"Aren't we going in?" Javan asked.

"We should. We will." She looked at Javan, terror in her eyes. "Will you go in first?"

"Okay. But only if you tell me what has you so freaked out."

She took a deep breath and slowly exhaled. "Your father's mother is in there. She blames me for your father's banishment to the Land of No Return."

Javan flinched at the first mention of his father. He'd hesitated to think or ask about him because he feared he would learn the man was dead. "Banished? So he's still alive?"

"That's my hope."

"Well...was it your fault?"

"In a way. We got married illegally."

"How do you marry someone illegally?"

"According to King Omri, marriages are not permitted until age 200, and then you're only permitted to marry the person his Marriage Council assigns you."

"Ugh. That's a rotten deal."

"That's what your father Dartez and I thought. When we met and fell in love, we got married. He was 158; I was 129. A few years later, I became pregnant with you. However, you're only allowed to have children if the Reproduction Council awards you a child permit.

"When King Omri found out about our marriage and my pregnancy, he enslaved me and banished your father. As with all illegal children, he would have claimed you as his own property and raised you to serve as a lifetime soldier in his army, so we faked your death the night you were born. That's why Kenton and Ravier took you away and hid you safely on earth."

Javan wasn't sure how to process this news. He thought he had been an unwanted child. Now he learns his mother gave him up to protect him from a lifetime of enslavement in some rotten king's army? As his way of saying thanks, he decided to defend his mother. "Sounds like grandma needs to blame the stupid king, not you."

Esmeralda chuckled. "I agree."

"Wait a minute." Javan scratched his head. "If you were living in this place hidden with an invisibility shield, how did the king find out about you and my dad?"

"We weren't in Gri at the time your great-grandfather Vince discovered our secret. He works for King Omri and turned us in."

"What a—ouch!" A sudden sting on his right shoulder made Javan flinch. Then the sting moved to his left shoulder. More stings pelted his arms and legs and back and face. He turned in circles, swatting at the air in an attempt to prevent any more attacks. But all he could see was a swirl of red. How much blood was he losing?

"Red rain! Get inside! Now!" Esmeralda grabbed his arm and pulled him into the restaurant.

The solid wood door closed behind them, and Javan turned to look outside the nearby window. Torrents of horizontal red streaks filled the air, obscuring the surrounding buildings and mesmerizing Javan.

"What is going on?" he asked.

"It's a red rain storm," Esmeralda said in an odd-sounding deadpan tone. "It sweeps across the land from time to time and stings something fierce when it hits your skin."

"No kidding. Are there any other weird weather storms I should know about?"

"Not really the time to discuss weather."

Javan turned around. Every customer in the packed restaurant was staring at him and Esmeralda.

But Esmeralda was staring at the tall, thickset woman with long, flaming red hair wearing an apron over her drab brown dress pointing a cross-bow contraption at them.

"Hello, Hannah."

"Goodbye, Esmeralda." The red-haired woman pulled the trigger. A streak of what appeared to be lightning zapped Esmeralda. She yelled and fell to the ground, jerking as though she had just stuck her finger in a light socket.

"Mom!" Javan dropped to his knees beside Esmeralda, not sure how to help her. He looked up at Hannah. "What did you do?"

"Are you with her?"

"Yes."

The woman pulled the trigger again. Thousands of volts of electricity pulsed through Javan's body. Before collapsing beside Esmeralda and writhing in pain, he couldn't help but notice the satisfied grin on the red-haired woman's face.

CHAPTER 8

A Second First Impression

As Javan slowly blinked his way back to consciousness, he became aware of three distinct noises: clanking dishes, pattering footsteps and a soothing hum that made him want to keep his eyes closed. His body lay on a hard, unforgiving surface, but his head rested on something soft and comforting.

Wanting to figure out where he was and what was happening, he rubbed his eyes and sat up.

The footsteps stopped when Ravier spoke. "The boy awakens. Finally."

"Javan, how are you feeling?" Esmeralda was sitting on the bench at the table in the living room beside him. It was her leg that his head had been resting on. She was the source of the soothing hum.

"Like I just got struck by lightning," Javan said, cocking his head from side to side. His skin felt hot to the touch, and the blood coursing beneath his skin seemed electrified. "What did that woman shoot me with?"

"That woman is your grandmother, and she shot you with a Jolt Blast," Esmeralda said. "The effects will wear off in another hour or so."

Javan turned to Esmeralda. "Please don't introduce me to any more family members. They keep trying to kill me."

Ravier stopped pacing and sat down across from Javan. He placed his hands on the flat surface in front of him. "We might have made a bad first impression."

"Correction," Javan said. "You *did* make a bad first impression. In case you forgot, last night you tried to take my head off with a sword, and today that woman zapped the life out of me."

Ravier sighed. "I apologize. I thought you were an intruder. For reasons you can't understand yet, we can't allow intruders of any kind."

"All right. I accept your apology. But what's her excuse?" Javan pointed to Hannah. "She recognized Esmeralda and shot us both anyway."

Hannah huffed and banged a cabinet closed.

Ravier spoke for her. "Your grandmother apologizes for shooting you with the Jolt Blast."

"No, I don't!" Hannah crossed the room and slammed an empty frying pan on the table. "Esmeralda deserved it, and I don't believe you're my grandson. Your eyes are the wrong color."

"You blasted me because you don't like the color of my eyes?"

"You're an imposter. I find that worse than rude!"

"Javan," Esmeralda said with a hoarse voice, "show her the true color of your eyes."

"No." Javan's heart skipped a beat at the thought of letting people see his emerald eyes. He didn't know how to function without the bright, clear, nearly glowing gemstone green disguised. "I like my brown eyes."

Ravier leaned across the table and stared into Javan's eyes. "How are you hiding the color of your eyes?"

"Contacts." Javan squirmed under Ravier's scrutiny. "If you stop staring at me, I'll take them out."

Ravier returned to his seating position and urged Hannah to sit beside him. They watched as Javan bent his head, removed his contacts and looked up.

Hannah gasped. "Oh my. You have eyes just like your father. Much brighter and greener, but you definitely inherited those eyes from Dartez!"

Before Javan could process the encouraging fact that he shared the same funky eyes as his father, Hannah had him pulled into a hug so tight he struggled to breathe. "I'm so sorry I hurt you," she said. "To make up for it, I'm going to fix you some lunch. What do you want? Stew? Steak? Lamb? Emu? Doesn't matter. I'll make it all. Then I'll take you on a tour of the farm.

"We raise okties here and supply them to the rebels. Our animals are the best flying creatures in all of Zandador. Except for dragons, of course. But not many people have dragons. You will, though. You're a Collector. We're going to have such a party when you collect your first dragon!"

"Can't...breathe..."

"Sorry again, dear." Hannah released him and put her hands on his cheeks. "Welcome home." She kissed his forehead and skipped to the kitchen.

Javan smiled. Apart from the weird talk about okties and dragon collecting, that was the kind of grandmotherly love he'd only dreamed of experiencing.

Then Ravier ruined it. He gripped Javan's shoulder and whispered in his ear. "Enjoy being pampered today. Tomorrow you're mine."

That sounded a bit ominous. What did that burly man have planned?

CHAPTER 9

Stalking the Stalker

"Wake up, kid!" Ravier threw some clothes at Javan's head, interrupting his pleasant dreams. After touring the farm with Hannah and Esmeralda yesterday and seeing dozens of the oversized dragonfly-like creatures they called okties, Javan found himself dreaming about soaring on the back of one of the okties. He had never felt so free as they flew over the meadows and through trees that covered the mountains in the distance.

Ravier's voice ruined his dream. "Put those on and meet me downstairs. And make sure you hide your eyes with those contact things."

Javan groaned and rolled out of bed. The sun wasn't yet streaming through his window to light the room, a sure sign that it was entirely too early to be up. But it did give Javan a chance to play with the lighting system.

Unlike the normal electricity Javan was accustomed to, this house was powered with energy from dragon scales. The hand-size triangular white and gray scales had been shaped into rings a little bit bigger than lifesavers. The rings were strung like popcorn, and the string ran along the perimeter of the room where the wall intersected with the ceiling. The end of the string hung down beside the door to a place halfway up the wall where a light switch would normally be.

The "switch" wasn't something you flicked up and down but was rather a triangle impression in the wall. To turn the lights on, Javan inserted a full-size scale into the wall. Once the main scale touched the string of scales, light flooded the room.

"That's so cool," Javan said, then dressed himself in the prescribed brown shirt and brown pants. He wasn't exactly the hippest teen when it came to fashion, but he knew enough to know this was a completely unstylish outfit.

When Javan met Ravier downstairs and saw Ravier wearing the exact same clothes, Javan had to protest. "Wearing these clothes is bad enough, but I'm not going anywhere being all matchy-matchy with you. I'm going to put my Earth clothes back on."

"No, you're not. We're leaving the protection of Gri today. If you're caught wearing any clothes other than these, you'll be beaten and thrown in prison."

"Seriously?"

"King Omri controls everything, right down to the clothes on our backs."

Javan scowled at his outfit. "This king has got to go."

"Glad you agree. To make that happen, you need to learn how to collect dragons." Ravier slung a long sword protected in a leather sheath over his shoulder so that it hung diagonally across his back. "Training starts now. The first step is to stalk a Stalker."

"That sounds dangerous. I should probably carry a sword, too." Carrying a sword across his back like that would add a touch of coolness to his uncool outfit.

"You've been trained to wield such a weapon?"

"How hard can it be to 'wield such a weapon?' You hold the dull end and slash with the pointy end."

Ravier huffed. "You don't get to carry a sword until you've been properly trained and know how to use it effectively."

"Then train me."

"In due time. Right now we need to fly south. I don't want to miss our chance to observe the Dawn Stalker at feeding time."

◇　◇　◇

"I actually get to fly on one of these things?" Javan stood at the entrance of the okty barn. The large, dully lit stone structure with a hard-packed dirt floor housed the okties. Wooden perches of varying heights hung from the ceiling by strands of rope. Many were occupied by okties calmly swaying back and forth while other okties lazily floated through the air from one end of the barn to the other.

"Unless you'd rather walk," Ravier said. "But that would take several weeks. These guys can get us to Dawn Stalker territory within hours."

"I vote for flying."

"Thought so." Ravier took a few steps into the barn and whistled. Four of the okties flying just over his head swooped down and landed side by side in front of Ravier. He tapped the heads of the two in the middle, and they flew away. "These two are our rides. You take the pink-winged one on the left."

"Sure," Javan mumbled, watching Ravier walk toward the green-winged okty on the right. "Give me the girlie one."

Pink Wings snorted at Javan as he approached. "Sorry girl." He only had to tilt his head slightly downward to look into her big ugly eyes. "Didn't mean to offend you."

She stared at him, nodded and let her ten-foot long wings rest on the ground. That seemed to be her invitation to climb aboard, but Javan wasn't sure how to go about riding the thing. "Um...how do I get on?"

Ravier was already sitting on the back of his okty. "Walk between her wings. Pull yourself up and straddle her body in the space between the wings. Like me."

"Flying bareback? I can do that on a horse with no problem, but we're gonna be in the air. Don't we need saddles? And reins?"

"Just get on."

Javan grit his teeth and skirted around his okty's front left wing. The top of her back only came up to his waist, so getting on her soft, fuzzy back wasn't a problem. Neither was straddling her since her body wasn't nearly as wide as that of Storm. It was the staying on without a saddle to hold him in place that he was worried about. Plus he had nothing to hold on to. How was he supposed to direct her flight?

"I'm on," Javan said. "What now?"

"Pat her back twice."

"Okay." Javan tapped her back twice, and Pink Wings lowered her antennae back to within reach of Javan.

"Your reins," Ravier said, grabbing on to his okty's antennae. "Use them to lead her, and follow me." Without another word, Ravier jerked his hands up. His okty lifted itself a few feet off the ground and darted out the open door.

"That looks like fun." Javan smiled and mimicked Ravier's movements. Pink Wings drifted up. And lingered. "Forward!"

They went nowhere.

"Fly!"

Still nothing.

"Why aren't you going?" Javan leaned forward, dug his heels into her sides and gently shook the reins. That was all the encouragement she needed. They sped out of the barn and up into the dark, pre-dawn sky. "Woohoo!"

Javan leaned to the left. Pink Wings flew left.

He leaned to the right. Pink Wings flew right.

Up. Down. Left. Right. Pink Wings flew wherever Javan directed her. What fun!

"Stop playing!" Ravier yelled at Javan in the air in front of him. "We have a long flight ahead of us and need to be on our way."

"I've never ridden one of these things before. I needed to figure it out."

"Got it figured out?"

"Think so."

"Then let's go." Ravier took off, and Javan had to concentrate to keep up with him. Thankfully the okty's wings created a green blur in the dark sky, and he used that blur to track Ravier's flight.

◊　◊　◊

Javan enjoyed the speed at which they clipped along. He wasn't sure how many miles they traversed, but according to his watch, he did know they flew for just over two hours before landing in a meadow beside a lake surrounded by a thick forest. Although the sun had yet to officially rise, hazy light flooded the land.

Once they dismounted, the okties buzzed across the water, flying circles around one another and occasionally sipping from the surface. Javan hoped they were trained to return to the people who rode them from place to place. Ravier didn't appear worried about being abandoned by their rides. Javan thus decided not to worry, either.

He was curious about their location, though. "Where are we?" he asked.

"Dawn Stalker territory. According to the Protector registry, five are still alive and living somewhere within this thousand-mile wide forest."

"Oh. So it's going to be really easy to find one and catch it."

Ravier failed to catch the sarcasm dripping off Javan's words. "It won't be easy," he said, "and we're not trying to *collect* one today. I simply want you to observe a Dawn Stalker feeding so you have a healthy respect for the animal."

"That means we have to find a Dawn Stalker to observe. How do we do that?"

"We wait by the water."

"Wow. Good plan. 'Cause I'm sure that of all the possible lakes in all this land, all the dragons are going to come here to drink."

"This is a spot in the northwest corner patrolled by Opny, the oldest of the Dawn Stalkers. Like all the Dawn Stalkers, he is extremely vain. When he gets hungry and his scales begin to change colors, he often pauses at this lake to observe his reflection in the water."

"If you know he's coming and you know his weakness is vanity, why can't I take advantage of that and just go ahead and add him to my collection?"

"Collecting a dragon—especially one as old as Opny—is not a simple task. To collect him, you have to ride him without falling for a distance of at least hundred miles, more if he refuses to submit to your control. Are you ready to hop on a hungry, wild dragon who spits acid and would enjoy eating you?"

"Not so much. Let's stick with your plan."

"Good." Ravier looked at the sky beginning to brighten with sunlight. "His six o'clock feeding time is approaching. He should be here shortly. We'll hide in the woods."

They set up a hiding spot behind a dense row of bushes fifty feet from the shore of the lake while the okties perched themselves in some trees above the bushes and dozed off.

"How long do you think we'll have to—"

"Shh," Ravier said. "He's coming and has incredible hearing. Not another word until he's gone."

Javan pretended to lock his lips and threw the invisible key over his shoulder. He started to yawn, but when a dragon appeared out of nowhere on the far side of the lake, Javan was too astonished to close his mouth.

The stunning creature was a good ten feet tall and fifteen feet wide with a long pointy tail and four muscle-bound legs that each ended with three sharp claws. Two spear-like antlers adorned the top of its head between its pointy, oversized ears and above its round black eyes.

This dragon had no wings, which Javan found odd. In his mind, all dragons should have wings and be able to fly.

The dragon's most striking feature was its scales. Many were a bright white, but more than half were dazzling colors of red, orange, pink and purple.

Apparently the dragon also thought his best feature was his colorful scales. He stared at his reflection in the water, mesmerized by his own beauty. As more scales slowly changed colors, he became more entranced by his reflection.

Then he struck a pose. He cocked his head down and to the left, bent his right leg so that his claw was just under his long snout and stuck his tail straight out so that it was parallel to his back.

Gorgeous, Opny, the dragon said, *just gorgeous. Your scales are looking especially bright and shiny today.*

Had Javan not been able to read the dragon's mind, he probably would have been able to overcome his amusement. But when Javan heard the fierce-looking dragon praise himself with such shallow vanity, a burst of laughter escaped from Javan's lips.

Ravier's hand immediately covered Javan's mouth.

Too late.

In less than a second, the dragon disappeared and reappeared right in front of the bushes where Javan and Ravier were hiding. He stepped on the bush in front of Javan and looked straight into Javan's eyes. *Humans*, he said. *You must die!*

With Ravier's hand clamped over his mouth, Javan couldn't respond. Fortunately he didn't need to employ any negotiation tactics. Ravier rolled them to the side behind taller and thicker bushes as Opny opened his mouth and sent a stream of putrid acid over the area Javan vacated.

A few stray droplets burned a strip through Javan's pant leg just below his right knee, singeing the hair off his leg and branding his skin. Javan yelped, curled himself into a ball and readied for an all-out acid attack while Ravier let out a shrieking whistle inches from Javan's ear.

Fools! You can't escape me. Opny beat back the bushes protecting Javan and Ravier. *I don't usually enjoy eating humans, but I'll make an exception today.*

Opny's claw was about to clamp down on Javan's head when the pair of okties swooped in, distracting the dragon. *Oohhh, tasty,* Opny said, watching the okties circle his head.

He swatted at them every time one buzzed by his head until they broke their flight pattern and flew back over the lake. They hovered over the water, taunting the wingless dragon.

Opny stared at them from the water's edge. He stood motionless and took a series of deep, heaving breaths.

Javan could sense Opny's darkening mood even though more and more of his scales were turning bright and vibrant colors of red and purple and orange and pink. Javan knew something dreadful was about to happen, but he still wasn't prepared for what he saw.

The dragon inhaled one final time. When he exhaled, he spewed a streak of acid that sailed through the air and drenched the okties. They let out an ear-piercing screech and dropped to the water. Before they splashed, the dragon popped to the middle of the lake, caught the falling okties in his mouth and immediately popped to the other side of the lake.

As he crunched his breakfast, half his scales reverted back to white. He looked in Javan's direction, shrugged as though the humans no longer mattered and vanished.

CHAPTER 10

Torix

"What just happened?" Javan asked. "How can he leap from one place to another so fast?"

"He doesn't leap; he teleports. All Dawn Stalkers have that ability." Ravier stood, jerking Javan up with him. "And what just happened is that my two best okties sacrificed their lives for us because you had to chuckle at a dragon."

"Sorry." Javan inspected the acid burn on his leg. It was only about the size of his pinky finger, but it sure stung. "I wasn't expecting to hear him talk so highly of himself to himself."

"Hear him? You can hear his thoughts?"

"Yeah."

"Hmmm. Interesting. So are your eyes. The left one is still brown, but the right one is green."

"Great. I must have lost a contact in all the commotion. It's gotta be here in these bushes somewhere. Can you help me find it?"

"No time." Ravier nodded toward Javan's leg. "That will leave a scar, but it's only a surface wound. You'll be fine. Soak it in the water for a few minutes. Then we'll get going."

"Going? Where? How? Our rides are gone."

"The nearest village is Torix. It's a good thirty miles from here. Hopefully we can arrange alternative transportation there. Until then, we walk."

"Can't we call somebody to come pick us up?"

"Call? I just told you Torix is thirty miles away. Nobody is close enough to hear us call."

"Don't you have cell phones?"

"Cell what?"

"You don't have phones in this place? Next thing you're going to tell me is that you don't have televisions or computers or the Internet, either."

"I have no idea what you're talking about."

"Oh, boy." Javan took his shoes off, rolled his pants up above his knees and stepped into the lake. The cool water instantly brought him some relief from the stinging burn, but he didn't know how he was going to recover from the no phones, no television, no Internet news.

◊　◊　◊

"Can we please take a break?" Javan wiped another round of sweat off his forehead. They had left the comfortable shade of the woods hours ago and were forging onward through endless meadows in the early afternoon sun.

Javan was sure he would faint from fatigue, exhaustion and just plain irritability if he had to take another step. He was grateful, however, that he didn't have the extra weight of a sword hanging across his back.

"No," Ravier said and kept walking.

Javan scowled at Ravier's back. Although Ravier had let them pause to snack on wild and oddly filling berries as well as to take quick sips of water at random stream crossings when in the forest, the man had been merciless in his quest to get to the village. They'd been walking for more than seven hours without any sit-down-and-rest-your-legs breaks. Maybe it was time to take a stand by sitting down.

"You go ahead then," Javan said, plopping down on the knee-high grass. "I'll catch up when I'm rested."

"The village is over that next hill," Ravier called back, quickening his pace. "Meet you there. But good luck getting in without the entrance tax or travel permit."

Javan rolled his eyes. "Stupid unfamiliar territory," he mumbled, getting to his feet. As long as he didn't know the lay of the land or how this world worked, his rebellious teenage attitude had no power.

At least Ravier wasn't underplaying the distance to the village. It was indeed located over the next hill. A wooden fence three times as tall as Javan formed the perimeter of the village, and they had to walk around the wide perimeter to get to the front gate.

Ravier pounded on the gate. A head-high slot opened, revealing the brown eyes of a man on the other side. "What's your business in Torix?"

"Seeds for my farm."

"Show me your permit."

Ravier pulled a postcard size piece of paper out of his back pocket and handed it to brown eyes through the slot. "How did you get this permit? Planting season for energy balls isn't for another month."

"Too many of the king's soldiers have vanished in time traps. He's demanding an increase in the production of energy balls to equip his army with. My farm has been commissioned to find a way to grow them sooner and faster."

"Time traps have been a growing problem. Lost a buddy in one." The man returned the paper. "Five ring scales."

This time, Ravier unhooked a necklace Javan hadn't even noticed he was wearing. It was a black string filled with ring-sized scales on it like the ones used for the lighting system at the house. Ravier slid five off, handed them to the guard and rehooked the string around his neck.

"You have one hour," the guard said. The slot closed, and the gate opened.

"Keep your mouth shut and your head down," Ravier mumbled as they walked through the gate. "Don't let anyone see your eyes."

Javan wanted to ask about energy balls and time traps, but he was too self-conscious about guarding his exposed eye to risk looking up at Ravier to ask him anything. Instead, he observed what he could about the town while keeping his head tilted toward the ground.

Two and three story stone buildings lined the wide dirt street that led straight through the center of the village. An impressive five-story stone mansion dominated the end of the street while narrow side streets led to rows of tiny wood huts.

Soldiers dressed in black uniforms patrolled the streets with silent scowls. The few villagers that were out and about walked with their heads down and were dressed in the same brown shirt and shorts Ravier had made Javan wear.

Although the soldiers stared at Javan and Ravier, no one greeted them or even looked up to acknowledge their existence. As Javan glanced in the windows of the buildings he passed, all he could see were the gloomy faces of brown-clothed folks diligently working as seamstresses, tailors, blacksmiths, carpenters, butchers or scribes.

No one spoke. No one smiled. No one laughed. This was not a happy place.

The clerks working in the store Ravier guided Javan into were just as depressed as everyone else. Javan could see why. It was a gloomy store, despite the sunlight streaming in through the windows.

Every item on every shelf was packaged in the same dull beige bag with boring black block lettering to identify the contents. Granted, the bags were different sizes, but that wasn't enough of a difference to make any product stand out. These people obviously didn't waste much money on slick marketing tactics.

Then again, they didn't seem to use money at all. If the tax paid at the gate was any indication, scales were the currency of choice. Javan made a mental note to ask Ravier about their "money" system later.

Ravier meandered through several aisles. Javan assumed he was searching for energy ball seeds. Javan, however, was more interested in finding food. His stomach was rumbling, and he needed something to eat.

"Here we go," Ravier said. He picked up a fifty pound bag of seeds and indicated for Javan to do the same.

"Seriously?" Javan whispered. "You want to buy one hundred pounds of seeds? You're not even an actual farmer."

"It's the reason we were allowed entrance into Torix." Ravier glared at Javan. "Remember?"

"Ah, right." Javan decided it was best to play along. Still, Ravier needed to learn how to communicate better; he could have used their seven-plus hour walk to explain to Javan what was going on. But no. He chose to sulk and say nothing the whole way here.

The bored, bearded clerk at the front counter looked at their bags. "Six ring scales."

Ravier extracted more scales from his necklace. "I'll give you eight if you tell me where I can find some transportation out of here."

That got the man's attention. He jerked his head up. "Make it ten."

Ravier counted the ten rings and put them in the man's hand. The man nodded, looked around and leaned over the counter. "Thirteen miles north of here deep in the quagmire. Guy runs an animal shop. Ask for Reese. Tell him Marty sent you. Just beware of the swallowing sand."

"Thanks." Ravier patted Javan on the back. "Carry those bags."

"Both of them?"

"Yes."

Javan sent Ravier the meanest scowl he could muster. It didn't change the fact he was stuck carrying a hundred pounds of seeds, but it did make him feel better.

He slung one bag over each shoulder and was about to follow Ravier when the clerk grasped his arm. "That eye," the clerk said. "You're a Collector. You're *the* Collector."

"Marty," Ravier said, keeping his voice low, "let the boy go."

"Is it true? Am I right? Will he be challenging the Dark King?"

"That's the plan, but the timing isn't right yet. We need absolute secrecy in order to train him properly. Can we trust you to keep quiet?"

"Of course." Marty nodded and let Javan go. Then he bowed down to Javan. "I look forward to serving you, my future King."

"Yeah. Umm, thanks." Having a stranger bow to him was weird. It just wasn't natural for one regular human being to bow down to another regular human being, especially when the one doing the bowing was so much older than him. If he did become king, he was going to make a law that banned people from bowing to him.

He rethought that bowing ban as he walked back through town following the unencumbered Ravier. Even with his new status as Ravier's pack mule, no one noticed him. He simply blended right in with everyone else, as invisible here as he was walking the halls of high school.

If he became king, people would have to notice him. He would finally stand out and be someone other people envied. That thought brought a smile to his downcast face.

"Halt." The guard at the gate made them stop. Javan kept his eyes averted while the guard inspected the bags resting on Javan's shoulders.

"Is this the only purchase you made?" the guard asked.

"That's it," Ravier said.

The guard nodded, opened the gate and let them through.

Once they had walked far enough along the straight dirt road to be out of earshot of the guard, Javan called out to Ravier. "Can I dump these bags now? They're heavy!"

"Deal with it. If we're stopped for any reason, that's our cover story. We can also use them as bargaining chips with the animal shopkeeper."

"Can you at least carry one of them?"

"I'm not the one who got our okties eaten."

"So this is punishment."

"You're quick." Ravier looked behind them. "Okay. I think it's safe to leave the road now. Make sure to follow my footsteps exactly. The landscape up ahead shifts from meadows to quagmires and swallowing sand. Your feet are going to get wet, but the earth won't suck you in as long as you stay away from any tan patches of sand."

"Got it," Javan said. "No tan sand." He tried to sound nonchalant, but where he came from, sand was tan. Trying to avoid natural-colored sand seemed like a tall order, especially if one misstep meant the earth would suck him in. That did not sound like a pleasant experience.

CHAPTER 11

Bargaining for Boundaroos

For a good nine miles, Javan didn't have to worry about where to walk. He just had to endure the burden of the bags of seeds. That burden seemed to multiply by a factor of ten once they entered the swamp.

Huge distorted trees with draping branches blocked most of the rays from the late afternoon sun as they walked through sticky red mud along the edge of moss-covered water. Stalks of bamboo forced them to zig and zag in and out of the water.

Unsettling creatures he couldn't see slithered through the water, cackled from the land and taunted from the trees.

It was an altogether creepy experience, and Javan wanted out. "I think that man back at the shop wanted us dead. Nobody lives in this place."

"Someone who wants to avoid the Dark King does. We haven't gone far enough in yet."

"I have. I'm turning around." Javan spun around but forgot to watch his step. Instead of landing on solid but sticky ground, his right foot sunk into a puddle of tan sand.

He lost his balance and fell forward, dropping the two bags of seeds. The earth instantly swallowed the bags whole. Had Ravier not snatched Javan's shirt, it would have swallowed him as well.

"I told you to follow my footsteps exactly," Ravier said, jerking Javan back onto solid ground. "Now we've lost our bargaining chips. Disobey me again and I'll purposefully find a patch of sand to throw you in."

Javan swallowed and nodded. It took several miles of trailing Ravier step for step for his heart to finally slow back down to its normal rate. This was his second brush with death in one day on the heel of two attacks from his family the day before. He hoped a devastating strike three wasn't around the corner.

Reaching a long, wobbly, wooden bridge lifted Javan's spirits. A man-made structure meant a man had to be around here somewhere.

The bridge led them to a circular clearing with one large square log building bordered by five smaller huts, all of which rested on stilts and were interconnected with a net walkway. Squeaks and squabbles and chirps and a symphony of general animal chatter emanated from the large building. But no people were anywhere to be seen.

"What is this place?" Javan asked.

"Not sure," Ravier said. "Whatever happens, do not let anyone see your green eye." He drew his sword and inched forward.

"You won't be needing that." A gruff man appeared in the doorway of the nearest hut holding a bow and arrow. The bow was loaded. The arrow was aimed at Ravier. Javan was somewhat relieved that the weapon wasn't pointed at him.

"We're not here to cause trouble," Ravier said.

"Then turn around and be on your way. We don't tolerate visitors." Seven more gruff-looking men dressed in swamp camouflage armed with bows and arrows appeared at ground level, surrounding Javan and Ravier.

Javan held his breath and bit his lip. Was this the inevitable strike three?

"Marty sent us," Ravier said. "Told us to ask for Reese, said he could help us acquire some transportation."

A tiny man pushed past the warrior in the hut doorway. "I'm Reese." The three-foot tall man looked terribly out of place. He was clean-shaven with short, dark hair and wore white slacks with a purple silk shirt. He signaled for his men to put their weapons down. They obeyed. "If Marty sent you, that makes us friends. Put your sword away and come up to the animal house."

Reese waddled across the net walkway while Javan and Ravier climbed the ladder hanging down from the porch of the big building. They walked inside to find a warehouse filled with rows of cages. All sorts of animals from chickens to foxes to birds and snakes occupied the cages.

And those were the animals Javan recognized. Many of the creatures with their prickly hair or furless bodies or abundance of legs Javan had never seen before. Those were the ones who captivated him. "What's with all the animals?" Javan asked, spellbound by the new species he was discovering. He wanted to be able to check them out with both eyes but was careful to keep his right eye closed and covered with his hand.

"It's one of the many services I provide for my friends," Reese said. "If you need dinner or a pet or a ride without first getting the king's permission, I'm your man. The king doesn't take kindly to those who operate outside of his system, though, so I have to be careful whom I help."

"We're not part of the king's puppets, either," Ravier said. "We could use some reliable okties to get back home."

"Okties?" The man chuckled. "I don't operate that far out of the system. I do have some phenomenal mrickers that can get you from point A to point B in the blink of an eye."

"They can't hop over the river. We need to fly."

"Heading into North Zandador? That does make a difference." Reese tapped his fingers across his chin. "Like I said, I don't have any okties, but I do have two boundaroos that will get you home just as fast. I wasn't planning on selling them, though."

Smooth, Javan thought. This guy would make a good used car salesman.

"What's your price?" Ravier asked.

"Ten triangle scales." Reese paused. "Each."

"For boundaroos?" Ravier whistled. "Ten for both is way too much."

"You don't seem to be in much of a position to bargain."

"That's where you're wrong," Ravier said, putting his hand on Reese's shoulder. "You look like a man who appreciates the finer things in life. What if I told you I had a device you could wear on your wrist that tells you exactly what time of day it is at any moment of the day?"

Javan cocked his head at Ravier's description of a watch, especially since Ravier wasn't wearing a watch of his own.

Reese's eyes widened. "I'd say you could have as many boundaroos as you want."

"Good," Ravier said. "Javan, give him your time device."

"Excuse me? I'm not giving up my watch. I earned this two years ago for helping a guy tame his wild horse. It's engraved and everything."

"You call it a watch?" Reese seized Javan's left wrist and inspected the gold watch. "Fascinating. I'll take it."

"Give it to him," Ravier ordered.

"Fine." Javan glared at Ravier with his one open eye as he unclasped the band and handed the prized watch to a giddy Reese.

"The boundaroos are in the back right corner," Reese said, strapping the watch on his wrist and dismissing his guests.

Javan hated the idea of leaving his watch with the midget in exchange for some weird-named creature. That watch belonged on his wrist, not the animal salesman's. Only he didn't have a chance to protest. Ravier grabbed his arm and dragged him to the back of the building. At least he no longer had to worry about hiding his eye.

The cages and animals got bigger and bigger the farther back they walked. By the time they made it to the back right corner, the animals were as tall as or taller than them.

"I hate boundaroos," Ravier said, stopping in front of two red-furred creatures jumping and spinning and turning and twisting in their cages while hooting and snorting at the top of their lungs. "They're wild, stupid, irritating, loud and obnoxious, not to mention uncomfortable to ride. But they are fast and can swim."

"You sure we can ride these things? They look a little out of control."

"I told you they're wild. They're easy to control, though, once you grab hold of their ears."

"And how are you supposed to do that?" The animals were so busy spinning that Javan couldn't even tell where their ears were.

"Watch." Ravier clanged both cages and let out a shrieking whistle. The animals stopped, stood on their hind legs and stared at Ravier. Their eyes were level with Ravier, and they looked like giant Tasmanian devils with the long ears of a rabbit and the pouch and tail of a kangaroo.

Ravier opened the door of the first cage, grabbed the tip of the animal's ear and led it out to Javan. "Hold this."

Javan took charge of the furry ear while Ravier extracted the other from its cage in the same way. "What now?" Javan asked.

"Keep hold of her ears and step inside her pouch."

"Huh?" They were going to ride under the animal? That didn't seem like a good plan.

"Just do what I do."

Ravier positioned himself under his boundaroo's head and snagged the other ear so that he was holding one ear in each hand beside his face. Then he stepped inside the pouch which covered him almost to his waist. "Use the ears like reins to tell the boundaroo where you want to go."

"Okay." Javan mimicked Ravier. He stood under his boundaroo, clutched the other ear and stepped inside the gooey pouch. He cringed as slobber dripped on his face. "Ugh."

"Brace yourself," Ravier said. "It's going to be a long ride home." Ravier tugged his boundaroo's ears forward. The animal charged down the aisle, through the front door and leapt off the porch.

Javan closed his eyes and mumbled, "I do not want to do this. I do not want to do this. I do not want to do this." He inched his right eye open, held his breath and jerked his hands forward.

The boundaroo screeched, spun in a circle and bounded down the aisle after Ravier. Without pausing, the animal sailed off the porch, spinning and slobbering and jostling Javan around the whole way down.

They landed with a thump, found the waiting Ravier and bounded through the darkening swamp at a pace that would make a galloping Storm look like he was standing still.

CHAPTER 12

A Smashing Return

"Slow down!" Javan tugged on the boundaroo's ears, but it was too late. They crashed through the large door of the okty barn, sending splinters of wood in every direction. The collision threw the boundaroo off balance, and it slid sideways to the middle of the barn.

He took advantage of the opportunity and scrambled out of the oversized pouch onto the dirt floor. Free of its human cargo, the red boundaroo began bouncing about and badgering the okties. The poor okties started swishing around and banging into each other while trying to avoid the pest.

"I told you to make your boundaroo stop, not break my barn door!" Ravier stepped out of his overactive boundaroo. He let it join its buddy and marched toward Javan. "Now it's going to take me hours to calm these okties down and round up the escapees."

"I told you that I tried to make it stop, but that stinky animal wasn't in a cooperative mood." His pants, sticky with boundaroo goo, suctioned themselves to his legs. A combination of water, slobber and dirt dripped from his disheveled hair and onto his ripped shirt. "Guess it wasn't happy after I made it run through a swamp, swim through a river filled with biting fish, crawl through pitch-black caves, climb up and down steep hills, weave through a thick forest and carry a person in its belly!"

"None of that would have been necessary if you would have kept your mouth shut when we were watching the dragon!"

"How was I supposed to know the dragon could teleport, spit acid and devour okties? You're supposed to be the teacher," Javan said, pointing his finger and poking Ravier in the chest, "and you did a terrible job of teaching me."

"Don't touch me again."

"Oh? You mean don't do this?" Javan pressed both of his hands onto Ravier's chest and pushed.

Ravier didn't budge. He did, however, push back, sending Javan to the ground with a flick of his wrist. "You don't want to fight me," he said.

"I think I do." Javan jumped to his feet and rushed shoulder first into Ravier. It didn't knock Ravier off balance like he intended, but judging by the angry face and fisted hands, he did succeed in making Ravier more angry than before.

"Enough!" A sharp whistle from Esmeralda's lips for ten straight seconds stopped the fight.

The boundaroos stopped bounding.

The okties stopped flying.

"Now that I have your attention," she said, entering the barn and taking each boundaroo by the ear, "Ravier, I want you to feed these things, then set them free in the woods. Javan, I want you to go inside, shower and go to bed. Hannah, you're going to account for all the okties and find any that flew away. In the meantime, I'll rig a door so no more can escape."

When no one moved, Esmeralda handed off the boundaroos to Ravier and shouted, "Go!"

Ravier grunted and took control of the boundaroos. He led them to the corner feeding trough while Hannah wandered off, mumbling something about recovering the escaped okties because she wanted to, not because Esmeralda told her to.

The only one who didn't move was Javan. "Well," she said, "go shower."

"I want to watch you fix the door. I've never seen anyone use magic before."

"Magic?" Esmeralda laughed. "There's nothing magical about pounding nails into wood. What makes you think I am going to use magic?"

"Gee, I don't know," Javan said. "I just figured that a place with dragons and portals and invisible shields had magic to go along with it. Any earthling who has read about fantasy worlds like this would logically conclude that magic is involved. I've kinda been wondering what my magical powers are and how to use them."

"First of all, this isn't a fantasy world. It's a real place in a real dimension that is just different than yours. Second, what you see as magical is nothing more than scientific scalology in action. Scalologists have worked for thousands of years to figure out how to use the scales the dragons shed every ten years to give us energy, medicine, portals and even invisible shields.

"And third, you don't have any magical powers. You do have a unique talent that allows you to communicate telepathically with dragons, and once you begin collecting dragons, you'll be able to tap into and use the speed, strength, invisibility and teleportation abilities of your dragons.

"But you, my son—like every other person in this dimension—have no magical powers. If you did, you wouldn't need to go through with the very human, very mundane activity of taking a shower. Please go do that now. You're filthy, and you stink."

"Don't you want to know why I'm filthy?"

"I look forward to hearing the story tomorrow when you're clean, and I'm rested." She pointed to the door. "Go."

"Good idea," Javan said. If life in Zandador was going to involve more days like the one he just lived through, he wanted no part of it. "Tomorrow is day three, and I've made my decision. I want to go back to Earth."

◊   ◊   ◊

"Whoever those scalologists are," Javan said, shivering and burying himself under the covers on his bed, "they need to figure out how to get hot water in their showers."

At least the contraptions they called showers encouraged quick cleaning and minimal water waste. But it sure was a miserable experience stepping into that steel closet punctured with holes on three walls, the ceiling and floor.

Had he known what was coming when he stepped on the pedal on the floor, he would have braced himself for the onslaught of frigid water rushing at him from the hundreds of holes around him. Instead, he was caught off guard, jumped, slipped and bruised his rear.

Showers here were cold, painful experiences. On the plus side, he did like the soap and shampoo; he smelled like he just stepped out of a rain forest.

The fatigue didn't take long to overpower the cold, and Javan soon drifted off to sleep.

He had no idea how long he had been sleeping when a noise from the porch below startled him. He tried to check the time, but considering his earlier "gift" to Reese, his watch was no longer on his wrist, and the room didn't have a clock.

Javan stayed in bed with his eyes closed trying to force himself back to sleep. He could tell, however, that someone was pacing on the wooden planks, and he could hear the sound of muffled voices. Curious, he got up, opened his window and listened.

"Fail, fail, fail," Ravier was saying. "All that kid did today is fail."

"Oh, it couldn't have been that bad." Esmeralda's voice. His mother was defending him.

"Really? He had no respect for the dragon, got our okties eaten, made eye contact with the clerk in Torix, lost our seeds and nearly himself in swallowing sand, forced us to travel by boundaroo and whined and moaned and complained like a childish brat all day."

"Ravier, give him a break. He's young, he's in a strange new place, and he hasn't learned how to handle himself in Zandador. That's your job: to teach him."

"I pass. He's not the one. He can't be the one. If he is, we have no hope." Ravier's voice lowered, and Javan had to strain to hear. "Besides, we're asking the impossible of him. The only dragons remaining in Zandador are hundreds of years old. Collecting a yearling is tough enough; collecting four dragons—all more than 500 years old—can't be done."

"It can if he's trained properly."

"The first dragon he tries to ride is going to eat him alive no matter how well he's trained."

Javan gulped. That did not sound pleasant.

"You're wrong, and there's something you need to get through your head right now." Esmeralda spoke with an intensity Javan hadn't heard in her voice before. "Dartez isn't here. As much as you and I wanted him to be, he's not the one. Javan is. And he needs your help."

"He's not going to get it. I'm done with him. Take him back where he came from tomorrow. I'll meet with the men of the village; we'll figure out another way to overthrow the Dark King."

"There is no other way."

"There has to be. That kid is not man enough to be a Collector or a King."

Javan heard the front door open and slam shut, but it was the harsh words of his grandfather that caused Javan's knees to buckle and his body to slump down to the floor.

He wanted to get angry.

But he couldn't.

Not when he knew his grandfather was right.

CHAPTER 13

Return to Obscurity

The sun was high in the afternoon sky by the time Javan rolled his stiff, sore, beat-up body out of bed. He had traversed entirely too many miles on foot yesterday, and now he was feeling the consequences of that abuse. He just hoped he would be recovered enough by tomorrow to reclaim his insignificant place on his football team.

He was ready to slip back into his comfortable world where no one expected anything of him or from him. Here, he was nothing but a disappointment. He couldn't be who these people wanted him to be. He wasn't king material.

He didn't even know how to be a son or grandson. He was better off being a lonely orphan back on that ranch in Montana.

Javan cringed in pain with every tiny move he made as he dressed in a clean t-shirt and shorts from his stash of colorful earth clothes, covered his eyes with his contacts and wandered downstairs, his packed backpack slung over his shoulder. If all went well, perhaps he could be back at the ranch in time to soak his overused muscles in a warm bath before dinner tonight.

Then again, he might not be hungry later.

Hannah was waiting for him in the kitchen and had the long table covered with all sorts of delicious smelling food. "You're up," she said, smothering him with a hug. "I know you didn't eat much yesterday, poor thing, so I made everything I had." She led him to the table, sat him down and started piling food on his plate. "Eat!"

"Thanks." He bowed his head, thanked God for his food, then wondered if God even heard prayers from people in this dimension.

Did they worship God here? Javan didn't recall seeing any churches. It didn't matter. He was going to keep praying to the one God he knew regardless of his dimensional location.

He took a bite of something that resembled roast beef. The savory, tender meat practically melted in his mouth. He took another bite. And another.

For the next twenty minutes, he gorged himself on the various meats, vegetables, breads, potatoes and sweets Hannah provided. When his appetite was finally satisfied, he had the sense to realize no one else was around. "Where's Esmeralda?" He didn't really care where Ravier was.

"I think she went for a walk earlier." She sat on the bench beside him. "You don't have to go back, you know. This is your home. We're your family. We want you here with us whether you collect dragons or not."

"I don't belong here," Javan said. He didn't really belong in Montana either, but at least that place was familiar. "It's time for me to go back."

Hannah wrapped his left hand in both of hers. "Please stay."

Javan looked at his grandmother and was surprised to find tears in her eyes. He almost wanted to give in to her plea, to find out what it was like to be part of a real family. But this family wanted him to be someone he wasn't. He couldn't meet their expectations. He needed to return to a place where no one expected anything from him.

"I can't," he said, standing. He had to get out of here before he started crying, too. "Thanks for the food. It was all really good."

"You're welcome, dear." Hannah stood as well and gave him one final hug. "And you're always welcome here if you ever change your mind."

"Thanks." He wouldn't be changing his mind. Blinking back a few tears of his own, Javan grabbed his backpack and walked outside.

The bright afternoon sun gave him an excuse to shield his eyes, a good thing since his mom was sitting on the porch steps.

"You look like you're ready to go," she said.

"I am. I told you I'd give you three days. This is my third day, and I don't want to stay."

"Fair enough." She stood and slung a leather bag over her shoulder. "We'll say goodbye to your grandfather and be on our way."

"That's not necessary. He doesn't like me very much, and he's probably just going to get mad if he sees me again."

"Then let him get mad, but you're going to say goodbye."

"Fine." Javan hung his head and followed Esmeralda to the garden behind the barn.

At least Javan was thankful for this final chance to walk through the head high nectar-producing plants the okties fed on. He recognized many of the flowers, but he had never seen them so big, so colorful and so breathtaking.

He took deep breath after deep breath as he walked through the rows of bright orange butterfly weeds, deep purple and bright white bushes, copper and brass marigolds, red and yellow milkweeds, velvet and lavender lilies and golden dandelions. Half a dozen okties flitted from bush to bush, drinking in the nectar.

This would be one of his favorite memories from Zandador.

Then Ravier, who was pruning some of the bushes, ruined it. "What are you still doing here?"

The snippy tone of Ravier's voice sparked Javan's temper. He made no attempt to keep the anger and sarcasm out of his own voice while pointing at Esmeralda. "She wouldn't let me leave without saying bye to you, dear grandfather."

Ravier sighed and put down his pruning shears long enough to huff one word. "Goodbye."

"There," Javan said, turning around. "We can go now."

"No we can't," Esmeralda said, spinning Javan back around. "Hug him. Then we'll go."

"What?"

"You heard me."

"That's not necessary, Esmeralda," Ravier said.

"Yes, it is." She took the sharp shears out of Ravier's hands. "Whether you like it or not, you two are family. You're never going to see each other again, and the last memory you have of one another is going to be a pleasant, loving one. Now hug!"

Javan and Ravier both jumped at the shrill command and complied. Javan wrapped his stiff arms around Ravier's stiff body for the briefest of seconds. They backed away from each other just as quickly.

"There," Esmeralda said, handing the shears back to Ravier, "now we can go."

"Finally." Javan gladly followed Esmeralda out of the garden, through the village and into the woods past the protective shield.

CHAPTER 14

A Hint of Attachment

Javan much preferred walking through these woods during daylight hours. He was able to drink in the pristine beauty of the odd-shaped trees and enjoy watching the birds and squirrels and other cool creatures he couldn't identify scurry about rather than being able to see nothing in the dark and feel like he was about to be attacked by packs of wild animals at any second.

The more they walked, though, the more Javan realized this was the last chance he would ever have to spend with his mother. And he knew almost nothing about her. The time they had spent together on Saturday evening was focused on her and Hannah learning about him and his world. He hadn't bothered to ask many questions about her.

If he didn't ask now, he would have nothing to hold on to when he returned to Montana. He wasn't sure where to start, so he blurted out the first thing that came to his mind. "Where did you grow up?"

Esmeralda paused, then talked as she walked. "I grew up in the region of Madai in northeast Zandador in the city of Oer."

"Is that close to here?"

"Not really. We're in northwest Zandador right now in the region of Gomer. It would take about half a day by okty to get there."

Javan wanted to know if he had aunts, uncles, cousins and another set of grandparents somewhere in this dimension. "Is your family still there?"

Esmeralda halted. Her whole body went rigid, and her single word reply sounded robotic. "No."

Trying not to hound her but wanting to know the story behind her answer, Javan whispered, "What happened to them?"

Minutes passed.

Javan waited.

Finally, she started walking and talking again. "First you have to understand what growing up in Zandador under the rule of Omri is like. We call him the Dark King because he has a way of making life feel dark and depressing despite the beauty of the land around us. Anyway, as a child, you're required to spend the first twenty years of your life in school learning what the King wants you to know about Zandador and all the territories of the Great Rift to the north and south of us.

"Then you spend the next eighty years away from your family working in assigned apprenticeships that each last a decade in areas like government work, teaching, farming and ranching. You're only allowed to return home to visit for the final two weeks of each year.

"Once you reach the age of 100, you're required by law to spend the next century of your life serving in the king's army to enforce all the laws you've been conditioned to follow throughout your childhood."

"Hold up," Javan said. He had a hard time comprehending how different life could be when the average lifespan lasted nearly a millennium rather than a century. "You're telling me a century of life is considered childhood? On Earth, I'll be considered an adult and able to serve in the Army in three years."

"At eighteen? Strange. But I suppose you do have to grow up faster when your life doesn't last as long."

They walked a few steps in silence before Javan prompted his mother to continue. "What happens when you turn 200?"

"Once you complete your century of service, you're either assigned to a lifetime of work as a soldier or to a job that you showed the most aptitude for during your apprenticeship years."

"That's a rotten deal. You mean nobody gets to decide what they want to do?"

"It's worse than that. You can't even decide what to believe regarding God. Omri sees himself as god and is the only authority he allows anyone to serve. He thus banned religion and had all churches demolished. He tried to burn all the religious documents brought here from Earth, but those of us who believe in the God who created us have done a good job of preserving our Bibles.

"In essence, you're told who to be, where to live, what to wear, what to do, who to marry and how many kids you can have. Omri doesn't tolerate people who think for themselves and has worked hard to erase and retell the true history of Zandador.

"He wants to rid the land of all dragons except his own and annihilate the Collector and Protector Bloodlines." Esmeralda took a deep breath before continuing. "My parents were both Protectors. Despite the Dark King's mandate, they refused to deny their heritage and passed on everything they knew to me and my younger sister, Merissa."

Javan had an Aunt Merissa! He wondered if he looked older than her, too.

"My sister and I both loved to sing," Esmeralda said, plucking a golf ball–size blackberry from a shrub, "but that's also something that's forbidden under Omri's rule. Unless, of course, you're singing for his entertainment." She bit into the berry and handed Javan the other half.

He popped it into his mouth before the juice had a chance to drip all over his hand. The warm, sweet liquid drenched his tongue. "That's good," he murmured between chews.

"They're called gooey globes. Here. Have another." She picked two more, giving one to Javan and keeping one for herself.

They walked for a bit as they enjoyed the gooey treats. Then Esmeralda resumed her story. "Anyway, when I was 129 and Merissa was 118, we did what we usually did when we arrived home for our yearly visit: we sang. We sang hymns of praise to God. We sang romantic ballads. And we sang songs of our true Zandadorian history taught to us by our parents.

"What we didn't know was that the king's youngest son Micah was patrolling our city at that time. Reports of our singing by those loyal to the king made their way to Micah, and he reported us to his father.

"The next night, I snuck out of the city to collect shed noon stalker scales from the dragons my family protected." Esmeralda was starting to choke on her words. She stopped at a fallen log and sat down. "I returned a little past midnight to the sight of my city being ravaged by the king's Midnight Stalker. My house had been leveled, and only pieces of my family remained."

Tears streamed down her face. Javan had no idea how to help his crying mother tell this terrible story. He sat awkwardly beside her, hoping that would somehow help.

"I had never been filled with so much pain and rage and anger and guilt," she said. "I knew that dragon was sent as punishment because of me, and I was determined to send that dragon home with a scar before it destroyed me and the rest of my city.

"I dug through the rubble, found my sword and marched through the street after that black dragon. It was about to devour my father's best friend, so I did the only thing I could think of: I ran my sword through his back claw, temporarily tying him to the ground. That dragon screeched, dropped his snack and turned on me.

"I was prepared to die." Esmeralda reached for Javan's hand. "I would have, too, if your father hadn't shown up riding his own Midnight Stalker."

"My dad saved you?"

"Oh, yes. Dartez was my hero that night. He and his dragon Kandorg fought off Serenity, the king's dragon, before Serenity could kill any more people. After the battle, your father returned for me and took me to the safety of his home.

"I left shreds of my clothing so that I would be presumed dead in the attack; had I remained, I would have been carted off to prison. Ironic since I ended up a prisoner anyway, but not before I fell in love with your father, married him and became pregnant with you." Esmeralda squeezed Javan's hand and stood. "We're almost to the portal. It's time to return you to the safety of your home."

Javan wanted to learn more about her and his father. But he shouldn't get too attached. This wasn't his world. These weren't his people. So he refrained from asking any more questions as they walked the rest of the way to the portal.

CHAPTER 15

Captured

The windy path led them downhill and to an open shoreline with a rocky cliff wall to Javan's right and acres of trees to his left that ended in another span of sheer rock walls.

Now that Javan could see the portal area in the full afternoon sun, he could appreciate the beauty of the spot. The same wide, clear blue river he crossed by boundaroo yesterday stretched before him. He could barely make out the flat, grassy shoreline on the other side and felt small compared to the cliff he found himself standing beside.

The end of the cliff jutted inland at a sharp right angle and had a slanted overhang that looked like a fun challenge for a skilled rock climber. The tricky part would have been climbing up the first thirty or so feet that was as slick as glass and thus offered no sort of hand or foot holds.

The slick part of the cliff was where Javan expected the portal to be, but he didn't see the colorful octagon glowing in all its dragon scale glory. "You sure this is the right spot? I don't see the portal."

"It's here," Esmeralda said, laying her bag on the ground. "The portal on this side is cloaked and only appears when you insert the four scales in the proper place on the wall."

"How exactly do you know where that is?"

"I can't reveal all my secrets." She winked at him, took the four scales out of her bag and tossed a handful of stalker dust on the rock wall. "Ah! Found it!" Esmeralda began inserting the scales into the newly revealed circle on the wall. Once she added the fourth scale, the octagon appeared.

"That is so cool," Javan said, admiring the shimmering wall.

"It is beautiful." Esmeralda spun the dial to the left, to the right and back to the left again. She was paying attention to the number of clicks as she turned the dial, but Javan didn't bother counting. He was too distracted by a dull buzzing sound and looked around to try to figure out where the noise was coming from.

"Do you hear that?" he asked.

"The clicks? Yes."

"No. The buzzing. It's getting louder."

"Buzzing?" Esmeralda looked over her shoulder and pointed to three dots over the river flying toward them. "Okty riders. Great. The king's soldiers patrol this area. We have to hurry."

When she finished all the necessary spinning and clicking, she pushed the dial in. Javan recognized the hum and the flickering scales. He couldn't make out any sort of pattern between the flickers, but his mother apparently could.

"What happens if they catch us?"

"Activating the portal is a crime punishable by death."

"They'll kill us?" He could now make out the figures of the three men.

"Not here." She tapped a grey scale once, the other grey scale three times, and both of the white scales six times. The scales whirled and twirled and eventually melted together to create the watery rainbow of the activated portal. "They'd take us back to the capital city of Japheth and make an example of us there by executing us in public. Omri likes to vary the execution methods. His favorites are death by dragon and death by decapitation."

Javan gulped at the prospect of losing his head and instinctively protected his throat. "Then you have to come through with me." He grabbed Esmeralda's hand and stepped toward the portal.

"No." She jerked her hand away. "My home is here; yours is on the other side. I'll be okay, but you have to go. The portal will only stay active for a few minutes, so they shouldn't be able to follow you. I love you, my son." She kissed his cheek, quickly wrapped her arms around him and walked straight toward the men who landed on the shore fifty feet away.

The leader was a tall, muscle-bound black man with deadly brown eyes and dreadlocks that cascaded past his shoulders. He wore a sword across his back and a belt with a variety of handheld weapons around his waist. To Javan he only looked to be about seventeen or eighteen, but age was a hard thing to gauge in this place.

The other two men were also tall and ripped and carried weapons, but they weren't nearly as intimidating.

"Boys," the leader said, approaching Esmeralda, "we have come across a prize that will earn us a feast tonight."

"Stop right there, Micah." Esmeralda pulled a dagger out of her boot and held it to her throat. "I won't be much of a prize if you don't return me to your father alive. I will slit my throat this instant if you even think about touching that boy."

Micah stopped, crossed his arms and studied Javan. "The King doesn't need to know about some skinny boy who slipped through the portal."

"You're going to let him go?" One of the sidekicks was not happy.

Micah turned to the sidekick. "Do you have any idea who that kid is?"

"No."

"Me, either." He pointed at Esmeralda. "Do you know who this woman is?"

"Of course. She's Esmeralda, the escaped prisoner with the biggest bounty on her head."

"Would you rather take a dead Esmeralda and a live nothing boy back to the King or present to him one live, prized prisoner?"

The sidekick hung his head and shuffled his feet. "The live, prized prisoner."

"Good answer." Micah turned his attention back to Esmeralda. "Put the knife down, come with us and we'll let the boy go."

Esmeralda looked at Javan. "Go," she said and dropped her dagger.

"No!" Javan charged toward his mother, but he was too late. Micah already had her in his grip. "Let her go!"

"Javan, this isn't your fight," she yelled. "Go home!"

"Not without you!" He rammed into Micah, trying to make him loosen his grip. It didn't work.

With his free hand, Micah latched on to a handful of Javan's hair and pulled him back. Javan was forced to look up as Micah spoke. "This woman just saved your life. But if I ever see you again, I won't hesitate to kill you on sight."

He released Javan's hair, punched his nose and kicked the back of Javan's knees, sending him crumpling to the ground. Micah gave Javan one final kick in the ribs before he carried Esmeralda to his okty and flew away with his buddies.

CHAPTER 16

The Decision

J avan coughed away the warm blood that oozed into his mouth from his busted nose and grimaced from the pain that shot through him as he stood. He had to get word back to Ravier.

Ravier had to save his mother.

But Esmeralda said the portal would only be active for a few minutes. If he didn't go through it now, he might never have another chance to return to Earth.

Javan stumbled to the portal. One more step and there was no turning back.

Comfort or challenge?

Obscurity or purpose?

Loneliness or family?

Family. He was part of a family. A family who lived here. In this dimension. A family who needed him now.

Could he really turn his back on a mother who willingly surrendered her own life to save his? Is that the kind of man he wanted to be? A selfish coward who only protected himself?

She did, however, give herself up so he could go back home through the portal. Would he be letting her down by staying here?

What if he couldn't save her? Then she would be dead and he would be stuck.

Unless he did what she brought him here to do in the first place: collect dragons and overthrow the Dark King.

She had risked everything for him. It was his turn to risk everything for her.

Javan snatched the four scales from the wall, deactivating the portal. He picked up his mother's bag, slung it over his shoulder and took off at a dead sprint through the woods toward the hidden village of Gri.

◇　◇　◇

It was dark by the time Javan returned to the village, but he wasn't going to let that stop him from carrying out his newly devised plan.

He charged into his grandparent's house and found them eating quietly at the table. "Good. You're here. Ravier, I need your sword, an okty and directions to the city of Japheth. Grandma, I need you to pack me some food for the trip. I don't know how much time I have and need to be on my way as soon as possible."

"Javan!" Hannah jumped up and hugged him, then inspected his face. "What happened, dear?"

"I got beat up by some bully named Micah." Javan noticed the look of alarm Hannah and Ravier shared. "You know him?"

"Yes," Ravier said. "He's the youngest of the king's thirteen sons and a vicious Dragon Hunter. He's destined to take King Omri's place one day, but his father won't allow him to hunt dragons and thus dethrone him until the king is on his deathbed. In the meantime, Micah practices by hunting people."

"He took my mom."

"Took her? Oh, dear. Where were you when he found you?" Hannah asked while she led Javan to the table.

Javan sat down and cleaned up the dried blood on his face with a wet towel Hannah gave him. "At the portal."

"Was he waiting for you there?" Ravier took over the questioning as Hannah scrambled to get a place set for Javan.

"No. He showed up with two other guys right after mom activated the portal."

"She activated it?" Ravier leaned forward. "Why didn't you go through?"

"I almost did. After all, Micah let me go because my mom gave herself up if he would leave me alone."

"What made you stay?"

"I realized I'd be running away from home, not back to it. Besides, my mom brought me here to collect dragons and overthrow the king. That's what I intend to do, hopefully with your help. First, I need to rescue her before the king kills her. Thus the need for your sword, an okty and directions."

Ravier leaned back and crossed his arms. "I like this spunk. I wasn't sure you had it in you. I'll help you. But not by sending you off with a sword you don't know how to use to a city you know nothing about."

"You're going to get some people together and save her yourself? Good." Javan stood. "Just let me come with you."

"Sit down and eat. We're not going anywhere tonight."

"We have to! I told you, that Micah guy took her, and the king is going to kill her."

"Not right away. You see, King Omri likes to make a spectacle of people like Esmeralda. He can't send his dragons to destroy her family and friends because he's already done that. Instead, he'll have her toted around in chains through every city and every village in every region in Zandador while proclaiming the fate of her public execution. He wants to remind the people what happens to those who defy him."

"So we're going to rescue her when he brings her to one of the villages close to here?"

"No."

"No?" Javan could feel his blood starting to boil. "Why not?"

"Because we need save her on the day she is scheduled to die."

"Isn't that cutting it a little close?"

"No. The best way to save her is to introduce you as a challenger in the Battle for the Throne. The best way to introduce you is in front a crowd forced to gather by order of the king to watch a beautiful woman die for committing the 'crime' of personal liberty, something most of that crowd secretly longs for but lacks the courage to pursue."

"How is introducing me as a challenger going to save her from being executed?"

"It might not, but it's our best chance. You'll understand when the day comes. I figure we have about four weeks to get you ready and perfect our plan."

"Shouldn't we come up with a plan B, just in case?"

"A contingency plan. Good. You are thinking like a leader. We'll work on it. But our primary focus is preparing you to collect dragons. Understood?"

Javan nodded. "Understood."

"While in training, there are rules to follow." Ravier stood and looked Javan in the eye while ticking off his rules on his hand. "No whining. No complaining. No arguing." He poked Javan in the chest. "You do what I say, when I say, how I say. Do you have a problem with that?"

He did, but if he could learn how to fight in order to protect those he cared about and avoid another beating like he got earlier, he could keep his mouth shut. "Are you going to teach me how to fight?"

"That's part of the training."

"Okay. I'll follow your rules. When do we start?"

"Now. Get some food in you, then meet me in the barn for your first lesson."

Javan wanted to protest and eat after the lesson, but he decided arguing with Ravier's first order would not be wise. He thus sat and ate the bowl of stew his grandmother put in front of him while dreaming about what it would be like to confront Micah, pull his dreadlocks and bust his nose.

Then he wondered if he would ever be strong enough and brave enough to make a dream like that come true.

CHAPTER 17

Omri's Orders

M icah gripped Esmeralda's arm and barged into the banquet hall. "I demand a place at the table for the prize we bring you." He shoved the prisoner toward King Omri, who sat alone at the head of a long table lined with mounds of food.

Omri hadn't permitted anyone the honor of his presence at dinner since Esmeralda had escaped. No one could tell him how she had gotten out, so he refused to let anyone join him for the evening feast until she was returned.

Micah would have an invitation at the dinner table for years to come as a result of this find.

The King carefully wiped his mouth with his napkin and slowly pushed back from the table. His sense of power rose with him. He wasn't as broad-shouldered or as strong as Micah, but his commanding personality towered over his son.

Unnerved by his father's silence, Micah spoke. "I caught her attempting to open the portal to Earth."

Omri kept his deep brown eyes on Esmeralda as his feet clapped toward her on the marble floor. Micah watched his father intently, waiting for his words of praise for bringing Esmeralda back to where she belonged.

As Omri circled Esmeralda, he looked neither pleased or upset. Why hadn't he praised Micah yet?

Without warning, Omri grabbed Esmeralda's braid with his left hand and his dagger from his boot with his right hand. He cut the braid off at the base of her neck, and her hair fell in short, ragged strands around her face as she gasped.

"Never return a prisoner with her dignity intact." He draped the long black braid over Micah's shoulder.

"Father, I—"

"You are not to speak."

He flinched and braced himself for the verbal beating.

"This woman has made a mockery of me," Omri said. "Even after she broke the marriage and child-bearing laws, I allowed her to live in my home as a servant rather than a prisoner in the dungeon because she could sing like no other. How did she repay my kindness? She ran away and broke another law by attempting to open the portal. Her singing voice cannot save her now. Zandador must witness what happens to those who dare defy me.

"You are to take three teams of the Justice Unit with you to every village, town, and city in the Land of Zandador. March her through the streets with chains on her hands and feet. Make her sleep in the open in the town squares. Beat her in front of everyone in every place you go. The next time I see her, I don't want to recognize her. Keep a little meat on her bones, though. I want Vasilis to having something to munch on when I feed her to him upon your return.

"Make the people feel my power. My rage. My wrath. If anyone even glances at this woman with pity, whip them. Remind them that I am in control every chance you get. Understood?"

"Understood."

"Good. Now go."

Micah glanced longingly at the food-covered table. He was so hungry. But he had been given an order. His stomach would have to be satisfied with whatever scraps he could find in the kitchen tonight.

◊　◊　◊

Unsure what he was walking into, Javan eased open the door of the dark barn and peeked inside before entering. "Ravier?"

No response.

He stepped inside and meandered across dirt floor. "Hello," he called. "I'm here. Ready to get started. This is where you said to meet."

"Down here."

Javan followed the faint voice to the end of the barn and noticed a light coming from a hole in the floor in the corner. A flat piece of wood the size of the hole was leaning against the wall. Javan bent over the hole and saw a ladder that led to the underground room. He climbed down, turned around and gasped at the sight of the vast space.

It was a good twelve feet high and looked to be about twice the length and width of the gym-sized barn above. Shiny weapons from swords to spears to bows and arrows covered the long wall to his right. A target area filled the space to the left.

Some were shaped like humans, some like animals and some were simple circles attached to the wall with a bull's eye in the middle.

The wall behind Javan was painted with a giant map of what Javan assumed to be Zandador while the far wall was divided into two sections. The left held floor to ceiling bookshelves filled with old, thick books; the right was simply a blank black slate. Several rows of chairs faced the slate wall, and a podium as well as a desk faced the chairs.

Ravier was standing behind the podium. "Come." He pointed to a chair. "Sit."

"This is a neat room," Javan said as he walked toward Ravier. "Can I shoot that bow?"

"Not tonight. Tonight you sit and you learn."

"Learn how to fight, right?"

"Eventually." He handed Javan a notebook with thick, rough paper and a pencil. "First, you need to learn about Zandador and the basics of dragon collecting."

Javan sighed. This was starting to sound way too much like school. He felt like he was going backwards when he wanted to be moving forward. "You mean I have to sit here and listen to you lecture?"

"While taking notes, yes." Ravier picked up a piece of chalk. "This type of teaching bores me, too, but in order for your active training to make sense, you must have a fundamental knowledge of Zandador as well as how and why collecting dragons is necessary."

Javan sighed, opened his notebook and readied his pencil. "Fine. Tell me what I need to know." He wanted to get this book training over with so he could learn how to use some of those weapons.

CHAPTER 18

The First Dragon Collector

Ravier picked up a piece of chalk. "Let's start at the very beginning."

"A very good place to start." Javan couldn't help but notice Ravier's unintentional reference to the song Do-Re-Mi from *The Sound of Music*, his high school's spring production last year; he had helped build the set. Now the song was playing on an endless loop in Javan's mind, making it more difficult to concentrate on Ravier's history lesson.

"When God created the world, the Earth was one large supercontinent." Ravier drew a circle on the slate and outlined the edges of the supercontinent within the circle. Then he began drawing lines that divided the supercontinent into sections. "Large beasts such as dinosaurs dominated the region now known as Africa. Snow tigers and lions lived in the European and Asian regions while quaggas, monkeys and lions dominated the South American region.

"The most feared, most respected, most honored creatures—the Dragon Stalkers—ruled the mountains and plains of North America."

"Ummm...what about humans?"

"I'm getting to that." Ravier starred the land in the middle of the map. "Mankind settled in the Middle East. Now, the rich oxygen atmosphere allowed man to live an average of 900 years, but instead of using those years to live for and grow closer to their Creator, they turned from God. They became consumed with their desires for selfish pleasures and grew extremely corrupt over the course of nearly 2000 years. Angered at man's defiance, God sent judgment on the Earth in the form of a worldwide flood."

"Hang on." Javan raised his hand. "I know this story. God had Noah build an ark. The flood wiped out everything and everyone except Noah, his family and all the animals Noah brought on the ark."

"You are correct."

Javan smiled and put his hand down. He wasn't sure why he was proud of being right when he was the only student in the class.

"The flood didn't just wipe out the human and animal populations; it changed the face of the earth." Ravier erased his supercontinent and redrew the land to look like the map of earth Javan knew. "It was so powerful and so devastating that it caused the supercontinent to break apart into seven distinct continents.

"The very atmosphere changed as well. God knew that with decreased levels of oxygen in the post-flood world, many of His creatures would not be able to survive. So in the Great Rift between the Americas and Europe/Africa, He created a new dimension, a dragon dimension. The extinct animals of the post-flood earth would reside here, and the dragons, with their unique gifts, would rule the land."

This was not part of the Biblical flood story Javan had heard before. "How did the animals get from earth to here?" he asked. "Why are humans here if dragons are supposed to be in charge?"

"Let me finish telling the story before you ask any questions."

"Okay. Sorry. Keep going."

"Thanks." Ravier rolled his eyes. "God chose one man to work with the dragons to build the portal and round up the animals that needed refuge in the new dimension."

"That man had to have been Noah."

"No. It was Japheth, Noah's youngest son." Ravier sounded rather smug, like he enjoyed telling Javan he was wrong. "Before the flood, Japheth gathered eight baby dragons—a male and female of each kind—then cared for them on the ark."

"There were dragons on the ark? They must not be that ferocious if they were able to co-exist with other animals and humans."

"God had a hand in keeping the dragons from devouring the other animals and all the people by enabling Japheth to telepathically communicate with the dragons. Once the floodwaters subsided and everyone was able to leave the ark, Japheth learned that if he was able to ride a dragon, he gained that dragon's loyalty. It would go anywhere he directed, follow any orders he gave and protect him from any threats.

"His brothers referred to his dragons as his collection, so he began referring to himself a Dragon Collector."

"Okay. This collecting thing is starting to make a little more sense," Javan said. "Just to make sure I'm clear, let me ask this. If I get my own collection of dragons, I'll be able to tell dragons what to do, and they'll have to do it?"

"They're not your slaves, but yes, you will have their complete loyalty." Ravier crossed his arms. "Can I get back to the story?"

"Sure." Javan began to wonder what other benefits came along with dragon collecting. Would having his own dragon collection turn him into a babe magnet?

Surely chicks would dig the chance to ride around on the back of a ferocious dragon that only he could tame.

Ravier turned back to his Earth map and drew a triangle off the coast of Florida. "Following God's directions and with his collection of Stalkers, Japheth flew across the Atlantic on the back of Zandador, his male Midnight Stalker; the other flying dragons carried the wingless dragons.

"They landed in what is now Puerto Rico, then Bermuda and finally Miami. In each place, Japheth plucked scales from the backs of his dragons and fused them to rock walls in a huge octagonal shape. He also carved out a circle in the wall next to the octagon that was just big enough to fit four dragon scales into.

"I would explain the science behind how the portal works, but I don't understand it. It's a complicated system that the Protectors would eventually study, record and master, so you don't need to worry yourself with the details of portal codes. I certainly don't waste my brain power on it.

"With some Divine guidance to help him, Japheth figured out the portal activation process. Once he had the portal set up, he returned home, gathered all the endangered animals that were living near the ark and used the teleportation abilities of the Dawn Stalkers to teleport the animals to the portal."

Javan raised his hand. "Question."

"What?"

"Why take the time to fly across the ocean if he could have teleported there in the first place?" He crossed his arms. "Teleportation seems like a better, faster way to travel."

"Dawn Stalkers can't teleport to a place they've never been before."

"Oh. Good to know."

"So, with the portal activated, any animals that swam into the triangle were transported to the dragon dimension; the land creatures went through the wall. After all the animals went through, the leader, young Zandador, invited Japheth in.

"Although he was tempted to see the wonders of the alternate dimension, he refused. He needed to remain on Earth to have sons and daughters and help rebuild after the flood. Zandador thus left Japheth with scale keys to access the portal if he ever changed his mind. He then left Earth and entered the Great Rift."

"And the Great Rift is this place we're in now?"

"Yes. It's a dimension roughly the width and length of the Atlantic Ocean and is made up of seven distinct regions. Let me show you."

Ravier and Javan crossed the room to look at the map on the wall.

An odd-shaped island in the midst of red and purple seas filled the wall. It was divided by thick black lines marking the borders of the different regions. The northern most tip, Xyies, looked like a giant thumb covered by a white, icy-looking landscape. Ravier pointed to the thumb. "This is Xyies, a cold, barren land; the only habitable places are in underground caves."

Javan shivered just thinking about living in such a cave. He liked the warmer look of the land below Xyies, though. It spread out like the palm of a hand and was covered with pictures of thick clusters of trees. He pointed to it. "This looks more human friendly."

"It is. That's Gibbet. The weather is warmer, but the thick jungles make building there challenging. And the abundance of monkeys are annoying to deal with."

Javan moved his finger to the wide open area south and east of Gibbet. "What is this region?" It was more than twice the size of Xyies and Gibbet combined. The northern corner of the region was filled with pictures of volcanoes while most of the rest of the area looked to be a bleak desert. The only exception was the far eastern shore that was filled with a picture of a huge lake and trees and open space.

"That's Tirza, the country just north of Zandador. An extensive mountain range separates our border from theirs while a desert separates us from our neighbors to the south." Ravier drew an air circle around Zandador with his finger. "We're in the middle of the Great Rift. The weather is near perfect all year, and the land is the most habitable in the entire Rift. The river that runs through the middle of Zandador breaks off into various streams, allowing us to set up cities and villages pretty much wherever we want.

"North Zandador, where we are now, is hilly and mountainous. South Zandador is swamp land along the river, then turns into rolling meadows and farmland."

Javan noticed four distinct areas separated by dotted lines on the map of Zandador. "What are these sections?" he asked, indicating the areas.

"Those are Dragon Stalker territories. The Midnight Stalkers own the mountains in the north. The Noon Stalkers own the north eastern shore from the river to the mountains. The Dusk Stalkers own the south eastern shore from the river to the desert. And the Dawn Stalkers own the south western shore from the lake down to the desert; that's where we went yesterday."

"Got it." Javan was starting to understand the lay of the land. The rest of Zandador was divided into different sections the way America was divided into states. Right in the middle of the country just north of the river was a picture of a castle and the name of the capital city, Japheth. That's where his mother was. That's where he needed to go.

"Now to finish our little geography lesson." Ravier shifted his hand to the land south west of Zandador decorated with colorful trees and flowers. "This is Keckrick, a lush rain forest. Wonderful plants grow there that we use in many of our foods and medicines. A giant canyon divides Keckrick from Varzack, a mountainous and rocky region to the southeast of us."

Javan noticed that the canyon looked like a sideways Y and also separated Keckrick and Varzack from a blank, white land on the southernmost part of the Great Rift. "What's this place?" Javan asked, pointing to the white land.

Ravier flinched, clenched his fingers into fists and said, "That is the Land of No Return."

"The Land of No Return?" Why did that place sound familiar? Because his mother had mentioned it. "That's where the king banished my dad to?"

"Yes."

"Do you think it's possible he's still alive?"

Ravier stared at the map. "No one who's ever been sent there has ever come back."

"That's not what I asked. I asked if you think he's still alive."

Ravier shook his head. "No." He clapped his hands and rubbed them together. "Back to the chalkboard. You have more history to learn."

Javan, angry with his grandfather for giving him no hope and dropping the subject of his father so carelessly, returned to his seat.

He would sit and listen to Ravier lecture.

But when the lectures were done and he had a dragon to ride, Javan planned a trip to the Land of No Return.

He would find out for himself if his father was alive or dead.

CHAPTER 19

A History Lesson

Ravier resumed his place behind the podium and rubbed his eyes. "Where were we?" he asked.

"Zandador and Japheth parted ways." Javan yawned. "It's getting late, and it's been a long day. Can we please pick this up in the morning?"

Ravier slapped the podium at the same time he yelled, "Do you want to save your mother?"

Javan jumped in his seat, banging his knees on the underside of the desk. "Yes. That's why I'm here."

"Then pay attention." Ravier erased his map of Earth from the chalkboard and continued his lecture. "Zandador took charge of the Great Rift and dispersed the animals to the region best suited to their well-being. Stalkers were given the task of patrol to ensure no predators ever made their way back through the portal.

"A hundred and six years passed. Man multiplied on the earth. Animals multiplied in the Great Rift. All the animals except the dragons."

"Why not dragons?"

"For some reason, dragon eggs wouldn't hatch. So it was left to eight dragons to fight against hostile and growing populations of dinosaurs, flying lions, six-legged bears and giant spiders, to name a few. Two dragons were killed; the other six were in dire need of help.

"Zandador opened the portal, flew across the ocean and attempted to telepathically connect with his rider. But Japheth was no longer alive, and the only one who could hear Zandador was the middle of Japheth's seven sons, Javan."

"Whoa. What was his name?"

"Javan, your namesake. He was the first human leader of the Great Rift."

"So my mom didn't give me some weird, random name. Nice."

Ravier took a deep breath. "Moving on. Javan ignored Zandador's telepathic plea, certain he was imagining the voice he was hearing even though his father had passed along the scales and tales of Zandador and the Great Rift to him.

"At about that same time, a turning point in human history occurred. Man—who at this point still all spoke one language—was not dispersing and filling the Earth as God commanded. God intervened by introducing new languages and creating confusion."

"Now you're talking about Babel." Javan was familiar with this Bible story, too. "That's where people started speaking different languages and couldn't understand each other."

"Exactly. Javan and a small number of others, including his daughters and nephews and their families, spoke English. As a group, they decided to band together, follow Javan to the Great Rift and answer the dragon's cry for help.

"Each of the nephews were sons of Javan's brothers, so each of Japheth's seven sons were represented. They built a boat and used Zandador's wings as sails to speed their trip across the Atlantic.

"Once they entered the Great Rift, Javan ordered the people to find dragon eggs so they could take them back to Earth to hatch. But the only one who had any luck finding eggs was Greshon, son of Tiras, Japheth's youngest son. He and his family became known as the Protectors and oversaw the transport of the eggs to Earth. After the dragons hatched, they transported them back to the Land of Zandador.

"With the new influx of dragons, Javan chose four stalkers to ride and became the leader of his own collection. He and other Collectors worked with the dragons to fight the dinosaurs and won back control of the land."

"Where did the dinosaurs go?"

"They migrated north to Tirza, turned on each other and wiped themselves out."

"Bummer."

"Bummer? What does that mean?"

"It means I was hoping to see some dinosaurs. They're extinct on Earth, too. Oh, well." Javan shrugged. "What happened after the dragons beat the dinosaurs?"

"For the first 599 years, Javan led the people. He started by dividing the Land of Zandador into eleven regions: four stalker territories and seven human territories. To honor his brothers and father, Javan named six of the regions after his brothers and the seventh—the capital city—after his father.

"The dragons taught the humans how to use the resources of the land—including their own scales—to build houses and power them. In exchange, the humans worked with the dragons to transport one egg to Earth a year to hatch. Once it hatched, they brought it back to Zandador to live. They also helped protect the dragons from predators during shedding seasons."

"Shedding seasons? What's that?"

"Once a year for the first ten years of its life, a dragon sheds its scales. Then the shedding time is reduced to once every ten years. It takes about three weeks for a dragon to grow a new set of scales, which also double as a defensive shield. Without its scales, dragons are helpless against attack."

"Did not know that." Javan decided that was a good thing to write in his notebook.

"As I already mentioned, those who took the eggs to Earth became known as Protectors. They would also bring back earthly news to Zandador when they returned home."

"Is that how you know so much about Earth?"

"Yes. Our worlds are similar, especially in the way we measure time. That's why we mimicked the calendar system Earth developed. We use the same days, weeks and months as Earth; the major difference, however, is the year. Our historical timeline began when the first fortynine entered the Great Rift."

"Got it. That means this is August like it is on earth. But what year does that make it here?"

"It's 4200, a Battle for the Throne year. No one has entered the competition, though."

"Not yet."

"Right. Not yet. And you can't until you have a better understanding of our history."

Javan groaned. He wasn't sure how much more of this history he could handle. When would Ravier stop talking so they could start fighting? But the dull pain that lingered from the shot he took to the nose earlier reminded him he wasn't ready for action. He slumped back in his chair and listened to Ravier teach on.

CHAPTER 20

Bloodlines

Ravier turned back to the chalkboard and wrote as he talked. "In the beginning, the people in Zandador lived by a simple code of conduct that included five things to do and five things not to do.

"The positives: honor God; love and respect each other; live with integrity; work for what you own and eat; help those in need. The negatives: do not steal; do not murder; do not commit adultery; do not build in the dragon territories; do not hunt in the dragon territories."

"Good rules. But from what I understand about the guy who is king now, he doesn't follow those rules."

"No, he doesn't. You see, when Javan suddenly died in the year 599 from a spider bite, the people disagreed about who should take his place as leader and how humans should interact with the dragons."

"What do you mean, how humans should interact with dragons?"

"Four factions developed: Collectors, Protectors, Hunters and Destroyers. Each descended from one of Japheth's seven sons."

"Seven sons? Four factions? That math seems a little off."

"Not if you know that the descendants of three of the sons—Magog, Tubal and Meschech—wanted nothing to do with the conflict. Magog's sons were adventure seekers, built ships and sailed off into the ocean. To this day, no one knows what became of them.

"Tubal's sons developed a genetic tendency toward dwarfism. They were tired of being overlooked because of their height and moved north to set up their own secluded community in the Thickets of Gibbet."

"Dwarves? Oh, like that dude we met who now has my watch."

"Exactly. Not many dwarves live in Zandador, but some like to make their home in this land."

"What about the third group?"

"They were descendants of Meschech and were the intellectuals of the bunch. They had a peculiar genetic feature as well."

"Let me guess. Giants?"

"No. Albinos."

"Not as neat as giants, but okay."

"They moved to the region of Xyies and made their homes in the underground caves."

"I don't think I'll be visiting them."

"No one does. Anyway, the Collectors you're familiar with. They were direct descendants of Javan and tend to have tan skin and dark or red hair like us. They're also the only ones with the ability to communicate telepathically with the dragons. They believed man should work with the dragons and that the dragons were able to thrive when given a purpose: to serve and protect man. Riding dragons and thus gaining their loyalty gave the dragons that purpose without the dragons having to lose their free will."

"Their free will?"

"If a Collector asks one of his dragons to do something the dragon does not agree with, the dragon has the right and ability to refuse."

"Oh. Okay." Javan nodded. "What about the Protectors? What did they believe?"

"The Protectors, brown-skinned peoples with black hair, brown, or red hair, were direct descendants of Japheth's youngest son, Tiras. They thought dragons should be free and have no one to look after except themselves. They believed man should protect the dragons—especially when they were most vulnerable during shedding seasons—not the other way around."

"These were the people who worked the portal, right?"

"Yes. They were the only ones with the knowledge to activate the portal and became responsible for transporting dragon eggs to Earth, then bringing the hatched dragon back to Zandador."

"All right. Collectors can talk to the dragons, and Protectors can work the portal. What's unique about the Hunters?"

"The Hunters, dark-skinned peoples, had an insatiable thirst for power and control. They were direct descendants of Japheth's oldest son Gomer and discovered that a dragon would become subservient to anyone who cut off the tip of its tail. They believed dragons were to be used, not be useful. Their goal was to enslave all dragons, and use those dragons as tools to gain power over man."

"Is there any way to free a dragon if its tail has been chopped off?"

"Only if its master dies. But with no one to take orders from, the dragon usually dies soon after its master."

"That's sad."

"The Destroyers, who grew to be unusually tall, were worse. They were the direct descendants of Japheth's third son, Madai. They hated dragons, wanted nothing to do with dragon scales and wanted to wipe out all dragons by beheading them."

"Why?"

"They built one of their first villages on Dawn Stalker territory, something Javan strictly forbade. The Dawn Stalkers showed their disapproval of the encroachment by attacking the village and killing the inhabitants."

"Guess those people should have listened to Javan."

"They should have." Ravier put the chalk down, wiped his hands and leaned on the podium. "Since these four factions, or Bloodlines, couldn't agree how to govern, they chose to fight it out. Whoever collected, protected, hunted or destroyed four dragons first would assume the throne for 100 years. Then, in the last year of the king's reign, another dragon battle would ensue to determine who would rule for the next 100 years."

"What if no one won?"

"Then the current king would keep the throne for the next century."

"So that's how the guy who is king now has kept the throne for 500 years."

"Right. After Omri's first century, a handful of participants from the varying Bloodlines entered the competition. He had them and their families all killed and threatened anyone with death who dared challenge him again."

"And this is the guy you want me going up against? He's going to kill me the instant he learns about me!"

Ravier looked Javan in the eye. "I won't let that happen."

Javan gulped. For the first time, he felt like his grandfather just might care about him.

"Now," Ravier cleared his throat and continued, "when Addin, a Collector, won the first battle, the Collectors remained in Zandador."

"Where did the losers go?"

"The Destroyers moved north to Tirza. The Hunters moved southeast to Varzack, and the Protectors moved southwest to Keckrick."

"But my mom's a Protector, and she said she grew up in a city in Zandador."

"Some people from all the bloodlines remained in the land and stayed in the cities they had already established. Most of them, however, were bitter and wanted to leave the land. Still, they would send representatives back to Zandador every 100 years for the Battle of the Throne."

"If someone other than a Collector won, did the Collectors have to leave the land?"

"No. A wave of people from the winning Bloodline would take over the capital and surrounding cities, but for the most part, homelands became pretty entrenched."

"Why didn't they set up their own countries with their own kings?"

"The Hunters tried that. They kept to themselves at first but soon realized they needed the food resources Zandador provided. Farmland is scarce in Varzack, so they had to maintain ties with Zandador and submit to the rule of the king."

"Were most of the kings Collectors?"

"For the first three hundred years of the competition, yes. Then a Protector won the throne in 900 and ruled from 901–1000."

"Hold on. How can a Protector win?"

"What do you mean?"

"A Collector has to ride the four dragons, right?"

"Yes."

"Hunters chop off their tales, and Destroyers chop off their heads."

"Correct."

"So what do Protectors do?"

"A Protector 'brands' a dragon as protected by plucking the scale between its eyes."

"Say what?" Javan tried to imagine ripping a scale from Opny's face and shuddered at the idea. "How do they manage to do that without being eaten or drowned in acid like I almost was yesterday?"

"They don't deal with full-grown dragons. Remember, the Protectors are the ones who take the eggs to Earth, have them hatch, then return the baby dragon to Zandador. It takes about a month for a dragon to fully develop its scales.

"If the Protector is able to bond with the dragon and pluck its scale as soon as it develops, that dragon becomes the Protector's responsibility. It can still be hunted, collected or destroyed, so it's the Protector's job to, well, protect it and allow it to remain free in its own habitat. But to this day, no Hunter, Destroyer, or Collector has ever attempted to win a protected dragon knowing that dragon's loyalty lies with the Protector."

"Got it."

"The first Protector king, however, was not a very wise man." Ravier pulled up a chair and sat down in front of Javan. "Up until this point, the portal was activated once a year. Only one Protector with one dragon egg was allowed to go through, so the dragon population only grew at one per year, except in a battle year."

"What happened in a battle year?"

"Eight eggs, two of each stalker, were allowed to hatch. But this king, Yinsur, ordered one egg a week through the portal to hatch."

"That's a lot of dragons to hatch over the span of a hundred years."

"Exactly. There were too many dragons and not enough Collectors to ride them, Hunters to enslave them or Destroyers to kill them. So when the competition for food within the stalker territories became too fierce, the dragons broke the borders and started making meals of humans. The people were getting annihilated and looked to the Destroyers for help.

"That's when a Destroyer, Coredum, rose to power next. He didn't stop with beheading his four dragons. He killed hundreds on his own and built the first Destroyer army. His entire reign was dedicated to eradicating the dragons, and he blocked access to the portal to ensure no new dragons would hatch.

"Meanwhile, the Hunters were determined to prove that their way—enslaving the dragons—was the right way to deal with the dragon population. They trained a band of Hunters during Coredum's rule, and one of them, Ompar, finally won the throne in 1100.

"Ompar used his dragons to hunt the other Collectors, Hunters, Protectors and Destroyers. Nevertheless, Geoff, a Collector, won the throne in 1200. He ruled for 200 years, restoring order and prosperity to the land following the devastating rules of the previous three kings. Then a Hunter followed by three Protectors each ruled for 100 years.

"The Protectors re-opened the portal but permitted no more than four dragons a year—one of each stalker type—to hatch. The dragon population was growing again, but not at the alarming rate it was under the first Protector king."

"The Destroyers probably didn't like that much."

"No, they didn't. They came close to gaining control of the throne next, but a Collector, Benjamin, beat them to it. He ruled from 1801-1900. Then the millennium of Destroyer domination began."

"That doesn't sound good." Javan leaned forward. His fatigue had faded, and he wanted to know more.

CHAPTER 21

Javan's Family Tree

"It wasn't," Ravier said, confirming Javan's suspicion. "The Destroyers, including the first female to ever rule, kept the throne in their Bloodline for 1000 years, starting with Rehoboak. He was brutal and kept the throne for three hundred years. His successors became more and more ruthless, each trying to outdo the bloodbaths of the previous king. Or, in Mari's case, queen. She actually ruled twice, but not in successive years. She lost the throne in 2600 but regained it in 2700.

"By the year 2900, the dragons were in danger of extinction. Had Victoria, a Protector, not rescued four eggs, snuck through the portal and became the Protector of those four baby dragons, we wouldn't be sitting here today." Ravier paused. "Your mother can trace her heritage back to Victoria."

"I have royalty in my blood from both my mom and dad?"

"Yes, you do. But that doesn't mean anything. Here, you have to earn royalty, not inherit it."

"Got it." Javan nodded, but he still liked the idea of having royal blood. "How long did Victoria keep the throne?"

"A century. Then Itrich, a Collector, took over, followed by two Hunters—who were brothers—and Calvin, another Collector. He was my great-grandfather's great-grandfather."

"So that would make him my great-great-great-great-great...nevermind. I need to see this family tree for myself." Trying to figure out how many generations separated him from the Calvin guy was too confusing without writing it. "Help me figure this out."

Javan snatched the chalk from Ravier, erased the board, and wrote his name. "My parents are Dartez and Esmeralda. You and Hannah are my dad's folks. Who is your father?"

"Give me the chalk. This will be easier to explain if I can write it for you." Ravier scribbled for several minutes. When he stepped back, Javan saw his father's family line traced back to Calvin:

Javan
Parents: Dartez and Esmeralda
- Dartez banished to Land of No Return
- Esmeralda alive in Zandador
Grandparents (Dartez's parents): Ravier and Hannah
- both alive Zandador
Great-grandparents (Ravier's parents): Vince and Kaylin
- both live in the city of Japheth and work for Omri
Great-great-grandparents (Vince's parents): Riztish and Meguth
- Riztish killed by Omri
- whereabouts of Meguth unsure (579 years old)
Great-great-great grandparents (Riztish's folks): Kenton and Carolin
- Kenton (699 years old) hiding on earth with two dragons
- Carolin killed by Omri
Great-great-great-great grandparents (Kenton's parents): Leo and Ruth
- alive (in their 900's) but unsure of whereabouts
Great-great-great-great-great grandparents (Leo's parents): Calvin and Jenna
- Calvin reigned as King of Zandador from 3301-3400
- no Collector King has reigned since Calvin
- both deceased

"This is unbelievable." Javan traced his fingers over the names. "I have a...family. A family with history. I'm part of a family's history." He wiped unexpected tears from his eyes and turned to Ravier. "Tell me more. What about aunts, uncles, cousins. And what about my mom's side? What does the family line back to Victoria look like?"

"We don't have time to deal with extended family, and you'll have to ask your mother about her family line once you rescue her." Ravier put the chalk down and wiped his hands. "Can we get back to our story?"

Javan sat down with a renewed interest in learning about Calvin. "Please continue."

"No one won the Battle for the Throne in the year 3400, setting Calvin up for a second term. But a Destroyer, who had come the closest by slaying three dragons, made Calvin his fourth kill and usurped the throne. His son Lancert ruled next, and Lancert's son Quartu ruled from 3601–3700. The combination of their three-hundred year reign led to a massive decline in the already small dragon population.

"In 3700, less than fifty dragons remained, and Kenton and Omri were among those who battled for the throne."

Javan sat up straighter in his seat. Ravier was starting to use names of people who were still alive and whom Javan recognized. "Kenton, as in the dude I met on Earth, and Omri, the jerk who's king now?"

"Yes."

"What happened? Please tell me Kenton won first and that Omri's only king now cause he won the next competition."

"That's not what happened."

"Our guy lost?"

"In a way."

"How can you lose 'in a way'?"

"With a week left in the competition, both men were tied at three stalkers each. Kenton needed a Dawn Stalker, and Omri needed a Dusk Stalker. Kenton found and rode his Dawn Stalker, finishing his collection first. He was on his way to the capital to claim victory when Omri stopped him.

"Instead of capturing his required Dusk Stalker, Omri had captured Kenton's wife Carolin. He had a knife to her throat and threatened to kill her unless Kenton traded Eli, his Dusk Stalker, for Carolin."

"Kenton made the trade, didn't he?"

"Yes. But even though he cut off Eli's tail, he's never had complete control over that dragon. He keeps it locked away, knowing its true loyalty lies with Kenton."

"We have to rescue that dragon."

"The only way to do that is to win the throne by gaining your own dragon collection."

"Then enough of this history stuff." Javan closed his notebook and stood. His mother, father and now this dragon were depending on him. "Teach me how to collect dragons. Now."

CHAPTER 22

Collecting Basics

"This is stupid." Javan stood ten feet off the ground on one of the lowest okty perches in the barn. He was swaying back and forth on the round piece of wood barely wider than his foot and clinging so tightly to the rope attached like a trapeze swing to the high ceiling above that his knuckles were turning white.

Thanks to Ravier and one tiny little pebble he used to disturb the slumber of one big okty, all twenty five okties that lived in barn were now flitting and floating all over the spacious place.

"This is practice," Ravier said. He was sitting in a chair by the wall sipping a cup of water.

"I'm supposed to land on the backs of one of these okties as they fly by?"

"Yes."

"That's crazy!"

"That's what Collectors do. Only when you're attempting to ride a dragon, you're in a tree hundreds of feet off the ground. You have to stay there for hours or days on end without giving away your position while waiting to land on the back of an unsuspecting dragon who would like nothing more than to tear your skinny little body to shreds."

"Dragons are bigger and easier to land on than these okties."

"They can also fly, teleport and run with incredible speed. Trust me. These okties are much easier to ride." Ravier put his cup down and crossed his arms. "Jump on the next one that flies by. If you miss, don't break any bones when you hit the ground."

"Thanks for the advice." Javan was hoping for more helpful instructions like how to time his jump or how to choose what okty to ride.

At least Ravier wasn't making him practice from one of the twenty or thirty foot perches. Javan was much more likely to break a leg falling from that height.

Minutes passed. All the okties that flew near him were either too high up to jump on or at the wrong angle for him to be able to land squarely on its back.

Finally, Javan noticed a pure white okty floating near ground level under the frantic flying of all the winged creatures above her. He knew it was a female because her wings were round; the male wings were more angular.

"Come on, come on," he said, waiting for her to coast under his perch. The second he saw her head under his feet, he took a deep breath, closed his eyes and jumped.

She must have seen him coming because she spiked upward. His hands grazed her wing, but the rest of his body missed the animal completely. He slammed into the hard dirt floor, his right side taking most of the hit.

Ravier leaned forward in his chair. "You missed."

"Glad you noticed, O great teacher." Javan spit dirt out of his mouth. "I don't know what happened. I should have been able to land right on her back."

"You spooked her, made too much noise getting off the perch. You lack stealth."

"I can be stealthy."

"Prove it. Get up and try again."

Ravier whistled, and a pink okty with one dotted black streak across her left wing landed in front of Javan. "Here we go again." Javan hopped on, rode back up to the perch and transferred himself to the wooden swing. "Be stealthy," he said, working to stabilize himself.

He was just about to launch himself onto an orange and black male okty when a giant of a man burst through the door. The man filled the doorway from top to bottom and side to side. Scraggly red hair and a beard to match hung just past his wide shoulders.

"Where's the kid?" His booming voice flustered the few okties who had settled back onto their perches. "Hannah told me I needed to come meet the kid."

"Hamilton, would you get in here and close the door?" Ravier waved his hand around. "I don't want any okties escaping."

"Sure, sure." He stepped inside and closed the door. That's when he noticed Javan. "You must be the kid."

"Yup."

Hamilton, whose head was only a few feet lower than the perch, walked over to Javan and reached up to shake his hand. "Hamilton's the name," he said. "My sweet granddaughter Hannah talked her tongue off bragging about you, kid. She said you're going to collect dragons, save your mama and win the throne of Zandador."

The more he talked, the faster he talked. The faster he talked, the harder he shook Javan's hand. Javan had to fight to keep his balance, and that made it hard to focus on anything Hamilton was saying.

"We haven't had a good battle of the throne in centuries," Hamilton continued, "and I had to come be a part of it. I'm here to help with your training, kid."

As Hamilton let go of Javan's hand, Ravier stormed up beside him. "Not necessary, Hamilton. I can handle his training."

"I'm sure you can." Hamilton slapped Ravier on the back. Javan chuckled when Ravier stumbled and nearly fell from the friendly blow. "I'm only here to assist. What do we have to work with here? How's the kid in hand to hand combat?"

"Useless. No experience."

"What about weapons? Better with blasters or swords?"

"Neither. No experience with anything."

"A Collector who doesn't know how to fight? Seriously?"

Ravier shrugged his shoulders. "He's been coddled on earth. His weak upbringing leaves us with a pretty hopeless Collector competitor."

"Hey!" Javan said. "I'm standing right here!"

Yelling didn't do any good. The men ignored him and continued their conversation. "He might have some redeemable skills," Hamilton said. "How is he in the woods? Good instincts?"

"He walked right past ola berries when we had no food in the woods and nearly got himself sucked into a lake of swallowing sand in the quagmire."

"No survival skills, either." Hamilton shook his head. "What can he do?"

"I can take care of myself in the woods," Javan said. "I used to camp all the time back home in Montana." Once again, the men ignored him.

"Nothing."

"Surely he can do something." Hamilton snapped his fingers. "The four S's. How would you rate him in the four S's?"

"Okay. Let's see." Ravier held up his index finger to start counting. "First is strength. Look at him. He's a stick. He has no strength."

"Speed. What about speed? With his frame, he might be quick."

"Perhaps." Ravier shook his head. "I don't want to speculate. I've never seen him run."

"I'm fast," Javan said. "And agile."

Both men looked up at him, then looked at each other. "Kid says he's fast," Hamilton said. "That's a start. How about stamina?"

"Lousy," Ravier said. "We took a little walk the other day, and I thought I was going to have to tie him to my waist and drag him behind me."

"A little walk?" Javan had to defend himself. "That walk lasted the entire day, and I kept up with you."

Ravier scowled at Javan. "Barely. You sure did a lot of complaining along the way."

Javan opened his mouth to argue, but this time he had no defense. He wasn't exactly shy about letting Ravier know how much he hated having to walk all those miles to Torix.

"We'll give the kid credit for a little stamina."

"Fine," Ravier said. "But he gets no credit for the fourth S, stealth. He's so loud up there on that perch that no okties will come near him. Then he spooks the ones that do."

"We can work with this." Hamilton started pacing. "He's got speed and stamina. We can build strength and help him develop stealth. You're an expert with any kind of weapon, and no one's a better fighter than me. Between the two of us, we can teach him how to be a fighting machine."

"A fighting machine?" Javan nodded. "I like the sound of that. But who's going to teach me how to ride dragons?"

"That's where I come in." A small man with stooped shoulders, thinning white hair and spectacles spoke softly from behind Hamilton. "I can teach you everything you need to know about tracking dragons, surviving in their habitat, riding them and caring for them once you have collected them."

"Astor?" Ravier ran to the man's side and led him to the chair Ravier had been sitting in to watch Javan. "When did you get here?"

"Moments ago. I would have been here sooner, but Hannah had difficulty waking me." He chuckled and looked at Javan. "My apologies, young Collector. I'm a very sound sleeper."

"So you've collected dragons yourself?"

"Oh no, my child. I'm not from the Collector Bloodline, but I have assisted many Collectors in their quest to win the throne."

"Have any of them succeeded?"

"One. Calvin. I served on his counsel and helped care for his dragons during his reign. Another should have succeeded: Calvin's grandson, Kenton."

"Whoa. Kenton's super old, and you were alive to help his grandfather? You must be way super old." Javan said.

Astor chuckled. "I have been around for a while."

Javan wondered just how old Astor was but had a more pressing matter on his mind. Turning his attention to Hamilton and Ravier, he asked, "What about you two? Have either of you collected a dragon?"

"Well...ummm...no," Hamilton said, shuffling his feet and averting his gaze.

Ravier, however, stood straight up and looked Javan directly in the eye. "My father denied our Collector heritage and raised me according to Omri's rules. I never had the opportunity you have now to learn about collecting dragons."

Javan sat on his perch and swung back and forth. He bit his lip and studied his collection of teachers.

One was so old he couldn't stand for more than two seconds.

One was big and boisterous and was likely to squash the life out of Javan in the process of teaching him how to fight.

One was grouchy and bitter and didn't believe in Javan despite the fact they were related by blood.

And none of them had ever collected a dragon of their own.

Javan's chances of success seemed to grow more impossible by the moment.

CHAPTER 23

Target Practice

"Up! Up! Up!" Ravier flooded Javan's room with light and stripped him of his covers. "Enough sleep. We're wasting training time."

Javan squinted against the bright lights, curled into a little ball and checked his watch only to be reminded that he no longer owned a watch. Since he had yet to figure out how to read the triangle clock made of the four Stalker scales that apparently told time based on the color of the scales, he moaned and sat up. "What time is it?"

"Dawn Stalker feeding time."

"So that means it's what, six o'clock? Why couldn't you just say six?"

"You need to start thinking of time in terms of stalker feeding times. It's something you must constantly be aware of, especially when you have your own collection. Now get up, get dressed and meet me in the training room."

Ravier disappeared, and Javan collapsed back on the bed. He covered his eyes with his arm and wondered how he was going to survive the day.

Long after Hamilton and Astor left last night, Ravier had made Javan jump off that stupid perch dozens of times. He grazed a few okties, but not once did he land on anything except the hard dirt floor. His body felt like one giant bruise, and he was afraid he might cry if he had to try to ride another okty today.

But his mother's life was depending on him.

Replaying the sight of Micah carrying her away brought Javan to his feet. He was the reason she got caught. He thus had to do whatever it took to rescue her.

He just hoped he didn't end up with a body full of broken bones. That would make saving her rather challenging.

◊　◊　◊

The sun was beginning to rise as Javan made his way across the yard, through the okty barn and down into the training room.

The life-sized human and animal targets that were spread all over the place last night were now grouped together and shoved to the far left corner. That left a clear line of sight to the circular paper targets Ravier was attaching to the wall opposite the wall of weapons in a nice, neat chest-high row.

The man already looked irritable and grumpy.

"Where's Hamilton?" Javan asked. He had taken more of a liking to Hannah's grandfather than his own and was expecting the good-natured man to be around to help lighten Ravier's constantly dark mood.

"He'll be here later." Ravier finished hanging his last target and met Javan at the wall of weapons. "Our first order of business is matching you with the right weapon. Every Collector has one go-to weapon, and we have to find yours."

"Sweet." Javan's eyes lit up and his soreness faded away as he reached for the bow and the quiver of arrows. "I want to try this first."

Ravier nodded. "A classic choice. Many Collectors have been excellent archers, your father included."

Javan strapped the quiver across his back so that he could easily reach the feathered end of the arrows with his right hand. Then he inspected the long wooden bow that extended from his head to his thighs. "My dad shot this bow?"

"Yes. He shot with such speed, ease and precision that you didn't even realize he had taken the shot until the arrow was lodged in his target." The pride in Ravier's voice fell away when he addressed Javan. "Load the bow and shoot. Hit the target on the back wall."

"Which one?"

"It doesn't matter. Just pick one."

"No problem." Javan had learned how to shoot arrows at summer camp a few years ago. This bow was bigger than the one he used back then, but mastering this weapon should be easy.

Javan loaded the first arrow and attempted to pull the string back.

It wouldn't budge.

"Um," he said, "I think this bow is broken."

"It's not broken. Pull harder."

Javan bit his bottom lip and tried again. Nothing. On the third try, the string gave a little only to immediately return to its taut position. The arrow tumbled pitifully to the floor.

Ravier picked it up. "This isn't your weapon. Put it back. Let's try the spear."

"Give me one more chance." Javan took the arrow from Ravier, loaded the bow and pulled the string back as far as he could. That turned out to only be a few inches. His hands and arms started shaking. He could no longer pull or hold his current position, so he released the string and fired the arrow.

The arrow flew all of two feet.

"The sword," Ravier said, taking the bow and arrows from Javan and handing him a long, hefty sword. The tip of the handle to the tip of the sword spanned the distance from Javan's shoulders to his toes. "This is my preferred weapon. You were admiring it the other day. Now let's see if you're any good at using it."

Javan nearly lost his balance as he used both hands to pick the sword up. Well, attempt to pick it up, anyway. He could barely bring the tip higher than his knees, much less raise it high enough to fight with it. "This thing is heavy!"

"You're right. I should have known. You're too frail and don't have the strength for such a weapon." Ravier traded the sword for a weapon that looked something like a cross-bow. "The jolt blast might be a good weapon for you. It's something even your grandmother can shoot."

"I remember." Javan cringed. He did not want to be on the receiving end of this weapon ever again.

Javan inspected the black, warm rifle-type handle with his right hand and propped the flat, inch-wide shaft on top of his left hand. Two black triangular stalker scales were attached to one another above the handle; one pointed end faced Javan while the other pointed end faced away from Javan and had a hook carved into its tip.

A wide bow made of the same black material as the handle was fastened to the end of the shaft, and a golden string connected the tips of the bow. Javan pulled the string back, connected it to the hooked tip of the scale and looked at Ravier. "Don't I need arrows or something to load and shoot?"

"No. That's the great thing about this weapon. Because it's made entirely of Midnight Stalker scales taken from a stalker at the height of its feeding time, it generates its own ammunition: lightning bolts. All you have to do is hook the string to the scale and pull the trigger. The string scraping the shaft focuses the energy and sends a bolt of lightning in whatever direction you aim."

"Nice." Javan inspected the weapon with a new sense of admiration. "That is so much cooler than a sword or a bow and arrows."

He lifted the jolt blast to shoulder height and aimed at a target directly in front of him.

"It does have a little kick to it," Ravier warned.

"I can handle it." He narrowed his eyes, focusing only on the center of the target. After three deep breaths, he pulled the trigger.

The blast lifted him off his feet and sent him sailing ten feet backwards. His body collided with the wall while his head knocked into a sleek steel box hanging high on the wall.

Both Javan and the box plummeted to the floor. The long, thin box opened on impact, but the unconscious Javan didn't notice.

CHAPTER 24

Stun Balls and Stalker Swords

"Javan! Javan!"

Javan slowly became aware of Ravier shouting his name, slapping his cheeks and shaking his shoulders. "What happened?" Javan asked, rubbing his now throbbing head. "Did I hit the target?"

"No. But you did burn a hole in the ceiling."

Javan looked up and inspected his handiwork. A hole several inches deep and wide as well as a good fifteen feet long was seared into the dirt ceiling. "Oops."

"You're not allowed to shoot the jolt blast anymore." Ravier stood and took a long, thick wooden pole with a sharp iron point off the wall. "Get up. Try the spear. Maybe you can throw better than you can shoot."

"I can throw—wait a minute." When Javan moved to get up, his leg knocked the box that had fallen with him. "What's this?"

Javan pulled a leather belt out of the open box. What looked like tiny spiked footballs lined the back of the belt. Two black sheaths hung at an angle from either side of the belt, and each held a dagger roughly the length of Javan's arm. A spiked football like those on the belt topped the white handle of one dagger and the grey handle of the other.

"This is cool." Javan stood, strapped the belt on and drew the daggers. Based on the angle of the sheaths, he drew the dagger on his right hip with his left hand and the dagger on his left hip with his right hand. Much to his surprise, there was a half-inch gap between the end of the handle and beginning of the blade; only a thin piece of steel connected the two pieces.

Even more surprising, though, was the color of the sharp, simple, triangular blades. The blade on the dagger with the grey handle was black on one side and golden on the other. The blade with the white handle was streaked with red, orange, purple and pink on one side and blue, green, purple and pink on the other.

"Put those away," Ravier said. "They are useless toys, not weapons meant for a Collector."

Javan swished the daggers in the air, liking the balanced feel of the beautiful blades. "I can do some damage with these weapons. What are they called?"

Ravier sighed. "They're stalker swords and have been in the family for thousands of years. Kara, the wife of the third Collector king, made them as a way of honoring the four types of Dragon Stalkers. They're the only ones ever made and are for decoration, not for fighting."

"I'm not so sure." Javan studied the stalker swords in his hands. They felt strong and steady and ready for battle. "I could fight with these."

"Nonsense. Put them back in their sheaths, and take that silly belt off."

"Fine." Javan sheathed the swords. Before he took the belt off, though, he plucked one of the mini footballs off of it. It was sheer black with two rows of tiny white spikes: one where the seams would normally be on a football and another directly opposite it. He turned it over a few times, then gripped the unspiked sides using his first three fingers and thumb. One row of spikes faced his palm and the other faced out. "What are these?"

"More toys. They're called stun balls. They're only effective if you throw them with a precise spiral spin and deadly accurate aim."

"Hmmm. Interesting." Maybe all that football throwing practice he did this past summer wasn't going to be a complete waste after all. "What do they do?"

"If they're thrown with the right spin, claws come out of the tips mid-air. The claws attach to the target, and the spikes emit shock waves that render your target motionless for several minutes."

"Can I throw one?"

"Very few people have ever been able to make them work, which is why they are rare, useless, outdated weapons. Besides, you have to have a live target to make them work, and I don't want you throwing one of those spiked things at me whether it stuns me or not."

Javan was about to throw the ball at Ravier anyway when Hamilton's large frame spilled down the ladder. "Hello, boys! Great morning, isn't it?" He slapped his hands together and rubbed them back and forth. "I hope you're ready to do some fighting, kid."

Javan nodded toward Hamilton as he asked Ravier, "Can I throw it at him?"

Ravier shrugged. "Sure."

Hamilton dropped his hands. "Throw what at me?"

"This." Javan cocked his arm back and flung the stun ball. It sailed toward Hamilton in a perfect spiral motion, unlocking the claws in the tip. The claws locked into the center of Hamilton's chest followed by a high-pitched shriek.

Javan wasn't sure if the shriek came from Hamilton or the ball, but he was sure that Hamilton was suddenly as still as a statue.

◊   ◊   ◊

For several minutes, Javan and Ravier circled the stunned Hamilton while listening to the low whirr of the ball attached to his chest. Hamilton's eyes remained wide open as though he was frozen in time.

"I've never seen him this still or this quiet before," Ravier said.

"How long do you think he's going to stay this way?"

"I don't know. I've never actually seen one of these balls work."

"Should I take it off of him?"

"Not yet. Let's see if it comes off on its own. I think it's supposed to."

"You're the boss."

The longer Javan watched the frozen Hamilton, the more guilty he felt for attacking the man without warning. Just when he was ready to reach for the ball to revive the man, the whirring stopped, the claw retracted and the ball clunked to the floor.

"Was that a…" Hamilton shook his head and massaged his eyes. "Was that a stun ball?"

"Yes," Ravier said. "Sorry. I didn't think he'd be able to make it work."

"Yeah, sorry man," Javan said. "Didn't mean to hurt you."

"Kid, you didn't hurt me; you just stunned me." He chuckled and slapped Javan on the back. "Nicely done. And are you wearing the stalker swords? Wow. No Collector has ever used stun balls or the stalker swords as his weapon. Most go with the standard backsword or bow and arrow. You're just full of surprises."

"Don't be absurd, Hamilton. Not even the dragons will take him seriously as a Collector if he shows up to any fight with these toys. We're still trying to find his ideal weapon. He just happened to knock these down when he lost control of the jolt blast." Ravier held out his hand. "Give me the belt, Javan."

Javan hung his head and reached for the buckle. But giving up the belt didn't feel right. He knew he could learn to fight with these weapons. They were a much better fit for him than taut bows, mega swords and overpowering jolt blasts.

"No," he said, crossing his arms. "I've made my choice. Stalker swords and stun balls."

"No," Ravier said. He crossed his arms to match Javan. "I won't allow it."

"I won't fight with anything else."

"No."

"Come on, Ravier," Hamilton said. "It's brilliant. No one is going to be expecting him to use these antiquated weapons. The shock value alone could win him a dragon or two."

Ravier huffed, then relented. "You're sure these are the weapons you want to master?"

"I'm sure," Javan said.

"I know I'm going to regret this." Ravier hung his head. "Then stalker swords and stun balls it is."

"Great!" Javan turned to Hamilton. "Thanks."

"No problem, kid." His entire demeanor changed to stone-cold seriousness. "Now take off that belt. It's time to learn to fight with your fists."

CHAPTER 25

Fighting with Fists

"**H**it you?" Javan stared at the man twice his size standing in the middle of the training room coaxing him to attack. "That's nuts, Hamilton. You're way bigger than me. Can't I fight Ravier?"

"If you can learn how to fight me, you can learn how to fight any midget your own size."

"Don't we need protective gear or something?"

"Protective gear?"

"Yeah. Stuff to protect my hands and face, like boxing gloves and a helmet."

"I don't know what kind of sissy fighting you do on earth, but we don't have that stuff here. Just hit me. It's not hard."

"It's hard when you've never hit anybody before. Where I come from, hitting someone is not a good thing."

"In your situation," Ravier said from the sidelines, "it's a necessary thing. Now walk up to the man and hit him."

Javan swallowed, flexed his fingers and obeyed Ravier's command. As he approached Hamilton, he balled his fingers into fists and looked up. His head barely reached above Hamilton's wide waistline. This was going to be a disaster.

"Let's get this over with," Javan muttered. He swung his arm back and jabbed his right fist into Hamilton's gut. His fist bounced back as though it had slammed into a trampoline.

"Don't tap me," Hamilton said. "I won't break. Punch me."

"I did!"

"That was a punch? You can do better. Try again."

This time, Javan delivered a series of alternating punches with both his right and left fists. Hamilton just chewed on his fingernails like nothing was happening.

"You can start hitting any time," Hamilton said. "I'm ready."

Javan bit his bottom lip to keep his growing anger in check and looked back at Ravier. Seeing him laughing only made Javan more upset. "That's it," Javan said. "Forget the fists. It's time to tackle."

The only experience he had with violence was tackling in football practice. Granted, he was the one who got tackled, but he had been tackled enough to know how it worked.

He stepped back about five feet, then charged forward. He rammed his shoulder straight into Hamilton's left leg. When the man didn't move, Javan latched on and tugged.

"What are you doing?" Hamilton asked.

"I'm tackling you," Javan squeaked out as he strained to make Hamilton lose his balance.

"Oh." Hamilton crossed his arms and sighed. "Carry on."

"I will." Javan pulled and squeezed a little longer. No progress. Out of breath, he let go and stepped back. "New strategy," he said.

This time, he ran up behind Hamilton and leaped onto his back. He wrapped his arms around Hamilton's neck and screamed while swaying from side to side, trying to pull him down.

The new strategy was as ineffective as the first.

"Okay," Hamilton said. "That's enough." He leaned forward, grabbed Javan's waist and flipped him over his shoulder to the floor.

The collision knocked the breath out of Javan. So he just laid there, eyes closed, humiliated, trying to remember how to breathe. "Told you that was an unfair fight," he finally managed to say.

"It was only unfair because you had no idea what you were doing." Hamilton helped Javan to his feet and led him to the chair by the chalkboard. "Have a seat while I use Ravier to teach you a few things about fighting."

◊　　◊　　◊

Sitting down was both good and bad.

It was good because it gave Javan a chance to rest his weary body. It was bad because now he had nothing to do to take his mind off his splitting headache and aching muscles. The only thing keeping him glued to his seat and attentive to Hamilton's teaching was the hope that Javan would see Hamilton use Ravier as a live punching bag to illustrate his moves.

"When you're fighting a Hunter like Micah," Hamilton was saying, "there's only one rule: don't die."

"Good rule," Javan said.

"If you try to fight him like you just fought me, you're going to break that rule."

"I'll have stun balls and stalker swords to help me out."

"You have to know how to defend yourself if you get caught without your weapons."

Javan rubbed his temples. "I'm listening."

"When you're attacked, your best defense is to strike at one of your opponent's vulnerable points."

"What, like his groin?"

"Exactly."

Javan crossed his legs. "That seems kind of cruel."

"You're trying to survive here, kid." Hamilton leaned down. His frizzy hair grazed Javan's forehead while his naturally hazel eyes bore into Javan's contact-colored brown eyes. "You can't play nice."

"No playing nice," Javan said. "Got it."

"Good." Hamilton raised himself back to his giant height and put his hands on Ravier's shoulders. "A man's eyes, ears, nose, jaw and throat are ideal targets. You can scratch or poke his eyes, break his nose, tear or bite his ears, knock him out with a punch to the jaw or produce a choking pain with a chop to the throat."

Javan's hands instinctively moved to protect his throat. "What if he's much taller than me, and I can't reach his face?"

"You aim for lower vulnerable points like his feet, shins and joints. You can crush his toes, kick his shins or bust his kneecaps." Hamilton turned Ravier around and fake punched his lower back. "If you have a shot at his lower back, you can punch his kidneys.

"From the front," Hamilton continued, spinning Ravier back around and throwing a few more fake punches to the middle of his chest and stomach, "you can attack his solar plexus or abdomen to wind him."

"Think I got it," Javan said. He stood and pointed out all Ravier's vulnerable points as he spoke. "Poke the eyes, break the nose, rip the ears, punch the jaw, chop the throat, punch the chest, stomach and kidneys, bust the kneecaps, kick the shins, stomp the toes and crush the groin."

Javan watched the aggravation in Ravier's eyes grow to infuriation at the threat of being hit by Javan in any part of his body. He stood there silently fuming while Javan's smile grew broader.

"Good!" Hamilton slapped Javan on the back, knocking him off balance. Now it was Ravier's turn to smile at Javan's discomfort. Hamilton seemed oblivious to the tension between the two men and carried on with his lesson. "Your objective is to strategically attack those points with your punches, elbows and kicks while keeping your own body protected. First, though, all we're going to focus on is your punches."

"Okay," Javan said, turning his attention away from the glowering Ravier and toward Hamilton. "Teach me."

"There are four basic punches: the jab, the cross, the hook and the uppercut. You'll learn them all, but today I just want you to practice the jab and the cross."

Hamilton led Javan across the room to the cluster of targets. He pulled one out from the cluster, a faceless man that stood a foot taller than Javan. It had a thick torso and lifeless arms that dangled by its sides.

"To throw the jab," Hamilton said, "you start in the guard position." As Hamilton spoke, he positioned Javan in front of the target. "Angle your body toward the target with your left foot in front of your right and your fists raised to the side of your chin with your left in front of your right."

"Now what?" Javan asked. "I just hit the dude?"

"First you make sure you have a solid fist. Curl your fingers a little tighter and squeeze them between your thumb and tiny finger." Hamilton pressed Javan's fingertips into his palm and adjusted his thumb. "Make sure you keep your thumb pulled way back so you don't hurt it when you punch."

Javan inspected his fists and threw a few mini air punches while Hamilton continued his coaching session.

"You want to strike your target with your two biggest knuckles while keeping the back of your hand even with the top of your forearm. Keep your arm relaxed as you throw the punch. When your fist connects, that's when you tense your muscles and throw the hip of your punching arm forward. Remember to punch into the target; aim for a point inside the guy's body, not the surface."

"I can do this," Javan said, shuffling his weight back and forth between his feet. "Big knuckles. Hand even with forearm. Relaxed muscles. Hip forward. Punch into the body."

"You got it, kid. Now, you throw the jab with your forward hand and the cross with your rear hand. I'll show you." Hamilton stood behind Javan and grabbed a hold of his forearms. Like a puppet master, he guided Javan's left fist into the target's chest followed by his right fist. "Any questions?"

"Nope."

"Good. Throw a jab into your target's chest. It's a quick punch with your front left hand. When you connect, push the left side of your body forward, twist your fist into the target and pull back."

"Quick punch, quick punch, quick punch," Javan mumbled. He shrugged his shoulders, swung his arms and head from side to side to loosen up and shifted back into his guard position. Taking a deep breath, he locked in on the chest of his target and jabbed his left fist forward.

His knuckles connected with the punching bag-like surface and sprung back before Javan had a chance to try pushing the left side of his body forward and twisting his fist into the target. He grimaced and shook his fingers out to dull the minor pain. "Ouch," he said. "You sure you don't have boxing gloves I can use?"

"Why do you want to wear gloves to fight?" Ravier rolled his eyes. "That's ridiculous."

"That move needs work," Hamilton said, shaking his head. "First let me see you throw a cross punch. Get back in your guard position."

Javan quickly massaged his hands, then did as instructed.

"This time you'll use your rear right hand. Drive your right hip, shoulder and foot forward as you punch into the target."

Javan practiced the weight transference a few times. When he felt prepared, he set up in his guard position, eyed his target and punched. This time the blow had more of an impact on the target than on Javan.

"Hey," Javan said, smiling at Hamilton, "that was kinda fun."

"Not bad," Hamilton said. "You need to use your body more. Get your hip, shoulder and fist all working together, and imagine you're punching through the target's chest. You need more force."

"Okay." Javan threw another cross punch. He jammed his right fist into the target and actually made it shake. "Hah! It moved!"

"Nice work, kid." Hamilton rumpled Javan's hair. "Now do it a thousand more times."

"Say what?"

"Make that two thousand. I want a thousand jabs and a thousand cross punches."

"You can't be serious."

Hamilton crossed his arms and looked down at Javan through his bushy black eyebrows.

"A thousand jabs and a thousand cross punches it is," Javan said, resuming his guard position. This was going to be a very long morning.

CHAPTER 26

The Old Man's Warning

"**O**ne thousand." With a final jab/cross combination, Javan flung his weak and weary fists into the target's chest and dropped to the floor.

He leaned his back against his immobile target's legs, wiped the sweat from his forehead and closed his eyes. If it wasn't for Hamilton's voice still buzzing in his ears from the hours of constant coaching he had just endured, he would have enjoyed the respite.

"Nice work, kid," Hamilton said. "We'll do it all again tomorrow."

"He needs to get stronger," Ravier said. "Those pathetic punches aren't going to get him very far in any fight."

Javan's eyes flew open, and he sprang back into his guard position in front of Ravier. "Maybe after I hit you a few times, you won't think my punches are so pathetic."

Ravier laughed. "Go ahead. Try me. See what happens when your target punches back."

Javan tightened his fists, but Hamilton stuck his thick arm between the two men and pushed Javan back. "No fighting live targets yet, kid," he said, nudging Javan in the direction of the ladder. "Now get yourself up to the house. It's eating time."

Javan glared at Ravier, then looked at the ladder. He was hungry. And tired. Maybe fighting Ravier at the moment wasn't such a great idea. "Food does sound good," Javan said.

"Then go." Hamilton shooed Javan away with his hands. "We'll be up in a minute."

Driven by the thought of food, Javan climbed up the ladder and sprinted through the barn to the exit. He threw the door open but halted just before slamming into the frail Astor.

"Whoa!" Javan said, putting his hands up and sliding past Astor without knocking him over. "Sorry, man. I didn't see you there."

"You see me now," he said, adjusting his spectacles and handing Javan a ball of bread the size of a cantaloupe. "I was just coming to get you. Hannah made you a dragon's delight."

"What's in this?" Javan turned the brown bread over in his hands. It was heavier than he expected a ball of bread to be, and he was a little nervous about biting into it.

"It's filled with meats and leaves from animals and plants dragons feast on."

"Oh." The idea of eating unknown meat and random leaves caused Javan's appetite to suddenly diminish.

"It is healthy and filling. You can eat it on the way."

"On the way? On the way to where?"

"You and I are going to meet Mertzer."

"Who's Mertzer?"

"A Dusk Stalker." Astor put his hand on Javan's elbow and walked him back into the barn. "Come now. Pick an okty. You're going to need a brave one for the trip we're about to take."

◊   ◊   ◊

Micah flew above the farming village on the back of Serenity, his father's Midnight Stalker, and waited for the stragglers to join the crowd on the road outside the gate. The town center of the village was too small to hold all the people and a dragon, so Micah had ordered his men to gather the workers from the fields and bring them to this spot.

Esmeralda's cage dangled by a rope from the dragon's claw, and when Micah was ready to begin, he yelled at Serenity. "Drop her!"

The cage dropped ten feet to the ground and landed near the road with a thud. Esmeralda grunted but couldn't complain thanks to the gag covering her mouth. After one more circle above the area, Micah guided Serenity to land beside the cage.

"I am Micah, the strongest son of the great King Omri." He addressed the crowd from the back of the dragon to maximize the effect of his speech. "King Omri has ruled longer than any king in the history of our world. He deserves and expects your respect and obedience.

"Nevertheless, some dare challenge his laws. When that happens, they are to be punished in order to preserve peace in the land." As he spoke, he scanned the faces, looking for any hint of dissention. "This woman broke the law and will be executed for her actions. I bring her here today to remind you that King Omri does not tolerate rebellion."

Submission. Fear. Acceptance. These people had been trained well, which Micah found disappointing. He wanted to make an example of someone.

A dark-haired man glanced at Esmeralda with pity. Excellent.

"You!" He shouted and pointed at the man as he slid off Serenity. The people began muttering until Micah grabbed the offender and jerked him to the cage. "There is room in there for you as well. Would you like to join her?"

"No." He trembled. "No, sir. Please. Let me go."

"Then sympathize with the king and not the prisoner. Spit on her."

"What?"

"You heard me. Spit on her. Show her what disdain you have for those who defy the king."

Without any more prompting, the man spit on the chained, gagged, caged Esmeralda.

◊   ◊   ◊

Javan polished off the crunchy and sweet and not altogether horrible dragon's delight as he walked beside the slow-moving and silent Astor. The old man shuffled his feet as he walked, almost as though he no longer possessed the strength to get each foot completely off the ground.

The okty barn was behind them as they traipsed through the lush green and flowery meadows that ran parallel to the vast mountain range on their right that Javan had been itching to explore. The okties they had chosen were flying above them as they walked.

Astor was holding the antennae of the okties so Javan could eat while they walked. Since they were walking, Javan wasn't sure why they had the okties with them at all. Finally he had to stop and ask.

"Hold on," Javan said, stepping in front of Astor. "Wouldn't these okties be more helpful if we were, umm, actually riding them?"

"We will ride them soon enough."

"That sounds cryptic." Javan took a sip of water from the canteen Astor had provided and studied his travel companion. The top of his head was bald except for a few strands of wild white hair; thicker bunches of white hair filled in the sides and back of his head and hung just past his neck.

Round glasses perched halfway down his flat nose, a nose that barely reached as high as Javan's chest. He had a slight forward lean to him, his stooped shoulders leading the way. Red suspenders helped hold up his oversized black pants and did not go well with his striped orange shirt. Javan guessed old people could get away with wearing colorful clothes, unlike the boring brown garb Javan was sporting.

"The okties need to save their strength for the journey that awaits them." Astor pointed ahead. "Walk."

"Still cryptic," Javan mumbled and fell back into step beside Astor.

Their forward progress was painstakingly slow. It was even worse now that he had nothing left to eat and thus nothing to do to keep him from collapsing out of sheer boredom. "Okay, dude," Javan blurted, "here's the deal. I'm really tired, and if we don't talk or something, I'm going to lay down on this super soft grass and take a nap."

"I always welcome stimulating conversation," Astor said. "Talk."

"Great," Javan said. "I'm not sure if this counts as stimulating, but I have to know: how old are you?"

"One thousand one hundred and seventy seven years old."

"Whoa! You have to be the oldest guy on the planet!"

"Yes, but not by much."

"You mean there are other people as old as you still alive?"

"Seven to be precise. We're all in hiding. For the past 500 years, the Dark King has been seeking out and eliminating those in my generation and older."

"Eliminating?" Javan swallowed. "He's been killing the old people? Why?"

"We are a threat. We remember what life was like in Zandador when a Collector was on the throne. He wants to wipe out those memories and keep the people in fear of him."

"What was life like back then?"

"We were free, my son." Astor smiled as he spoke and shuffled along. "We were free to do the work we wanted. To build our homes where we wanted. To travel when we wanted wherever we wanted. To live in harmony with the dragons rather than view them as dangers to be disposed of.

"We were free to love. To marry. To raise as many babies as our hearts desired."

"Who did you marry?"

"Ahh, I was in love with Marissa, a black-haired beauty from Varzack. We were going to marry and have an army of kids." His words drifted off, and Javan noticed a tear stream down the old man's weathered cheek.

"Something bad happened, didn't it?"

Astor nodded, wiped his cheek and kept plodding forward. "White winds took her away."

"White winds?"

"Right. You're not from here. I keep forgetting." Astor took his glasses off and dried the lenses with his shirt. "White winds are powerful blankets of wind that sweep through without warning. They displace everything in their path and can throw objects hundreds of miles away."

"We have storms kind of like that. We call them tornadoes. So what happened to your Marissa?"

"The night before our wedding, white winds swept through her village. When I arrived the next day expecting to be married, her village was destroyed, and she was gone. I never saw her again."

"Dude, that is so sad. How old were you?"

"Sixty-three. I've been searching for her ever since. It's been more than a thousand years, but I'll die before I give up looking for her."

"I'm sorry, man."

Astor stopped and grabbed Javan's elbow, causing him to stop, too. "I don't need you to be sorry, my son. I need you to do whatever it takes to collect the four Dragon Stalkers and win the throne. No king has reigned as long as Omri, and there are darker days ahead if he continues his rule."

"Okay. Got it."

"I don't think you do." Astor grabbed the collar of Javan's shirt and pulled him down so Javan was eye level with the old man. "The freedom of the people of Zandador and the survival of the dragons aren't the only things at stake here."

"I know. My mom's life depends on me."

"Yes. As do the lives of all the people on Earth."

"Huh? What are you talking about?"

"Unless you succeed, your Earth is in danger of destruction."

"What do you mean?"

"The lure of Earth and the possibilities it offers have always been a threat to the Dark King. He's been devising a plan to abolish that threat once and for all. He's close to putting his plan into action. But he can't until he first secures the throne for another hundred years. It's up to you to stop him."

"No pressure there."

Astor let go of Javan's shirt and allowed him to stand upright again. "Now walk. We still have much to do today."

Javan sighed and followed Astor, desperately wishing he was back in Montana. Being an invisible second stringer on his JV football team was sounding much more doable and appealing than fighting to save his mother, two dimensions worth of people and an entire species of mythical creatures.

CHAPTER 27

The Zandadorian Portal

Astor's vast knowledge of the land had Javan's head swimming after walking alongside the old man for several hours. Every flower or plant they passed had a name and a purpose. Some could be eaten. Some could be used for medicine. Some could be used as poison.

When they weren't discussing plants, Astor painted detailed descriptions of the geography of the Dragon Stalker territories. He made Javan spew back the descriptions of the mountains and valleys in the Midnight and Noon Stalker territories as well as the woods and plains that defined the Dusk and Dawn Stalker territories.

Astor also instructed Javan on ways to find food, water and shelter in each of the territories and described the kinds of animals Javan was bound to contend with in his quest to collect dragons. Creepy crawly creatures, deadly flying insects and ferocious four-, six- and eight-legged monsters all roamed the territories and apparently did not appreciate intruding human guests.

The talk of such animals had Javan wondering why they were about to enter the Dusk Stalker territory unarmed. He was about to ask Astor if he could fly back to the barn and retrieve his stun balls and stalker swords when he noticed the landscape was changing.

The flowery, hilly meadows were giving way to flat, white, sandy land with squiggly knee-high trees that had green bark and brown leaves. Although Javan could see the trees grew taller and more dense up ahead, he stooped to inspect one of the trees at his knee. The leaves were shaped like a dog's paw print, as thick as the palm of his hand, as rough as sandpaper on top, as smooth as glass on the bottom and smelled like salt.

"What are these cute little trees called?" Javan asked.

"Shoreline trees," Astor said. "The leaves make a tasty soup."

Javan stood up so fast he nearly threw his back out. "Does that mean we're at the shore?" He had never been to the beach before but had always longed to visit.

"The ocean is about a half a mile away on the other side of the trees."

"Awesome!" Javan zig-zagged his way through thickening forest of shoreline trees. He could hear the rumbling of the waves and feel the salt in the breeze as the trees he passed grew taller and taller.

He finally broke through the tree line and found himself standing on a pure white beach with an endless red ocean stretching out before him. A wave higher than his head crashed on the shore and drew back. Another formed. Crashed. Drew back.

He stood there out of breath, transfixed, disturbed by the sight of the bloody red water and wishing it was the crystal clear blue he had always dreamed of seeing.

"You look distraught, my son." Astor's quiet voice broke Javan's trance.

"Yeah," Javan said. "This is wrong."

"I don't understand."

"The ocean. It's wrong." Javan ran his fingers through his black hair and shook his head. "Oceans are supposed to be blue."

"No," Astor said. "Rivers and streams and lakes are blue. The western ocean—this one—is red; the eastern ocean is purple."

"Purple? That's crazy!"

"It is the way it is."

"Not on earth."

"I should like to hear about your earth oceans," Astor said, nodding, "but first we have a trip to finish. Come. I have the okties waiting for us at the portal."

"There's another portal?" The red ocean no longer held Javan's interest. He turned from the mesmerizing sight and followed Astor back into the trees.

◊   ◊   ◊

Javan stood with his arms crossed staring at the massive white circle on the ground. One triangle-shaped hole marked the center of the circle, and nine similar holes with the tips of the triangles all facing outward spread out along the circumference of the circle.

Even though he had worked hard to sweep the sand away using shoreline tree leaves, the circle was still covered with a thin layer of the white dust. "This doesn't look like the portal I came through with my mom."

"That's because this is a Zandadorian portal, not an interdimensional portal."

"Say what?"

"The Zandadorian portal is made only of Dawn Stalker scales and utilizes their ability to teleport. From here, we can transport ourselves to any of the other regions in the Great Rift—except for Xyies—or one of four other places in Zandador where a linking portal exists."

"This portal can't take us to earth?"

"No. To get to earth, you have to travel through a portal made of all four scales. There is one such portal in North Zandador and another precisely 965 miles south of it South Zandador. Only Protectors know how to activate those portals, but anyone who has two seven-year Dawn scales can use the Zandadorian portal."

"Gotcha." Javan really had no clue what the man was saying, but he also had no desire to hear a more detailed explanation. "Where is this portal going to take us?"

"First you must see where we are." Astor pointed to the triangle directly to the left of the middle triangle. "We are on the western shoreline and will be transported to the eastern shoreline." This time Astor pointed to the triangle directly to the right of the middle triangle.

"What's this middle triangle all about?"

"That is the central portal, the one located in the heart of Zandador in the basement of the king's castle."

"You mean we could use this portal to break into the castle and save my mom?"

"No. That would be foolishness. Omri controls it, and his soldiers constantly guard it. He uses it to send his dragons throughout the lands to devour those who try to rise against him."

That gave Javan an idea. If he could collect this dragon they were on their way to watch, then he and his dragon could go through the portal together and rescue his mother. He wouldn't have to wait the month Ravier wanted him to wait.

"Foolishness." Javan nodded as if agreeing with Astor. "I don't want to be a fool. I do want to learn about dragons, though. How about we get this portal fired up and go meet this Mertzer you mentioned."

"Yes," Astor said. He looked up at the sun as if he was one of those wise old school guys who could tell time by the position of the sun in the sky. Then again, Astor was a pretty old guy; he probably did know exactly what time it was. "His scales are starting to change, and I want you to observe his feeding time."

Astor untied the okties he had strapped to a tree via their antennae and handed Javan the antennae to the one with the blue and yellow streaks. His name was, appropriately enough, Blue. "Get on and hover over the portal. Hold on tight. Okties don't like traveling by portal. He's likely to throw you off once we reach the other side if you're not careful."

"Don't worry. I can handle myself on one of these things."

Javan mounted the okty and rested his legs comfortably in the crook between the okty's two sets of wings.

"All set?" Astor asked.

"Think so." Javan pulled up on the antennae, and the okty drifted into the air. "That's it, Blue," Javan whispered. "You take care of me, and I'll take care of you. I'll even give you a better name once I get to know you a little bit."

They turned slow circles in the air while Astor inserted a dragon scale into the spot that represented their current location. He then tied his okty's antennae around his waist and shuffled across the portal.

"Aren't you going to get on your okty?"

"I will once we reach the other side. Putting a scale in the slot while riding an okty is tricky business for an old man. Now come down a little closer; you're too high."

Javan nudged his okty down. Once they were hovering just a few feet over the portal, Astor put the second scale in the destination slot.

A burst of bright pinkish blue light blinded Javan and spooked Blue. Javan leaned his body against Blue and felt his stomach drop as Blue skyrocketed upward, his little okty heart beating a million miles a minute against Javan's chest.

"Whoa, Blue! Whoa!" Javan pulled on his antennae, but that only freaked Blue out and sent him in the other direction, straight into a downward spiral. Javan held on for dear life as he blinked incessantly to regain his sight.

The world became blurry again, but part of the blurriness was due to the deathspin he was in. Javan wasn't sure if he could trust his eyes anyway. The only thing he could see with any clarity was a wall of purple that Blue seemed determined to crash into.

He could feel the panic overtaking the okty's mind. Javan had to gain control. Fast.

Javan closed his eyes and made himself relax. He rested his limp body against Blue's tense one. Eased his hold on the antennae. Whispered to his ride. "Pull up, boy, pull up." Then he gave a tiny tug on the antennae.

Blue responded.

Javan opened his eyes just as Blue skirted the surface of the purple ocean and resumed the calm, easy demeanor he demonstrated when Javan first mounted him.

"Guess we're on the eastern shore." Javan and Blue floated above the ocean while Javan drank in the beauty of the purple water lapping onto the bronze sand. Beyond the sand, he could see cliffs and waterfalls and rolling hills covered with a canopy of colorful trees. "This place is paradise. I wonder why nobody lives here."

"Humans are not allowed to live in Dragon Stalker territories," Astor said, flying up from behind Javan. "Now come. Mertzer is on the hunt. We'll track him from the air."

Astor sped away.

"For a slow-walking man, he sure is fast on that okty." Javan urged Blue to keep up while working on his plan to collect Mertzer. He would let the dragon eat, then leap from Blue to Mertzer when the dragon was full, tired from hunting and least expecting him.

It was a simple, foolproof plan. Why was everyone trying to make this collecting thing harder than it needed to be?

CHAPTER 28

Mertzer

The sun was fading from the sky as Javan and Astor flew further and further inland just above the treeline. They had slowed their pace, and the calm, steady speed of the okty flight is what allowed Javan to tune in to the sounds of the woods below.

Actually, it was the lack of sound that Javan noticed most. Near the coast and with the sun still prominent in the sky, birds chirped, insects sung and the four-legged creatures roamed without masking their tracks.

But all those noises had slowly died away the lower the sun dipped in the sky and the farther from the coast they flew. Now Javan could hear nothing, not even the rustling of leaves.

"There he is," Astor whispered. He halted his okty in mid-air and pointed to the ground below.

Javan brought his okty to a hovering stop above a thinning patch of trees. To the left of the trees, a rocky hill led to a valley plush with bushes, tall grass and a smattering of flowers. More bushes filled the green landscape on the other side of the valley where several wide, six-legged sheep grazed lazily under a cluster of trees.

"I see some weird-looking sheep," Javan said, "but I don't see a dragon."

"Those are gorzelles," Astor said. "One or two of them will be Mertzer's dinner. He'll probably also eat the snake curled on the edge of the hill and all seven of the raxens hiding in the valley."

"Raxens?" Javan scanned the valley and noticed a group of what appeared to be seven oversized rats huddled together near a bush. "Oh, I see them." He also spotted the coiled brown snake that looked huge even from the air. "But I still don't see Mertzer."

"Look below you. In the trees. He's preparing to make his move."

Javan flew in a slow circle around Astor while staring at the ground, trying to see what the old man saw. Finally, a streak of blue caught his eye.

The blue streak turned out to be the dragon's tail. As the dragon inched out from under the trees, Javan saw that the streak extended across Mertzer's back, over his head, between his green ears, down his short snout and ended at his two black nostrils. Horizontal streaks of green and pink scales colored the sides of his sleek, twelve-foot long body. Patches of purple and blue scales dotted his otherwise white legs.

"Aw, he's a pretty dragon," Javan said.

"He's deadly," Astor snapped back. "He moves with incredible speed; you don't know he's coming until he's already gone. By then it's too late: he breathes poison on his prey as he passes. The poison sinks into the skin, rushes through the bloodstream and strangles the heart. Death takes moments. Once his prey is dead, he comes back and takes his time eating his kills."

Javan gulped. This dragon wasn't as friendly and gentle as he looked. "No more gawking at the pretty dragon. Got it."

"When he's not in hunting mode, he can be a sensitive, caring creature." Astor lost some of the sternness in his voice. "The Dusk Stalker is the one with the strongest emotional connection with his Collector. All the Stalkers are loyal to their Collectors, but the loyalty of the Dusk Stalker is unmatched by the rest."

"I could use a loyal companion."

"You must also know that he has an irrational fear of water. He'll only drink from streams, never lakes, and he won't go near the ocean."

"Why is that?"

"I can't explain it. That's why I said it was an irrational fear." Astor put his finger to his lips to silence Javan. "Watch. He's ready to attack."

Javan looked down in time to see a bluish green blur dart to the snake, down the hill to the raxens, up the hill to the gorzelles and back across the valley to his starting point. It couldn't have taken him more than a minute to cover the tricky terrain and what had to be a total distance of more than a mile.

"His attack is over," Astor said. "Now he'll wait for his prey to die."

All seven of the raxens were laying in a motionless heap in the valley. One of the gorzelles had dropped to the ground while the other two ran away. As for the snake, it was still coiled. Javan knew, however, that it had been poisoned. Mertzer was confidently walking towards it, ready to make it the first part of his meal.

Javan was starting to feel a little queasy. He knew that animals eating animals was part of the natural order of things, but he preferred not to watch one animal devour another. "Do we really have to watch the dragon eat?" Javan asked.

"I suppose not." Astor yawned. "This old body of mine is exhausted. I do want to get back through the portal and into my own bed."

"I have a better idea." Javan couldn't go back, not without Mertzer. "Why don't we find a place to land and rest for a bit? I'm supposed to learn how to survive in the Stalker territories at night anyway, right?"

"I could use some sleep." Astor yawned again. "I know of a good place to rest that's not far from here. Follow me."

"Yes, sir." Javan would follow the old man, make sure he was settled and sleeping, then go collect himself a dragon.

CHAPTER 29

Tree Tremors

"You sure this is a good place to rest?" Javan asked. They had landed in a meadow near a stream and had tied the okties to some trees near the water. Darkness had settled in, and with it came a blanket of heavy fog. The not-too-distant sounds of howling wolves did nothing to settle Javan's uneasiness at losing nearly all visibility.

Somehow, though, Astor could see well enough to lead them into a patch of crooked trees. The trees grew at odd angles out of a ground so soft that Javan was sure he was going to sink right through it any second.

"We're in the safety of the slanted acres," Astor said. "We have plenty to eat: the leaves are delicious and nutritious. We can also rest without fear of attack. Animals dare not enter any section like this throughout the Dusk Stalker territory."

"Animals are scared to walk where we are?" That didn't sound like good news to Javan. He moved a little closer to Astor until he was practically breathing down the old man's neck. "That makes me feel safe."

"As it should." Astor stopped under a tree shaped like an S. Now that Javan's eyes were adjusting to the darkness, he studied the strange tree Astor was under. Most of the trunk was bare. The top curved section, however, had hundreds of thin, spindly branches on it. Those branches grew tiny, circular leaves. It was those tiny circles that covered the ground all around them.

Javan gulped and tried to keep his voice from cracking as he asked, "Out of curiosity, why does this place scare animals away?"

"Tree tremors."

"Should tree tremors scare us?"

"The threat is real. They can be deadly. So we'll stop here." Astor knelt down and gathered a pile of leaves into a makeshift bed. "We're far enough inside the slanted acres to keep us safe from animal attacks but close enough to the edge that we can get out if a tremor strikes."

"What exactly is a tree tremor? Is there any kind of warning before one strikes?"

"You'll know if it's happening when it happens." Astor yawned and curled up on his bed of leaves. "There are no warnings. But one is more likely to occur if you keep babbling and pacing. The slanted acres demand quiet stillness. Now goodnight, young Javan."

The old man was snoring before Javan could respond in kind. That meant now was his chance. He could tiptoe back out of the acres, retrieve his okty and fly around until he found Mertzer. Since Mertzer's scales should have reverted back to white by now, the dragon shouldn't be too hard to spot despite the darkness.

Javan suppressed a yawn of his own. Maybe getting a little rest first wouldn't hurt. Astor looked like he was going to be asleep for a while anyway. And the ground was so soft.

Careful not to disturb the quiet of the acres and cause a tremor, Javan eased to his knees and practically sunk into the ground. He assumed the layer of leaves gave the ground its cushiony effect. He was wrong. When he started scooping up leaves to make himself a pillow, he uncovered not grass or dirt but plush white cotton. The more leaves he moved, the more cotton he found.

"Cool!" He laid on his back and stretched out. This place was more comfortable than any bed he had ever slept on. Within minutes, he was as sound asleep as the old man beside him.

◊   ◊   ◊

"Achoo! Achoo! Achoo!"

The series of fitful sneezes forced Javan out of his deep slumber. Particles of the wispy cotton that covered the ground were tickling the inside of Javan's nose. He brusquely brushed them away, turned over and tried to get back to sleep without opening his eyes.

But the ground had lost its softness. Instead of the soft, cushiony cotton, all he could feel was annoying sticks poking and prodding his body from his toes to his shoulders. "Stupid sticks." With his eyes half closed, he sat up and patted the ground in an attempt to find and remove the offending sticks.

Apparently the sticks did not appreciate being called stupid because one of them reached up and smacked Javan across the face. "Ouch!" Before Javan had a chance to retaliate, another smacked him in the back. "Whoa! What is going on here?"

Fully awake, he sprang to his feet and let his eyes readjust to the darkness. The leaves on the ground seemed to be jumping all around him. As he bent down to investigate, he saw why: the roots of the trees were jerking themselves up from the ground at sporadic intervals and causing the leaves to jump. It was those roots that had been digging into his back. "Astor! Astor, wake up!"

There was no wind, but the strangely shaped trees started swaying. Tremoring. "Oh, we gotta get out of here." Javan rushed over to Astor and started shaking him. "Come on, man! Pretty sure we're in the middle of a tree tremor!"

Astor snorted, brushed Javan off and kept on snoring. Meanwhile, the trees that were once as stiff as trees should be were becoming bendy and quivering in the night like slinkies. They began clanging and banging into each other.

It was only a matter of time before Javan and Astor were caught between some unhappy, tremoring trees.

Despite the growing noise, Astor continued to sleep. "Really, dude? You're gonna make me carry you out of here?"

A root spanked Javan, and a branch from above thumped the back of his head. "That's it. We're leaving!"

Javan reached under Astor's shoulders, hooked his arms around the man's armpits and began dragging him. He ran as fast as he could.

But he was running backwards. In the middle of the night. Hauling the dead weight of Astor. Zigging to avoid tremoring trees. Zagging to keep from tripping on lurching roots.

Just as the thunderous noise from the banging trees was becoming unbearably deafening, Javan felt his right foot step from soft to solid ground. "I'm out!" He leaped back with his left foot and paused to catch his breath. "Made it."

Only his celebration was a bit premature. A particularly large tree slammed into the ground beside Astor, spraying leaves and cotton everywhere. It picked itself back up and was on a collision course for Astor's legs. "Uh oh."

Javan scrambled backwards, barely escaping the wrath of the tree. He shakily lowered Astor to the ground and perched himself against the trunk of a straight, solid, untremoring tree. From his seat, he watched the trees tremor themselves out and return to a state of pristine stillness.

Once the world was quiet again, he looked at Astor. The man continued to snore. "Unbelievable." Javan closed his eyes and rested his head against the tree.

"Ahhhh! Strolling into the acres was a bad idea!"

"Now you wake up?" Javan rolled his eyes and turned toward Astor. Only he was still sleeping. So who had said that? Who else was here?

Javan slowly stood. Maybe he had imagined hearing someone else speaking.

"How am I going to get myself out of this trap?" The male voice sounded stressed and strained, but it was real.

And Javan was the only one available to help whoever was stuck.

He had never met a Zandadorian on his own before. Would the guy see Javan as a fellow Zandadorian or realize he was an outsider from earth? Perhaps this would be a good test to see if he actually did belong in Zandador. Plus it wouldn't hurt to do a good deed and help the guy out.

Javan took a few steps forward and yelled, "Who's there?" He began skirting around the slanted acres, listening for a response. Whoever was talking had to be close.

"You can hear me?"

"Uh, yeah. Where are you?"

After a slight hesitation, the voice responded. "I'm trapped at the edge of the slanted acres. I got stuck during the tremor."

"Okay," Javan said, walking in the direction of the voice. "Keep talking, and I'll find you."

"I'm not talking."

"Hate to disagree, buddy, but I can hear you."

"What you hear, human, are my thoughts."

Javan halted in his tracks. "Mertzer?"

"The one and only."

Javan smiled. He was talking to the dragon he had come here to collect. Now the dragon was stuck in some sort of tree trap, making it impossible for him to run away. That meant all Javan had to do was hop on an immobile dragon's back, and the dragon would be his.

After just one day of training, he would officially be a Dragon Collector. He forged ahead, certain he was about to set the record for the fastest collection of a dragon ever.

Then he met Mertzer.

CHAPTER 30

Unqualified

One turn around a tree as round and as tall as a water tower suddenly had Javan face to face with the black-eyed dragon.

Mertzer's eyes and flaring nostrils were the only things black about him. His pointy ears, short snout and the rest of his sleek, twelve-foot long, wingless body were covered in stunning white triangular scales that shimmered in the moonlight. He was easily one of the most magnificent creatures Javan had ever seen.

Javan's first instinct was to hop on the dragon's back and ride him out of there just like he rode Storm back home. Except this dragon was about three times as tall as Storm; he'd be even taller when he stood. But since Mertzer was resting calmly with his front legs sprawled in front of him and his back legs tucked under him, it was hard to tell exactly how tall he was.

Diagnosing Mertzer's problem, however, was easy: his long tail was stuck in a tangle of trees just inside the slanted acres.

"Hello there," Javan said. He tried to keep his voice friendly and carefree, but his words to came out in an unnatural, high-pitched tone nevertheless. "Looks like you could use some help."

I am in no need of help. I especially don't need the help of a human. He huffed at Javan. *If you even think about chopping my tail off to free me and in so doing enslave me to you, I will smother you with poison before you can even unsheathe your sword.*

"No need to poison me." Javan took a step back and held his hands up. "See, I don't have a sword. Even if I did, I wouldn't use it to chop off your tail. I'm not a Hunter."

Mertzer cocked his head. *No. You're not. You wouldn't be able to hear my thoughts if you were. That must make you a Collector.*

"Right. I am. So I'll make you a deal. If I get you out of that tangled mess you're stuck in, you have to let me ride you."

How about I make you deal? Mertzer raised himself into a sitting position, dwarfing Javan. He then clenched his right claw around Javan's chest, picked him up and stared directly into Javan's eyes. *If you get me out of this tangled mess, I won't kill you.*

His gut told him that Mertzer really didn't want to kill him, but considering the intensity radiating from the dragon's eyes, Javan thought it best not to take any chances. "I think I like your deal better."

Smart. Mertzer eased Javan back to the ground, glaring at him the whole way.

Javan tried to act as if he was picked up and glared at by dragons every day. He disguised his shaky hands by straightening his shirt, shot Mertzer a "that's-what-I-wanted-you-to-do" look and strolled as casually as possible on his wobbly legs back into the slanted acres to inspect the dragon's tangled tail.

Three squiggly trees had collided, and Mertzer's tail was stuck in the middle of the ball of branches about five feet off the ground. Hundreds of the round leaves grew on the branches, masking the length of what seemed to be an endless tail.

"Wow." The more leaves Javan pushed out of the way, the more white scales Javan could see. What he couldn't see from where he stood was the tip of the tail. "This is crazy! How long is your tail?"

Long enough to get stuck while I was trying to escape a tree tremor.

Javan rolled his eyes and made a mental note: Mertzer was a humorless dragon who liked to state the obvious. He would state the obvious as well. "It looks like I'm going to need a chainsaw to cut you loose."

I am not familiar with that term, human. What is a chainsaw?

"It's a...nevermind." Javan shook his head. It was not even worth trying to explain since he had no access to a chainsaw anyway. "I'll just try to break off these branches by hand."

Javan grabbed the closest offending branch trapping the top of Mertzer's tail and began tugging. It bent but did not break. The second he let go, it snapped back into place. He tried breaking branches on the right side and bottom of the tail only to observe the same unbreakable results.

"Why...won't...they...break?" Beads of sweat formed on his forehead as he pushed and pulled and kicked and shoved the branches. Nothing helped. The dragon's tail remained immobile and immersed in the branches.

Keep that up, human, and you'll start another tremor.

"My name is Javan." Javan stepped back, wiped his brow and put his hands on his hips. "And that's not a bad idea."

You want to intentionally start a tremor? You and the old man almost didn't survive the last one.

"We made it out just—wait. How do you know about the old man?" Javan turned to face Mertzer, but the dragon refused to make eye contact. Javan, however, could still see the guilt that flooded the dragon's eyes. "You were watching us. You came in to the slanted acres, and you caused the tremor while we were sleeping."

Mertzer turned away from Javan and stuck his nose up in the air. *I was defending myself. I am the last of the free Dusk Stalkers and had to make sure you didn't have any weapons with which to hunt or destroy me.*

"We didn't come to hurt you." Javan pulled and pushed a few more branches. Then he realized that what hindered the dragon could help him. He could use the branches as a ladder to get to Mertzer's back.

Mertzer wasn't looking at him at the moment anyway, so Javan would be able to dart from the branches across Mertzer's back and to his neck. Once there, he just had to hang on while Mertzer yanked himself free from the branches or caused another tremor. In the meantime, he had to keep the conversation casual. "We just came to observe you."

That is not the only reason you came, Collector.

"You're right." Javan scrambled his way up the tangled branches. "I need your help."

Why do you need my help?

"My mother is being held captive by the Dark King." He stood even with the dragon's tail staring at his sparkly white neck. "I need your help to rescue her."

The Dark King is an evil man. Because of him, all Stalkers are on the verge of extinction.

"Exactly. He needs to be stopped. We can stop him." Ever so slowly, Javan stepped from the branches and onto Mertzer's rock-like scales. Mertzer didn't seem to notice he had a human standing on him. "I need to collect all four Stalkers in order to overthrow him and win the throne."

Yes, I am aware of your human laws. Javan felt Mertzer's body grow rigid beneath his feet. *My brother is the Dark King's Dusk Stalker slave.*

Javan paused before taking another step. "What?" For some reason, Javan took the news about Mertzer's brother personally. "Then we'll just have to rescue him, too."

You would help me free my brother?

"Uh, yeah." Javan inched along Mertzer's back. Surely the dragon would have tossed him off by now if he didn't want Javan to ride him. "That's what this whole dragon collecting thing is about, right? It would make us partners."

How many other Stalkers have you collected?

Javan reached the top of Mertzer's back and crawled up to his neck. He placed one leg on either side and rested his hands on Mertzer's neck. He was in place. For the first time in his life, he felt like he was precisely where he was supposed to be and doing what he was born to do.

He took a deep breath, smiled and said, "You make one."

UNQUALIFIED! Mertzer roared, launched to his feet and reared up on his hind legs. The abrupt movement sent Javan sliding straight down the dragon's back and onto the conglomeration of trees that had Mertzer's tail trapped.

Mertzer twisted himself around and pressed his cold nose into Javan's chest. *I can tell you have a good heart, young one, but I will not submit myself to your leadership until you have first collected another Stalker.*

With a flick of his snout, he tossed Javan off the trees.

Javan watched from the ground as Mertzer clawed at and bit the branches until he was finally able to jerk his tail free. He glanced back at Javan, nodded goodbye and zipped away into the darkness.

CHAPTER 31

Javan's Unique Gift

"Explain yourself!"

Javan lifted himself up on his elbows and looked around. Mertzer was gone, but Astor was standing in his place, arms crossed, looking angry.

"The dragon was stuck," Javan said. "He needed help. So I came to help him."

"That's not what I meant!" Astor charged over to where Javan was laying. He kicked Javan's legs and squinted at Javan through his thick glasses. "Explain to me how you were communicating with him."

"Umm..." Javan stood, trying to figure out why Astor was upset. If he didn't calm him down quickly, the old man was likely to have a heart attack. "The same way I'm communicating with you: by talking."

"Of that I am aware. I heard you. But you acted as if you could hear him speak to you."

Javan nodded and spoke slowly as though that would help the seemingly senile man understand him better. "That's cause I could."

Astor adjusted his glasses and softened his voice as he peered up at Javan. "You could hear his thoughts?"

"Yeah." Javan shrugged. "I don't get why you're surprised. I thought all Collectors could talk to dragons."

"No. Only a few have ever had that ability. And none have ever been able to communicate with dragons before making them part of their collection." Astor rubbed his hands back and forth and began pacing. "This is big. Oh, this is big. This is much bigger than we thought."

Javan stepped in front of Astor, grabbed a hold of his shoulders and forced him to stop. "What are you talking about?"

Astor looked up at Javan and gasped. "Did Ravier know about this?"

"About me being able to talk to dragons? Sure."

"He should have told me!" Astor slapped Javan's hands away and began marching back toward the okties.

"I don't get it," Javan said, struggling to keep up with him. "Why is it such a big deal?" And where was this crazy fast pace when they were walking to the portal together yesterday? Guess the old man just needed something to panic about.

Astor spun around and pointed at Javan. "Because it means that you, my son, are the answer to the prophecy."

"Oh. The prophecy. Right." This conversation was getting stranger and stranger. "And what prophecy would that be?"

Flinging his hands up in the air, Astor screeched, "THE prophecy!"

"You mean THE prophecy?" Javan mimicked Astor with his hands. "Good. Now I know exactly what you're talking about."

Ignoring Javan's sarcasm, Astor continued his tirade. "This changes everything. We have to get back right away." He turned around and pointed straight ahead. "To the okties!"

"I was kidding." Javan tried to grab Astor's arm, but the old man was surprisingly quick as he dashed ahead. "Hold up! I really have no clue what you're talking about. What prophecy?"

The shouting did no good. Astor was too focused on getting home to explain this prophecy thing to Javan.

Which Javan found quite rude. If he was the answer to some prophecy, he had the right to know what it was. Maybe Ravier or Hamilton would enlighten him when he got back. If not, he would go on strike. Either his dragon-collecting trainers would tell him about this prophecy or he would refuse to train.

Certain that he would be able to get his demands met, he reached his okty just behind Astor, climbed on and followed the old man back through the Zandadorian portal.

◊   ◊   ◊

The first rays of sun were poking through the early morning darkness when Javan and Astor landed their worn-out okties between the okty barn and the house. Astor had been muttering incomprehensible nonsense to himself the whole way back, making it impossible for Javan to learn anything about this prophecy he was supposedly the answer to.

Javan was thus happy to see Hamilton, Ravier and Hannah walking toward them from the direction of the house. Surely one of them would explain the prophecy to him. Considering the loving, sympathetic gaze of his grandmother, his money was on her to help him out.

The cold, angry look his grandfather shot him, however, offered no sense of help, care or understanding. Neither did the gruff tone in Ravier's voice as he spoke. "What took you so--"

"Silence!" Astor's booming reprimand stopped Ravier cold in his tracks. Astor approached him and poked his finger into Ravier's chest. "You knew and yet you did not tell!"

Javan grinned and watched the scene play out. He enjoyed seeing the normally stern and in control Ravier off balance and in the hot seat for a change.

"I...uh...I don't know what you're talking about."

"Your son may have had the right color eyes," Astor said, "but your grandson possesses the ability which supersedes eye color. We cannot properly train him if you keep such things a secret!"

"Ravier hasn't been keeping secrets." Hamilton looked and sounded confused. His confusion seemed to grow when he saw the obvious guilt drenching Ravier's face.

"Yes, he has," Astor said. "Tell him, Ravier. Tell him what your grandson is capable of."

"Ravier?" Hamilton stood between Javan and Astor. The three of them stood in a semi-circle and stared at the fidgety Ravier. Hannah stood beside Ravier, but the blank look on her face made it clear Ravier had no ally in this situation.

Finally, Ravier shrugged his shoulders, rolled his eyes and exclaimed, "I thought it was a fluke!"

"Thought what was a fluke?" Hamilton asked.

"No," Astor said, staying focused on Ravier's excuse. "You just didn't want to accept that your grandson—and not Dartez—is the answer to the prophecy."

"The prophecy?" Hamilton's voice squeaked. "You mean this kid from earth can fulfill THE prophecy? That's impossible. His eyes are the wrong color."

Ravier sighed. "No, they're not."

Hamilton and Astor turned to stare at Javan; they were particularly focused on studying his eyes.

"I know my colors." Hamilton bent so that his nose touched Javan's nose as he spoke. "This kid's eyes are brown."

"Ever heard of personal space?" Javan nudged Hamilton's head away as he took a step back. The sudden fixation on his eyes had him on edge. He had hoped he would never have to expose his glowing green eyes to anyone ever again. His brown eyes made him feel safe and normal. His green eyes made him look and feel like a freak.

A freak couldn't collect dragons and rule a country as its king.

"It's an illusion," Hannah said. She stepped beside Javan, put her arm around his shoulders and gave him an encouraging squeeze. "He's wearing what he calls contacts to hide the true color of his eyes."

"Show them, Javan." Ravier had regained his composure and was back to issuing commands.

Javan looked to Hannah. She nodded in agreement with Ravier, so he relented. "Fine." He bent his head, took his contacts out and placed them delicately in the palm of his hand. He blinked several times, then looked up. Astor smirked knowingly, but Hamilton was in awe.

"Whoa." Hamilton turned his big bulky frame toward Javan and bowed.

"Stand up, please," Javan said, stepping back to avoid bumping heads with the giant. "Would somebody tell me what my eyes and my ability to talk to dragons have to do with some prophecy?"

Hamilton's jaw dropped. "Did you say you could talk to dragons?"

"Yeah. I can hear their thoughts."

"Then you are the answer to the prophecy!"

"There you go with talk of the prophecy again," Javan said. "Would somebody please explain to me what this prophecy is?"

"You mean he doesn't know?" Hamilton asked.

"No, of course not," Ravier said. "I didn't think it was necessary. He's barely committed to becoming a Collector. He might turn and run if he learns more is expected of him."

"He needs to see the whole picture," Astor said.

"He is standing right here," Javan said, "and he agrees."

"As do I," Hannah said. "Come with me. I'll let you read it for yourself."

CHAPTER 32

The Prophecy

Back in the house, Hannah tasked Ravier and Hamilton with making breakfast while she and Astor sat at the table on either side of Javan.

"Your grandfather should have told you about this the minute he learned you could communicate with dragons," Hannah said. She had retrieved a book that looked to be a good thousand pages thick from her room and placed it on the table in front of Javan. "Sometimes that man can be infuriatingly dense."

Javan brushed the dust off the black leather cover and read the title: The Complete History of Zandador: Volume I. He felt like he had been transported back to high school and been given his history text book for the year. He cringed at the idea of having to read, discuss and take tests on the content within the book. He had never been much of a history buff and had no desire to become one now.

"Please tell me I don't have to start reading from page one," Javan said.

"You shouldn't have to read anything at all." Ravier stomped out of the kitchen area and over to other side of the table so that he was staring down Astor as he spoke. "We are wasting time. The boy needs to be training so he's ready for the battles that come with dragon collecting, not reading the ranting of some ancient Xyien who left Zandador thousands of years ago when he didn't agree with the political decisions of the Zandadorians."

"Vichar was a wise and respected man with a unique gift from God that enabled him to see and foretell future events," Astor said. "If we train Javan by ignoring the prophecy, we are sentencing him to failure."

"I'm not a fan of failure and would prefer to avoid it by not ignoring the prophecy." Javan resisted the childish urge to stick his tongue out at Ravier. Instead, he opened the book and started rifling through the pages. "At what point in history does this Vichar dude appear and make his eerie predictions?"

"After the first king died," Hannah said, motioning for Ravier to get back to the kitchen. Once he grudgingly acquiesced, she took control of the book and flipped pages as she continued. "After the first king died, the people disagreed how to determine who should lead them and how they should deal with the dragons."

"Hey," Javan said, "I remember Ravier telling me about that and how the different Bloodlines had different plans for the dragons."

"Good," Astor said. "Did he also tell you about the albinos?"

"Yeah. They were the smart people who moved up north into caves, right?"

"Yes. Vichar was the oldest and wisest among them. Before he left, he made a prediction. His prophecy is something that every Collector, Destroyer, Hunter and Protector knows by heart."

"It's recorded right here." Hannah had found the right page and slid the book back over to Javan. He smoothed the pages out and began reading aloud:

"The war between the Bloodlines will divide the nation and cause the people to scatter. Many kings will rise to power, but one who masters the dragons and their scales will remain on the throne for centuries. He will rule with a cruel hand, suppress the will of the people and seek to annihilate all dragons but his own. If his power remains unchecked, he will expand his rule to the world beyond the portal. Gaining control of that world and its resources will allow him to reign for a thousand more years, bringing death and destruction to those who dare defy him.

"All hope is not lost. A young Collector whose eyes shine like emeralds and whose ears can hear the thoughts of any dragon will enter the competition in the final months of a Battle for the Throne year. He will be the only one capable of dethroning the king and must collect all four Stalkers by sunset on the final day of the battle year. If he succeeds, however, collecting the four Stalkers will not be enough to defeat the king.

"The dethroned king will use his dragons and loyal subjects to wage a war unlike any Zandador has ever seen. The Collector must therefore unite the four opposing Bloodlines for only the united front of the four Bloodlines led by the young Collector will be strong enough to win a war against this most powerful of men.

"If such a war is fought, the outcome thereof will determine the fate of the dragons once and for all."

As he read the final sentence, Javan's tongue turned to sandpaper while his palms turned to liquid. He scanned the words again. And again. Could a second string JV quarterback from a tiny town in Montana really be the hero in a prophecy about a boy, dragons and a king?

He did have eyes that shone like emeralds.

He could hear the thoughts of dragons.

And he did want to dethrone the evil Omri more than he wanted to be the starting quarterback on the varsity football team.

After spending those few precious seconds on Mertzer's back during which had had never felt more alive or more sure of his purpose, he was certain he was up to the task of collecting the Dragon Stalkers.

But was he capable of uniting the Bloodlines? Waging a war? Leading an army?

"Look at him," Ravier said having marched back over to the table. "He's in shock. I told you he didn't need to know about the prophecy. Now he's going to want to run back to earth without even trying to collect any Stalkers."

"No," Javan said. "You're wrong." He slammed the book shut and stood, squaring his eyes with Ravier's. "I'm not going anywhere except back to the training room. You're going to teach me how to use the Stalker swords and stun balls. Hamilton's going to teach me how to fight. And Astor is going to teach me everything I need to know about dragons, Zandador and the Dark King."

Javan pushed back from the table. "Then I'm going to go collect me some dragons."

He wasn't going to focus on the war that would follow. Such thoughts were irrelevant if he had no Stalkers in his collection and no mother by his side to help him become the leader he needed to be.

Javan walked to the door, determination growing with each step. He expected the trio of men to be following him when he looked back, but they all remained planted in the places he had just left them. "Well? Are you going to help me or not?"

No one moved. They just kept staring, the same dumbfounded look on all their faces.

If Javan didn't exit forcefully and immediately, his newfound confidence might crumble before he ever got out the door. "Fine. I'll just go practice on my own while you boys sit and stare at each other."

He slammed the door behind him and walked on wobbly knees toward the training room. He was going to find a way to live up to the hype of that prophetic Collector one way or another.

CHAPTER 33

Training Days

The fatigue and hunger from the past twenty-four hours combined with the daunting mission of the days ahead overwhelmed Javan the second he descended the ladder and stepped foot into the training room. So instead of strapping on his Stalker swords, he dropped to his knees and tried to pray.

But no words came as he thought about what was required of him. People who had been alive for centuries were depending on him to free them from the rule of the Dark King. Dragons who were on the verge of extinction needed him to find them and ride them and save them. The world he grew up in was facing an unknown global tyrannical threat that only he could stop.

That was a lot of pressure for a teenager whose biggest concern last week was how to get the girl of his dreams to notice him despite his scrawny build and acne-covered face!

It was also a lot of pressure he wasn't prepared to handle on his own. He needed some help—human as well as Divine—to carry him through the tough days that were sure to follow. Finally, he was able to muster four emotion-packed little words. "God, please help me."

"Help is here."

Startled, Javan looked up to find Ravier standing beside him. "Thanks for coming."

"You won't be thanking me in a minute," Ravier said. "Get your swords. We have work to do."

Javan smiled, offered a quick thanks to God for sending him help and jumped up to retrieve his swords.

◊　◊　◊

"Again. But better."
"Again. But better."
"Again. But better."

Such were the words of Ravier's refrain. Over the course of the next four weeks, never did Javan hear Ravier say anything close to "Good job!" or "That's it!" or "Nice work!" after Javan executed a skill well with his swords or stun balls.

It was always, "Again. But better."

It was always spoken in a monotone.

"Again. But better."

It was always spoken no matter how many times he had done the same move.

"Again. But better."

So Javan would bite his tongue and practice the move again. But better.

He had decided that if Ravier wasn't going to offer any words of encouragement, Javan wasn't going to offer any words at all. He kept his mouth shut, did everything Ravier told him to do and got through each sword-fighting lesson in silence.

He'd wanted to talk back, argue and complain more times than he could count. But playing with his swords and stun balls was fun, especially when he bested Ravier at his own sword-fighting game during their sparring sessions.

Plus Ravier was an admittedly good teacher. He controlled his own sword like it was an extension of his body and masterfully pushed Javan to get better and better each day.

The way Ravier taught, Javan was forced to improve. And fast. They used real swords to practice with, and he didn't much like getting scrapes and cuts from the edge of Ravier's sword. More than that, he hated seeing the joy in Ravier's eyes when the slightest trickle of Javan's blood ended up on his grandfather's sword.

Training with Hamilton was an entirely different experience. Moments of silence during their training sessions were rare, and the jovial Hamilton had no shortage of praise for Javan. While Javan drove himself to improve with his swords by feeding off Ravier's negative energy, he drove himself to improve his fighting ability by feeding off Hamilton's positive energy.

When the two men worked together to train Javan in joint sessions in the evenings, Javan found himself ignoring Ravier as much as possible and focusing on pleasing Hamilton.

Then there was Astor.

The most intense physical work he did with the old man was walk through the woods, but it was his sessions with Astor that left Javan feeling the most drained. The ancient intellectual maintained a running monologue for hours that he expected Javan to not only retain but regurgitate at a moment's notice.

His body may not have gotten much of a workout, but his mind was saturated with an abundance of information he found it difficult to process. If he didn't get a nap after one of his dragonology lessons, Javan was useless for the rest of the day.

And his days became long, repetitive and predictable.

He was up an hour before Dawn Stalker feeding time so he could get in a five mile run around the shield-protected city of Gri before breakfast.

Breakfast was always followed by two to three hours of sword fighting and stun ball throwing, then another two to three hours of hand to hand combat. After a brief break for lunch at Noon Stalker feeding time, he would spend the next four hours with Astor training his mind to recognize plants and animals and trees, reading books and charts and maps to understand the land and Dragonology and learning how to stealthily track the animals in the nearby woods.

He would take a brief nap before dinner at Dusk Stalker feeding time, then spend his entire evening in joint training sessions with Ravier and Hamilton fighting his way through obstacle courses, weight lifting and practicing his dragon collecting skills on okties.

He was in bed by Midnight Stalker feeding time only to get up and do everything again the next day. But better.

Little by little, Javan felt himself getting stronger. Tougher. Smarter. The training regimen was physically and mentally grueling, but the side effects were worth it.

His pasty white skin that had never before managed to tan turned to bronze from the hours spent outside, making his green eyes appear to glow with a deeper intensity than ever before.

He packed on a good twenty pounds of pure muscle, and although it had nothing to do with his training, he hit a growth spurt and grew nearly two inches.

And thanks to a special cream Hannah concocted, his acne faded away. He had clear, tan skin and muscle on his bones for the first time in his life. He was starting to look and feel like the king Zandador needed him to be.

Except for the nightmares.

They didn't plague him every night. But they did plague him.

The most common one was the mental rebroadcast of the day his mother was captured.

He watched himself stand idly by as his mother walked toward the three armed soldiers, then hold a dagger to her throat as she threatened to kill herself to save him.

He watched himself do nothing as Micah analyzed him and deemed him worthless.

He watched his mother beg him to leave as she surrendered to her captor.

He watched himself refuse her desperate request.

He watched himself attempt to fight only to be soundly beaten, hurt and humiliated.

He watched himself groaning on the ground while his enemies whisked his mother away.

He watched himself fail again and again and again. So weak. So helpless. So defeated.

It was those emotional waves of devastation that always jolted him awake.

At first, he would sit in the dark for hours, wallowing in his own pity party because he lacked the ability to save her that day. Then he would wonder where she was. How she was doing. What she was enduring as a prisoner.

As the days wore on, however, the training began to change how he responded to the nightmares. When they woke him, he would forego his pity party and do something that made him feel empowered—push-ups, sit-ups, boxing moves, phantom sword fighting—while mentally reviewing all he had learned that day in training.

Or he would will himself back to sleep and change the end of his dream. In the revised version, his four Dragon Stalkers would swoop onto the scene. He would be armed with his Stalker swords and stun balls and lead his dragons in a charge against Micah and his two goons.

Micah would cower before Javan and his Stalker collection while Javan and Esmeralda would safely escape on the back of the dragon who once called him unqualified.

The experiences with Mertzer and Opny also sparked nightmares. He would dream that anytime he approached a dragon, it would laugh at him just before killing him with its specialized weapon of lightning bolts, fire, acid or poison.

Such fear fed his doubts about his ability to collect dragons. But it also fueled his desire to work harder the next day than the day before. He was determined to be prepared for Opny or Mertzer the next time they met.

On that day, no dragon would dare attempt to kill him or toss him aside as unqualified.

CHAPTER 34

Share the Secret

"Wrong! Wrong! Wrong!" Ravier pounded the floor with the point of his sword as he belted out each word.

Javan wiped the sweat from his forehead and glared at Ravier, a stalker sword in each hand. The change in Ravier's refrain and demeanor sparked Javan's temper, and he wasn't going to stand by and let the man berate him any longer. "How is that wrong? I did everything just like you showed me."

Javan's growing hunger didn't help calm his rising temper. They had started earlier than usual, worked straight through breakfast and were about to miss lunch as well. He was famished, but he didn't dare admit that to Ravier. He had made that mistake once at the beginning of his training and hadn't been allowed to eat for an entire day. Instead of eating, he had been forced to practice his stun ball throwing accuracy.

"Wrong!" Ravier pounded his sword into the floor again. "If you had deflected my attack like I showed you, you would have done it right. Instead, you angled your left sword too high and your right sword too low. Had this been a real fight, I would have easily ended you with a stab to the heart."

"No way." Javan repositioned his swords just to check his form. "I would have blocked your attack."

"It's that kind of attitude that's going to get you killed. The soldiers in the king's army have been training for centuries. You've been at it for a month. You may be quick with your lightweight stalker swords, but those men are deadly and trained to take advantage of the smallest weaknesses in your defense tactics. I know. I trained them. Now resheathe your swords. Let's start again."

Javan grit his teeth and was about to comply when his grandmother's voice caused both him and Ravier to turn around.

"No," Hannah said. She was standing at the base of the ladder with her arms crossed. "Javan, you take that belt off and come with me. You're done training for the day."

She was talking to Javan but staring at Ravier. Ravier stared back, and Javan wasn't sure which grandparent he should obey.

"Javan," Hannah said, still staring at Ravier, "you have ten seconds to get that belt off and get up this ladder, or I will carry you out of here myself."

"Yes, Ma'am." Javan nodded and obeyed her orders, deciding now was not the time to test his grandmother's resolve.

◊　◊　◊

"Ummm...you sure this is a good idea, Grandma?" They were approaching the restaurant in the middle of town. He kept glancing behind him as they walked through the empty, dusty streets, certain Ravier was going to appear and drag him back to the training room. "Ravier looked mad when we left."

"You let me worry about him, sweetie." Hannah put her arm around Javan and squeezed his shoulders. "He has been working you too hard, and I haven't had nearly enough time with you."

Javan admired his grandmother's confidence in her ability to handle Ravier, but he had a hunch he was going to pay for it when training resumed in the morning. As he reached the door, the thought of a brutal training session suddenly seemed much more appealing than walking into a room full of strangers with his eyes unprotected by his color-changing contacts.

"You know, Grandma," Javan said, turning around, "you're right. We haven't spent much time together. Why don't we go back to the house and have lunch, just me and you?"

"Nonsense." Hannah put her hands on Javan's cheeks. "We've been keeping you a secret, but it's time for you to start meeting the people you'll be fighting to save. If you don't like that reason, it's time for them to meet you. They need to know there's hope that they won't have to hide out here cut off from their families for the rest of their lives."

He'd always assumed grandmothers were good at laying guilt trips to get their grandkids to do what they wanted. Now that he was experiencing such a guilt trip first hand, he was both thrilled and frustrated. He was thrilled because he had a grandmother, yet frustrated because he couldn't indulge his selfishness and run away.

Instead, he nodded obediently, and she opened the door.

At first, nothing about his entrance or the place seemed unusual. Booths lined the walls, and square wooden tables that sat groups of two, four and six people were spread throughout the long room. With the exception of a handful of women seated here and there, most of the tables were occupied by men ranging from gruff and buff types to stooped shoulder, white-haired great-grandfather types.

Everyone was dressed in dull, ragged clothes. Apparently beards were cool, long hair was the fad and brushes were outlawed. From the looks of things, his first act as king should be to bring back the brushes and teach the people how to use them. Introducing scissors and the occupation of barber probably wasn't a bad idea, either.

No music played, but the hum of the lunch chatter seemed to provide a natural rhythm that made the room feel alive. It was almost like walking into the cafeteria at school. He wanted to be a part of the rhythm, to contribute his own chatter with his own significant group of friends.

But like at school, no one noticed him when he walked in the door. No one waved him over to sit in a seat saved for him. No one made him feel like this was where he belonged.

He hung his head and began making his way to an empty table in the back of the room. Halfway to his destination, though, one of the bearded men reached out and grabbed his elbow. "Who are you, and how did you get in here?"

Javan could feel the threat in the man's tone as silence overtook the room. This was a protected city. Unfamiliar faces automatically drew suspicion. He closed his eyes and took a deep breath before looking at the questioning man. "I'm--"

"Whoa!" The black haired bearded man with a short forehead and square cheekbones dropped his death grip on Javan's elbow and scooted back in his chair. "For a second I thought you were Dartez, but his eyes were never that green. That must mean the rumors are true. That must mean you're his son. That must mean you're the answer to the prophecy!"

A tidal wave of gasps flooded the room. Once it washed away, Hannah spoke. "Afternoon, everyone. Radic is right. This is Javan, son of my son Dartez."

"How can that be?" Another bearded man stood a few tables away from where Javan stood. His hair was brown, his shoulders were wide and his voice was filled with angry skepticism. "Esmeralda told me herself that her child died at birth. Even if he did survive, that was fifteen years ago. This boy is at least 140 or 150 years old."

"I can assure you that he is my grandson, Javan. Feigning his death was the only way to save his life. He looks much older than he is."

The man didn't seem satisfied with her answers, but he sat down anyway. Hannah thus continued, "We've been keeping him a secret so he can focus on his training with Ravier, Hamilton and Astor." She nudged Radic out of his seat, used the chair for a stepstool and climbed onto the table. All eyes were on her as she announced, "He will be leaving for Japheth in a few weeks to enter the Battle for the Throne—as a Collector!"

The place exploded in applause, but Javan was too stuck on the immediacy of his departure to enjoy the cheers. A few weeks seemed incredibly soon.

CHAPTER 35

Ravier's Problem

R adic cheered, slapped Javan on the back and practically pushed Javan onto the chair he had vacated. "Here. Take my seat. It's the least I can do for our future king!"

The other three men at the table got up as well, allowing Hannah to sit across from Javan. One by one, the men filed by. They shook his hand, wished him well and told him how grateful they were that someone was finally standing up to the Dark King.

Soon the faces and well wishings began to blur together, and Javan was starting to wonder if he was ever going to have a chance to eat. Just when he thought his stomach would never stop growling and the line of adoration would never end, both the scenery and conversation changed.

"What can I get for you?" A thin, unkempt girl with long, braided brown hair who looked to be about thirteen set two glasses of water on the table. She did so quite gracefully considering her wide blue eyes were locked on Javan's green ones.

Rather than squirm under the scrutiny, Javan drained his glass, wiped his mouth and said, "More water, please. A menu would also be helpful."

That brought the waitress out of her daze. "I'm sorry," she said. "A what?"

"A menu. It's a piece of paper that lists what food you serve. You do have menus, don't you?"

"Sweetie," Hannah said, "we only serve two things here for lunch: potato soup with salad or meat sandwiches with chips."

Javan scrunched his face. "Oh. Well, I'm not a big salad guy, but I do like meat. What's on the sandwich?"

"The R & R sandwich is the special for today," the waitress said.

Javan looked to Hannah for some interpretive help. Fortunately she understood his look of confusion and said, "Rabbit and raxen. The rabbit meat tends to be soft and sweet, but the tough, tart raxen meat compliments it well."

The waitress tapped Javan on the shoulder and smiled. "The meat is fresh. I caught and killed the animals myself this morning."

"That's impressive." Javan tried not to let the churning of his stomach show on his face. He couldn't imagine eating a cute, cuddly bunny or one of those oversized rats he saw when tracking Mertzer. "I am in training, though, and don't want to eat anything too filling right now. I think I'll go with the soup and salad."

"I'll have the same, Gesha," Hannah said.

"Great." Gesha looked disappointed but nodded and disappeared with Javan's empty cup. The fact that she didn't ask what kind of dressing he wanted on his salad made him a touch nervous. That probably meant they only had one option, and he had no clue what that option could possibly be.

He looked around to see if anyone else was eating the salad, but apparently the people of Gri favored the R & R sandwich. And staring at visitors. From the people in the booths to the groups of people seated at the tables throughout the restaurant, all eyes were on him even after they had filed by to say hello.

Is this what it felt like to be popular? People staring in awe at you wherever you went?

He thought he would enjoy being the center of attention, but it unnerved him. He shuddered, leaned across the table and whispered, "Everybody is staring at me. I don't like it."

"Tough," Hannah whispered back. "You're going to have to get used to it."

Nobody had trained him for this onslaught of attention. A grueling private session with Ravier was looking more and more appealing by the minute.

◊   ◊   ◊

The newness of his presence wore off by the time his salad arrived, and he was able to eat without feeling like he was being watched. The salad turned out to be quite tasty even if he didn't know what the white dressing that topped the lettuce was called.

The best part of the three-hour lunch was listening to Hannah tell stories about his adventurous father Dartez. The man was fearless and lived to explore. He'd been to every stalker territory within Zandador and every region in the Great Rift. He could survive anywhere from the jungles in Gibbet to the deserts of Varzack.

He had even collected both a Dawn Stalker and a Noon Stalker.

The more Hannah talked, the more convinced Javan became that his father had found a way to survive in the Land of No Return. Once Javan collected his stalkers and became King, he was going lead a search for his banished father. In the meantime, he had a more pressing problem weighing on his mind.

"Grandma," he said, taking advantage of a lull in the conversation, "why does Ravier hate me?"

Hannah pushed her plate aside, wiped her mouth with her napkin and looked around. The place had slowly cleared out, and she and Javan were the only two remaining patrons. Nevertheless, she leaned forward and spoke in a softer tone than usual. "You have to understand that your grandfather was raised by parents who were loyal to the Dark King."

"You mean Ravier grew up wanting to be a part of the king's evilness?"

"In a way. He grew up wanting to be part of the king's army. He wanted to protect the king he was taught to honor and punish those who dared rebel against him."

"He didn't have a problem with that even though he was from the Collector Bloodline?"

"No. But that's only because he didn't know anything about being a Collector. You see, when Ravier's father Vince was recruited by the king to work as a scalologist in the castle, he cut himself off from his father Kenton and the rest of the clan. Vince never spoke of his family to Ravier, never told him about their Collector heritage and never taught him to respect dragons rather than fear and enslave them."

Javan finally felt connected to his grandfather in some way: they had both grown up knowing nothing of their heritage. Ravier knew they shared that connection, so why did he still treat Javan with such emotional disdain? Perhaps the answer was hidden in the rest of Hannah's story. He had to keep her talking. "How did Ravier find out who he was? Did he join the army? And why didn't he ever try to collect any dragons?"

"Slow down," she said, smiling. "I'm getting to all that." She scooted her chair in a little closer and continued. "They had a good life. Vince was a brilliant scalologist and developed many new uses for dragon scales. He was well-compensated for his work, and they lived in the most luxurious section of the capital city."

"Ravier wasn't a science nerd like his dad?"

"Far from it. He was a soldier through and through. Thanks to his father's connections, Ravier was able to train with the best swordfighters in the country rather than serve in the internships prescribed by the king for the youth of Zandador. When he turned 100 and was officially old enough to join the army, he registered on his birthday."

"He joined the army on his 100th birthday? That's so weird."

"What's weird about it?"

"This age thing. You're lucky to live to be 100 on earth. Here, life is just getting started."

Hannah laughed. "Well, I think it's weird that you have such short lifespans on earth. That's hard for me at age 312 to comprehend."

"Wow. Old sure takes on a whole new meaning here."

"I guess it does." After they shared a laugh, Hannah resumed her story. "Anyway, Ravier loved his life. He proved to be a natural leader with a knack for strategy as well as an excellent warrior who was great with any kind of weapon."

"He is pretty good with his sword."

"The Dark King noticed that as well. Within two years, he had Ravier transferred from the general Patrol Unit to a member of the one of the specialized Justice Units. A year later, he was promoted to captain of one of the teams. By the time he was 110, he became the Commander of the entire division, making him the youngest Commander in history."

The pride in Hannah's voice was obvious, but the significance of such a rise within the Zandadorian army was lost on Javan. "That would probably impress me if I knew what the Justice Unit was."

"It consists of four teams of twenty-four soldiers plus one captain per team. Each team is assigned to one of the King's Dragon Stalkers. When the king sends one of his stalkers to a city to execute justice for breaking the law, the team travels with the stalker and fights the rebels who dare fight back."

"I don't get it." Javan sat back and wrinkled his nose. "If the Justice Unit kills people who oppose the Dark King, how was Ravier being the Commander of these teams a good thing?"

"Because that's how he met me."

Javan leaned forward. "Go on."

"He had just taken over as Commander and had been sent to my city with standing orders to kill me."

"This is getting good. Why?"

"I was suspected of protecting a dragon."

"You mean you're a Dragon Protector?"

"Yes. And the suspicions were true; I was protecting a Dawn Stalker. So the King sent Ravier with his Midnight Stalker to kill me and my dragon, Kalek."

"What happened?"

"I had taken refuge in the Dawn Stalker territory. It took Ravier a week to find me, but he finally cornered me under one of the waterfalls that territory is known for. I did a better job of hiding Kalek; Ravier never did find her.

"Rather than kill me right away, he marched me back to the capital city so I could be properly executed in public. Along the way, I learned he was an arrogant man who was completely loyal to the Dark King. But I also learned he had a weakness: me."

"You changed his mind about his loyalty to the Dark King, didn't you?"

"Yes, I did." Hannah beamed. "By the time we made it to the capital, I had managed to convince him that he was wrong, and I was right."

"So you ran away together, and that's how you ended up hiding here in Gri?"

"Not quite. We instead devised a plan that would allow Ravier to remain in his position while working for the underground rebel movement. Ravier convinced the king he deserved a token wife for his impeccable service even though he was far from 'legal' marrying age. The Dark King agreed and let him marry me, thinking marriage to a soldier loyal to a Hunter was a worse punishment than death for a Protector."

"Slick."

"We thought so. Dartez was born a year later, and I took him to visit Kenton in Gri as often as possible. There he learned of his Collector heritage, and we were all convinced he was the answer to the prophecy. He began training to collect dragons before he could walk and seemed to be a natural.

"We kept his training a secret and by all public accounts raised him according to the Dark King's rules. Like a loyal Zandadorian, he joined the army at age 100. And like a loyal Collector, he began collecting Stalkers in preparation for the next Battle for the Throne. He had just collected his Noon Stalker when Ravier told him of a city slated to be ravaged by the Justice Unit.

"He and his stalker swooped in and rescued many people that night, one of whom was your mother."

"She told me that story on the day she was captured."

"Oh. So you know he brought her to Gri, and they were married illegally."

"Yeah. She told me that."

"When she was pregnant with you a few years later, she and Dartez came to visit Ravier and me in Japheth to celebrate the Changing of the Year, the biggest holiday in Zandador. Ravier's father Vince learned of the visit and joined us without an invitation. That's when he realized Esmeralda was pregnant and married illegally to Dartez. He became furious and turned your parents in. Esmeralda became a prisoner, and your father was banished."

Hannah's voice grew softer and softer as she spoke and eventually faded away. She took a few long sips of water before continuing. "On the night you were born, Ravier called off a planned Justice Unit attack and abandoned the team he was with to help Kenton rescue you. He couldn't explain his actions without giving away the secret that you were still alive, so he and I went into hiding. He's been branded a traitor ever since."

"He helped save me?" Great. That meant Javan was indebted to him.

"Yes, he did. But in his eyes, it cost him his job, his purpose and his son. It was easy to blame you when you weren't around. Now you are, and it's taking him some time to realize how foolish he's been to hold a grudge against the most innocent person in all this—you."

"I guess I can understand why he doesn't much like me."

"He'll come around."

"I hope he doesn't kill me with his crazy intense training tactics first."

They shared a smile, but it was interrupted a second later when Ravier burst into the restaurant with Hamilton right behind him. "Get up, Javan. We have work to do."

Hannah stood guard. "Ravier, I already told you he's done training for the day."

"We're not training. We're headed to Japheth. We just got word Esmeralda's execution is scheduled for tomorrow."

"Tomorrow?" Javan gulped, but it didn't help alleviate the panic. "That's too soon! I don't think I'm ready."

"There's only one way to find out." Hamilton tossed Javan his belt loaded with his Stalker swords and stun balls. "Game on, kid."

CHAPTER 36

Keeping Watch

The stillness of the river water beneath the moonlit sky calmed Javan's shattered nerves. Since the time they left the restaurant late that afternoon, everything had been a flurry of activity.

Changing into the appropriate brown, bland attire. Packing supplies. Choosing okties. Flying in zig-zag fashion across Zandador to avoid detection. Setting up camp. Sparring with Hamilton, then Ravier. Being quizzed by Astor. Memorizing the plan to stop Esmeralda's execution and introduce him as a competitor for the throne.

They were tucked in a quiet spot half a mile from the road that led to Elieve, a tiny fishing town to the west. The capital city of Japheth was to their north, the River that Divides Zandador just below his feet. He was taking the first watch while his three older traveling companions were getting some rest.

He had volunteered to keep watch. With all he had learned about Ravier earlier in the day, the rushed trip and the impending execution of his mother, he was too wound up to sleep anyway. He also couldn't help but wonder how different his life would be once people knew who he was and what he was attempting to accomplish by collecting dragons.

He had lived in anonymity his whole life. Now all eyes would be on him. He was going to have people to lead. And enemies to fight. Was he ready for such a life? Was he ready for the spotlight?

What worried him more was whether or not he was ready for power. Could he handle it without losing his sense of self? Or would he let the attention and control change him and turn into an obnoxious, cocky, power-hungry scumbag like the Dark King he was going up against?

"One thing at a time, Javan," he told himself. "One thing at a time. First you have to survive the night."

A few deep, cleansing breaths eased his worries as he gripped the handles of his stalker swords girded about his waist and tuned in to the sounds of the night around him. He was on duty and ready to attack if any man or animal dared disturb his watch.

◊   ◊   ◊

As midnight approached, Javan struggled to stay vigilant. He had caught himself dozing several times. Fortunately he snapped to attention again whenever he heard the slightest sound, such as the breeze rustling the leaves or a small animal snapping a twig. But the noise that brought him back to attention at the moment was the sound of voices.

The voices weren't coming from behind him in the camp he was guarding; they were coming from the direction of the town down the river. Had some of the townspeople spotted the camp?

Without bothering to wake Hamilton, Ravier or Astor, Javan made his way through the woods alongside the road to investigate. In a matter of minutes, he found himself looking at the town of Elieve.

The dirt road he had been following snaked its way through a small cluster of log buildings situated along the riverbank. No light shone from any of the buildings, and Javan would have assumed the place was deserted if three men armed with swords weren't lingering at the edge of town.

Two of them were sitting on rocks and leaning against the side of the outermost building. The third had his back to Javan. He was picking up rocks and tossing them into the river.

Something about his muscle-bound physique and dreadlocks seemed familiar. When the man spoke, Javan recognized the voice. It belonged to Micah.

"Even though I'm going to miss toting her around and instilling fear in people, I am ready to see Esmeralda die tomorrow," Micah said, launching a rock into the water. "We haven't had a good execution in a while."

Javan's heart quickened. His mother was here. Probably in that building less than a hundred feet from where he stood. He could sneak in, rescue her now and avoid the potential fiasco of their plan falling apart tomorrow. He just needed to circle around and come at the building from the other side.

"I know what you mean." One of Micah's cohorts leaned forward. "Our jobs get boring when we have no one to torture or kill."

Micah chucked another rock. "My thoughts exactly."

"Don't worry boys," Javan muttered. "Your lives are about to get a lot more interesting." He crouched and was about to sprint across the road when a skinny kid who looked to be about ten came whistling along.

Javan immediately dropped to his knees behind a trio of thick trees and froze as he watched the kid continue his carefree journey toward the town. He had a quiver slung over his shoulder and was carrying a bow in one hand and the carcass of what looked to be an oversized badger in the other.

It was the whistling that seemed to get the attention of Micah and the other two soldiers. They spread out to block the road. Micah positioned himself in the middle and waited with sword drawn.

The happy tune of the whistling boy faded into the night as he approached the soldiers.

"What do we have here?" Micah said, circling the kid. "A lawbreaker who chooses to ignore the curfew?"

"I...I...was...hunting," he stuttered. "My family needed to eat. I couldn't return empty-handed."

"You will tonight!" Micah snatched the carcass and flung it into the river.

The boy gasped. Javan considered helping the boy out by retrieving the dead animal. But he had a hunch he could be of more help by staying put and seeing how things played out. He put his hands on his swords in case he needed to interfere in a hurry.

"The King's laws," Micah continued in his arrogant, judgmental tone, "are to protect you from the dangers that lurk in these lands. He demands you are back in your homes by nightfall in order to keep you safe."

"Yes, sir. I'm sorry, sir."

"I cannot allow this blatant disregard for the King's curfew to go unpunished." Micah stuck the point of his sword under the boy's chin. "On your knees."

The kid hung his head and obeyed. Micah cut the quiver off the boy's back and sheathed his sword. He then unclipped the whip that hung from the side of his belt.

"I don't think so," Javan muttered. He drew his stalker swords and started to charge when someone grabbed his arm and pulled him back.

"You cannot stop this," Ravier said, whispering in his ear.

The boy screamed as Micah lashed his back.

Javan cringed and pulled against Ravier. "That kid has done nothing wrong," Javan whispered. "I have to stop it."

Another lash. Another scream.

"You can't." Ravier tightened his grip on Javan's arm. "Nor can I, as much as I would like to. We need our presence to be a surprise tomorrow. Otherwise the plan will not work."

A string of lashes followed by a string of screams.

"There has to be something we can do," Javan pleaded, tears filling his eyes. He didn't have the heart to look at the beating taking place, but he could feel every agonizing sound. The whip whistling through the air. Leather cutting flesh. Screams of the victim. Laughs of the lasher.

"He'll survive," Ravier said. "Your mother won't if you help him now."

"This isn't right!" Javan tried to move forward. Ravier pulled him back and hugged him, covering Javan's ears. When the beating stopped, Ravier let go.

Javan forced himself to look up. Watching Micah kick the bleeding boy and send him crumpling to the ground sickened Javan.

"Get him out of my sight," Micah said, recoiling his whip. The two soldiers standing by picked the kid up and dragged him down the street while Micah clipped his whip back on his belt and resumed tossing rocks as though nothing had happened.

"Someday," Javan said quietly, glaring at Micah, "I'm going to hold him accountable for what he just did."

"You can't unless you're king," Ravier said. "Come. Let's get back to camp. You need rest. Tomorrow's a big day."

As they walked away, the kid's agonizing screams echoed in Javan's mind. That wasn't a sound he would soon forget.

◊　◊　◊

Throwing rocks in the river hadn't settled Micah's nerves after delivering that beating. He hoped food would help. When it didn't, he offered the midnight meal to the prisoner.

"Eat up." He removed Esmeralda's gag and handed her the plate of food through the bars. "It's the last chance you'll have to eat before the dragon eats you."

As he walked away, he heard her speak. "I know it's an act."

He stopped. Keeping his back to her, he said, "What are you talking about?"

"You. You put on a tough show with that whip of yours, but hurting people bothers you. You don't want it to, but it does."

How did she know? He had never told anyone that secret.

"You're not your father," she continued. "You don't have to be so cruel."

"I disagree." He whispered his next words. "Mastering the art of cruelty is the only way to survive when you're a son of the Dark King."

CHAPTER 37

Execution Day

S ubdued conversations, shuffling feet and the rustling of papers eased Javan out of a deep sleep. Considering he had slept under the stars with nothing but a thick blanket separating him from the hard ground, he managed to get a decent night of rest once he returned to the campsite. Blocking out the memory of the beating he had witnessed proved to be a bit challenging when he first closed his eyes, but the physical fatigue was so overwhelming that it had conquered the emotional trauma.

He stretched, sat up and took note of the overcast sky. A few breaths of the humid morning air filled his nostrils with the smell of rain. The plan didn't account for rain. Would it matter? What adjustments would they need to make? And was it the normal, just-get-you-wet kind of rain, or were they in for an ouch-this-stings red rain storm like he had experienced when he first arrived in Zandador?

Then again, perhaps public executions were postponed when it rained. Or maybe it didn't matter. Maybe they operated football-game style and followed through with the killing regardless of weather conditions, even if the precipitation stung. Before Javan could work himself into a proper panic over the implications of the weather, Hamilton noticed he was awake.

"Morning, kid!" Hamilton broke away from Ravier and Astor who were studying papers and talking quietly on the other side of the small clearing. Hamilton didn't seem to think their conversation was all that important and plopped his massive body beside Javan. "Ready for your big day?"

"If I say no, does that mean we can go back to Gri?"

Hamilton smiled and slapped Javan on the back. "Not a chance."

"That's what I thought." Javan rubbed his neck. Sleeping without a proper pillow left his neck a little sore. The personal massage helped eased the soreness, and he nodded toward the other two men. "What are they talking about?"

"Oh, just finalizing plans. You remember what to do, right?"

"Yeah. I remember." At least he knew what to do right now. But what if his mind went blank come crunch time? A touch of queasiness gripped Javan's stomach. Now that game day was here, he was getting nervous. If he botched the play, it's not like his team would miss out on a touchdown. If he screwed up, his mother would lose her life.

"Any questions?"

"Not at the moment." None that he wanted to voice, anyway.

"You'll do fine, kid. Plus the three of us will be there to back you up. Now get up. Pack your stuff. Grab yourself a bite to eat out of that bag of deliciousness Hannah packed us." Hamilton stood. "I'm off to feed the okties. We leave in fifteen."

The mention of okties sent the butterflies in Javan's stomach fluttering. He wasn't sure he was ready for this. He wasn't sure he was ready for this at all.

◊　◊　◊

After a short flight north, Javan, Ravier, Hamilton and Astor stashed their okties beside a lake five miles outside of the city. The lake was a good mile or so from the gravel road leading into Japheth, so Javan had already worked up a sweat by the time they reached the edge of the road.

"Javan, put your hat on and stay behind me," Ravier whispered, donning a brown leather hat with a wide round brim. "Astor, stick by Javan's side. Hamilton, you walk behind us, and don't let either of these two get lost in the crowd."

"Yes, sir," Hamilton said. He took up his position in the rear while Javan secured his own wide-rimmed leather hat on his head.

Astor moved to the side of Javan and linked his right arm in Javan's left. "This way I'll make sure you keep up with me," the old man said, smiling.

"I was worried about that," Javan said, returning his smile. But all smiles disappeared when Ravier looked back, nodded and led the way forward into the crowd. They merged into the traffic on the road looking as if they got there like everyone else: on foot.

Javan was starting to wonder how much further they would have to walk when he spotted the high stone wall that protected the capital city. The wall was wide enough for soldiers to walk on, and Javan could see through the sunglasses he was wearing to hide his eyes that armed archers were stationed about every ten feet.

From what Javan understood, they were trained to shoot anyone or anything that flew over the walls and into the city's air space.

The road itself was packed with swarms of people all dressed in drab brown clothes. Everyone who was able had been ordered to march in from the surrounding towns and cities. And the closer they got to the gate, the entrance to the city became one giant pedestrian bottleneck. Javan was feeling claustrophobic just looking at the crowd.

They would be entering the city unarmed. No one was allowed entrance into the city while carrying a weapon. Ravier figured the guards would be extra vigilant about that rule today, so he had decided not to risk getting caught with weapons and left them hidden with the okties. The plan thus called for relying on the power of persuasive words to save Esmeralda rather than brute force.

Javan had grown accustomed to wearing his stalker sword belt and felt helpless without his swords and stun balls strapped around his waist. He hoped Ravier's words were as persuasive as he imagined they would be.

They stayed along the edge of the road and shuffled in silence toward the iron gate. No one around them spoke, either. Were they quiet because it was such a solemn occasion, or was there some law against talking while entering the city?

Since he couldn't gauge the mood of the people by their chatter, he studied their faces. The young faces around him looked eager, like they were about to walk into Disney World for the first time and experience the wonders of a whole new world.

The faces of their parents were more stoic. They had been here before. They had seen the sights. They knew what they were about to witness.

Javan only spotted a few older people in the crowd. They simply looked resigned. Beaten. Defeated. They looked like they were walking to their own execution.

In a way he supposed they were. Everyone was. That was the purpose of the day. To kill the spirits of the people.

Hannah was right. The people did need hope. He looked forward to seeing their faces when they discovered they had something to hope for.

"File into lines!" The command from a soldier in a black uniform marching along the entrance into the city jerked Javan's attention straight ahead. "Prepare to be searched! No one enters the city without being searched!"

In front of him, the crowd began dividing into dozens of lines that spanned the width of the arched opening. A soldier was assigned to each line. Unlike the guy barking orders, they were wearing red uniforms.

One by one, the people stepped forward, spread their arms and let the soldiers pat them down from head to toe. No one argued. No one complained. No one dared make a sound. They just followed the rules like good little sheep.

At least the unquestioned compliance allowed the lines to move quickly. Ravier made it through his inspection without a problem. Then it was Javan's turn.

He stepped up and spread his arms. But the soldier, a woman with short dark hair and a square nose, paused her systematic pat-down procedure to question him. "Why the hat and glasses? The sun isn't even shining today."

He watched Ravier tense in front of him. They were all supposed to make it into the city without being noticed, and now Javan was being called out before he even stepped a foot inside the gate. If he didn't play this right, their entire plan would be ruined.

"I'm sensitive to the light," Javan said, dropping his arms and shrugging. "I usually stay indoors all day, but my grandfather insisted I come. He wanted to make sure I saw firsthand what happens when you disobey the King."

The soldier squinted, cocked her head, then said, "Arms up."

Javan obeyed. He had to hold his breath to keep from laughing as she patted under his arms and down his sides. It was times like this he hated being ticklish. Once she finished checking his hips and legs to make sure he wasn't hiding any weapons, she let him through with a nod of her head.

He waited with Ravier as Astor and Hamilton endured their inspections. They made it through without any trouble and once again fell into step with the forward-moving crowd. This time, though, Astor acted as a tour guide as they walked.

"This is the outer city," Astor said. "It's three miles wide and wraps all the way around the inner city. Millions of people live in these houses and work in the factories that make things like clothes, shoes and construction materials."

Side street after side street looked the same. Tiny wooden shacks with flat roofs built within arm's length of each other lined the pebbled streets. The even smaller yards were nothing more than patches of dirt. No grass, shrubs or trees were anywhere in sight.

"This place is depressing," Javan said. "Do people really live here on purpose?"

"If they're assigned to factory life, yes."

"That's miserable. Does the inner city look like this, too?"

"Not at all. The inner city is flush with fountains, trees, flowers and rolling hills of thick green grass. The buildings are also much nicer, and it's a beautiful place to live."

"If factory workers live here, who lives in the inner city?"

"Those favored by the Dark King. Mostly the scalologists, intellectuals and artists."

"This is my first visit to Japheth, too." A hunched over man missing his two front teeth who was walking beside Javan joined the conversation. "Exciting, isn't it? Finally having a chance to visit the capital city?"

"I think so," a lady somewhere behind them said. "I'm glad this Esmeralda woman was stupid enough to break the law. They're letting everybody who's nobody into the city today, and we didn't even need travel papers!"

That sparked conversations throughout the previously silent crowd. Javan had to work to ignore the hateful and demeaning things they were saying about his mother for the next few slow-moving miles. They were marching to watch her die, and none of them seemed to have any problem with that.

It angered Javan, but it also helped him focus more intensely on his mission and what he needed to do to help change their warped perspectives.

The chatter ceased once again as they approached the gates to the inner city. Soldiers were posted on these twenty-foot high stone walls as well, but this time the people didn't have to separate into lines to be searched. They were allowed direct access beneath a golden arch, and it was the awe and wonder of the visitors to the city that caused the calming of the chatter.

The streets were paved with slate. Those that branched off the main road led to spectacular houses that sat atop slight hills covered with grass, flowers and trees. Lakes dominated the valleys between the hills, and each one was enhanced by stunning fountains in the middle of the water.

The most breathtaking sight of all, however, was the castle. It was straight ahead, a black stone building perched on the highest hill in the middle of the city. An array of towers—some round, some square—of differing heights enclosed the main building that, based on the windows Javan could count from the distance, was ten stories high and twenty rooms wide.

Javan imagined the stone sparkled on a sunny day, adding to the castle's mystique. "Are we going to the castle?" Javan asked. He wanted an up close and personal view of the place. He had never seen a castle before and was itching for a tour. As big as the place was, a tour would probably be an all-day adventure.

"No," Astor said. "Executions take place in Stalker Square, right outside the castle gates."

Disappointment washed over Javan as they walked up the gradual hill. He watched the castle get bigger and bigger the closer they got to it, and the desire to explore within its walls also grew with each step.

Then he caught sight of Stalker Square.

CHAPTER 38

Stalker Square

Javan had been so focused on the castle dominating the distant hill that he overlooked the crowd coming to a standstill as they reached the crest of the hill they were traveling on. It took Hamilton nudging him from behind to redirect his gaze to the world in front of him.

"That's Stalker Square," Hamilton said, pointing down.

Javan found himself standing at the top of an amphitheater. Countless rows of stone steps wrapped three quarters of the way around a square paved with Stalker scales that was half the size of a football field. The steps dead-ended into a wall on the far side of the square. Arched openings that served as box seats were built into the wall, and a gate in the middle led to the castle grounds.

Four fountains with life-size statues of Dragon Stalkers as centerpieces decorated the four corners of the square. The statues depicted the dragons at the height of their feeding times. Rainbow-colored Dawn and Dusk Stalkers thus each filled a fountain in the front two corners while a golden Noon Stalker and a black Midnight Stalker each filled a fountain in the back two corners.

A platform about the size of a theatre stage and supported by four tall, round columns marked the center of the square. It was accessed by regal spiral staircases on both the front and the back.

His mother would soon be standing on that stage. According to the plan, he would need to be as close to the front left column as possible. But right now, no one was even occupying the stairs of the amphitheater, much less the territory right near the stage. All access points were roped off and guarded by soldiers.

"Is this as close as they'll let us get?" Javan asked. He was on the brink of panic. He couldn't save his mother from here. If he had his stun balls, he might be able to make a go of it, but unarmed, he didn't stand a chance.

"Relax, kid," Hamilton said. "They'll let us fill the place up soon."

As if on cue, the castle gates opened. A man wearing a white shirt and black pants and carrying a trumpet walked through the gates, across the square and up the spiral stairs to the stage. He blew three long notes that reverberated throughout the stadium. Once the echoes died down and the crowd packed around the top of the steps hushed, the man spoke.

"Execution ceremonies are to begin in two hours." No microphone enhanced the man's voice, but Javan could hear every word as clearly as if the man were standing beside him. "Soldiers, let the people in!"

The soldiers unhooked the ropes, and the people flooded forward. Ravier led the charge down their row of steps, and Hamilton picked Astor up to keep the old man from getting trampled in the sea of people descending toward the square. Javan stayed between Ravier and Hamilton but had to keep his elbows up to keep from getting battered on his right and left during the surge.

He almost tripped on the steep steps several times and was relieved when they made it to the flat ground of the square. Then the battle for positioning began.

They, along with thousands of other people from every direction who wanted to watch from the front row, sprinted toward the stage. Javan kept his eyes on the front left column as he ran. That's where he wanted to be. That's where he had to be in order for the plan to work.

Ravier and Hamilton, however, needed to be near the front staircase. Javan thus kept plowing forward when Ravier split to the right. He didn't look for him again until he reached his intended spot.

Hamilton, still toting Astor, filed in right behind him. "This is where we part ways, kid," Hamilton said, setting Astor on his feet beside Javan. "Stick with Astor, and don't let anyone get in your way."

"Yes, sir," Javan said. He tracked Hamilton's walk to the bottom of the front staircase and watched him meet up with Ravier.

So far, so good. Now all they had to do was wait.

◊   ◊   ◊

After two straight hours, Javan had had about enough of being pushed and pulled and poked and prodded as he fought to retain his position. The task of holding his position became more and more difficult as more and more people packed into the square like sardines. The bigger, stronger men were forcing their way to the front lines with their wives and children in tow. He and Astor thus lost ground with each new wave of people, and he found himself constantly inching his way back to the front while pulling the old man with him.

When they made it to the front yet again, he took a moment to catch his breath and study his surroundings. The entire amphitheater was so packed with people all decked out in brown clothes that the square looked like a giant mud pit while the seating area appeared to be more like a dirt hill with a pulse rather than rows of stadium seats occupied by individual people. And they were all here for one purpose: to watch his mother die.

"Look! The gates are opening!" a nearby spectator said. "The show's about to start!"

All eyes turned toward the castle gate, and the crowd parted to form a pathway from the gate to the platform. Whispers spread throughout the finger-pointing crowd, and Javan strained his neck to see what they were all pointing at. It took several agonizing minutes, but he finally saw Esmeralda come in to view about halfway between the gates and the stage.

She wore the same plain brown dress as the rest of the women in the crowd, only hers was about five sizes too big and overwhelmed her emaciated frame. Her long black hair had been chopped off and hung in uneven patches above her shoulders. Her hands were clasped in front of her, which was only natural since her wrists were tied together. She walked with a limp, favoring her right leg.

As she drew closer, Javan also noticed dark circles under her eyes and a strangely pale complexion despite her naturally tan skin. Nevertheless, she walked with confidence and kept her head held high as she moved forward and ascended the steps to the stage.

Javan tried to catch her eye, to let her know he was there, to give her hope. But she was too focused on the path ahead to look into any of the faces of the crowd below her.

Six soldiers all carrying trumpets followed behind her. She took her place on the center of the stage while the soldiers fanned out beside her, three on each side. They simultaneously lifted their instruments, played a series of triumphant-sounding notes and said in unison, "Prepare the way for Dahlia the Dawn Stalker and Viviana the twelfth queen, mother of the thirteenth son!"

The twelfth queen? Javan coughed to cover his surprise. How many queens were there? Were all thirteen sons hers? Or did some of them belong to some of the other queens? Javan was thoroughly confused and wished learning the hierarchy of the royal family had been part of his training.

He was about to ask Astor for a quick lesson when the castle gates opened once again. The crowd gasped and pushed back to form an even wider walkway than the one they formed for Esmeralda, allowing Javan to easily see the white-scaled Dawn Stalker from where he stood. Standing atop the dragon and holding its reins was a dark-skinned woman with a long black braid draped over her right shoulder. She wore a flowing purple gown, jeweled necklaces and a diamond-studded golden crown.

She slowly guided the dragon forward, soaking in the reverence of the bowing crowd as she proceeded. The dragon kept her nose stuck in the air just like the queen. Javan wasn't sure if that was because the dragon was a snob or because that's how the queen forced Dahlia to walk by the way she held the reins of the halter. Then he heard the dragon's thoughts.

That's right, people. Back away and feast your eyes on my magnificence. I know I'm beautiful now, but I'm even more stunning when my scales change colors. Dahlia stuck her nose even higher in the air and walked a little slower. *But at least I do get to enjoy the admiration without wanting to eat everyone.*

Javan could practically feel the dragon's arrogance the closer she walked to him. As self-absorbed as she was, Javan wondered how she functioned without a mirror to stare at herself in wherever she went.

When the queen reached the stage, she turned the dragon around to face the gates. That's when Javan noticed Dahlia's tail ended in a ragged stump rather than its naturally thin point. He felt a stab of sympathy for the vain dragon and wondered what it was like to be marked as a slave who was stripped of all free will.

More triumphant notes sounded from the stage followed by another announcement. "Prepare the way for Eli the Dusk Stalker and the thirteenth son, Micah the Mighty!"

"Eli?" Astor said, sounding surprised.

They hadn't expected Eli, the dragon who was once a part of Kenton's collection and Mertzer's brother, to make an appearance today. Javan took a few steps to his left and strained his neck around Dahlia's massive body to catch a glimpse of the dragon Omri had used to cheat his way into power.

At the castle gates, Micah stood at the base of the stalker's neck. Micah's black skin and even blacker uniform contrasted sharply with the white scales of the Dusk Stalker he stood upon. One hand held the reins of the halter while he pumped the other in the air in victory fashion. The crowd erupted in applause, and Micah forced the dragon to trot forward.

The dragon was not an impressive Stalker specimen. His long body was thin and gaunt with patches of missing scales. His vacant eyes and defeated posture didn't exactly strike fear in the hearts of the onlookers. Nor did the halter the dragon was forced to wear.

While Dahlia's halter looked similar to the halter he used on his horse Storm, Eli's had a muzzle attached to the noseband which prevented him from opening his mouth. The leather strips also weren't sitting flat against Eli's scales thanks to spikes on the underside of the halter. The cruelty of the halter reminded Javan of Micah's cruelty.

The image of Micah whipping the boy last night played in Javan's mind. Hearing the crowd praise a man who would do such a despicable thing made Javan want to knock Micah off the dragon and talk some sense into this senseless crowd.

The only thing that kept him from taking such action was looking up and seeing his mother. She was ignoring the fanfare behind her and staring straight ahead. She appeared unmovable. Unflappable. Unshakable. If she could be a vision of strength on the brink of death, he could be strong enough to not move or act until Astor gave him the cue to do so.

Micah steered Eli to the stage beside his mother and her dragon, climbed up his dragon's neck and deposited himself on the platform. Amidst the cheers, Javan tuned in to the dragon's conversation.

Well, well, Dahlia said, *look who got to come out and play today.*

Not my choice, Eli said.

Nor mine. You are a miserable excuse for a dragon and belong in that dark little dungeon where the Hunter keeps you.

You're just bitter the Hunter didn't think enough of you to let you lead the execution.

I am the favored one! He knows I--

"People of Zandador," Micah said, now standing in front of Esmeralda. His booming voice quieted the conversation of the dragons and the cheers of the crowd. "People of Zandador, welcome Serenity the Midnight Stalker and your King, King Omri the Omnipotent!"

Micah turned and pointed up to the sky in the direction of the castle. The trumpeters played loud, bold notes as a dark grey spot in the light grey sky grew bigger and bigger.

Omri was approaching on his winged dragon just as they expected. Javan's heart began to beat a little faster. The arrival of the Dark King signaled the start of their plan.

CHAPTER 39

The Dark King

Serenity spewed a string of lightning bolts as she flew the Dark King over the castle walls. The brilliant flashes of bright lights were met with shrieks of both terror and awe from the crowd below her.

The shrieks didn't stop the trumpeting soldiers from playing. They maintained their tune and their focus even as they moved to the back edge of the stage to create a landing space for the Midnight Stalker.

Esmeralda wasn't as accommodating. Despite Omri and the Stalker hovering above her and the wind from the dragon's wings blowing her already disheveled hair, she maintained her position. Javan was sure he saw her smirk until Micah snagged her arm and forced her to the front of the stage.

With the landing area cleared, Omri masterfully landed the massive dragon onto the platform. The entire platform and the columns it rested on shook from the weight of the grey-scaled beast. The stage was long enough to hold the twenty-five-foot long dragon, but not long enough to hold her stumped tail. It hung over the edge and came close to scraping the ground near where Javan stood. Had its tip not been cut off, it would have easily reached the ground.

Serenity snorted several puffs of electrified smoke as she brought her pointy wings to rest alongside her body and bent her tall, fifteen-foot high frame to allow Omri an easier path of descent. The Dark King took his cue and slid down the dragon's right front leg. The moment his feet touched the stage, he lifted his hands in the air, palms to the sky and shouted, "Welcome!"

The crowd roared to life in response. Whistles. Shouts. Cheers. Applause. And the rumbling of stomping feet all along the stone stadium steps. Like an orchestra director, Omri kept his hands lifted, encouraging more and louder noises.

The people responded. Javan could sense the desperation they felt to please the tall, broad-shouldered black man beckoning them to praise him.

Unlike his queen, he wore no crown.

And unlike his son, he wore his black hair in short, tight braids rather than long, loose dreadlocks. His hairline was beginning to recede on either side of his brow, his dark brown eyes looked almost black against the whites of his eyes and the nostrils on his wide, flat nose flared in tune with each pump of his hands.

His boots added to the clamor as he paced from corner to corner of the platform in his black pants, white shirt and long black leather coat. The man must have prided fashion over comfort because it was way too hot out to be wearing such a warm coat.

The man radiated more arrogance than that of his narcissistic Dawn Stalker. He knew he controlled the crowd, and the crowd knew they were at his mercy. The plan to challenge this man suddenly seemed suicidal.

Omri stopped his pacing at center stage so that he stood in front of Esmeralda and Micah. He slowly scanned the crowd, then quickly snapped his hands into fists. The noise immediately ceased.

"Good people of Zandador," Omri said, his voice vibrating throughout the square, "you have done well to come here today. Your willing obedience to the Laws of the Land have allowed our nation to prosper, have kept our cities safe and have contributed to longer lifespans. It always pains me to have to send my Dragon Stalkers on city raids when I learn someone has broken one of my laws, but your compliance these past few decades has prevented many such punishments, so I thank you."

I thank you, too, Eli said. *I despise the taste of humans.*

You despise being a dragon. Chills shot through Javan when he heard the eerie voice of Serenity respond to Eli. *It's the fear of humans that makes them the most fun prey to consume. I wish I was the one who was hungry right now. These people would make a splendid feast.*

Compared to the other dragons he had encountered so far, this one was different.

More menacing.

Almost evil.

"But there is one," Omri continued, channeling the menacing evilness of the Midnight Stalker, "who has refused to obey." Anger coursed through his words and darted out of his eyes. "Even after she broke the marriage AND child-bearing laws, I showed her mercy. I allowed her to live a comfortable life as my servant in the castle. I even allowed her to use that beautiful voice of hers to sing for me.

"And how did she repay me for my merciful kindness? She ran away. Worse still, she put our entire world in danger when she attempted to activate the portal that leads to earth."

Attempted? She didn't just attempt that feat, Javan wanted to say, she did indeed activate the portal. But Javan could tell by the way Micah shifted his feet and averted his gaze that he hadn't shared the entire truth about Esmeralda's capture with his father.

"Disobedience is not tolerated in my kingdom," Omri said. "We are here today to remind you of that fact and to remind you what happens when you rebel."

Omri motioned to the trumpeters. They played three sharp, unnerving notes.

"When you rebel, my stalkers deliver justice," Omri said. "Today that honor falls to Vasilis, my Noon Stalker!"

The Dark King turned and pointed to the sky in the direction from which he had flown in on moments ago. The crowd began to murmur as the golden dragon appeared in the distance.

Javan had to take action before the dragon arrived. He stepped forward, but Astor caught his arm. "Not yet."

Micah moved to the far front corner of the stage while Omri moved to the corner above where Javan stood. That left Esmeralda all alone at the front and center of the stage, easy prey for the hungry Noon Stalker on his way.

The dragon passed the castle walls.

Javan looked to Astor. He shook his head, telling him to wait.

Wide-eyed and anxious, Javan held himself back and watched the dragon float over the crowd. Just as it was about to reach the stage, Astor let go of Javan's arm. "Now."

"Finally," Javan said. He sprinted the five steps to the column in front of him and touched the stone seconds before the dragon's claws snatched Esmeralda.

CHAPTER 40

The Contenders

The stone Javan expected to feel as he pressed his palms against the column wasn't stone at all. It was actually a soft, malleable surface that lit up and vibrated when he touched it. A perfect mold of his hands remained once he stepped back. The vibrations stopped but the glow lingered, and a vertical line of four triangles the size of dragon scales appeared above his handprints.

"Halt!" The Dark King ordered Vasilis to a hovering standstill above Esmeralda and peered over the edge. "Who touched the column?"

The people around Javan jumped back, sweeping Astor with them. How they were able to create a fifteen foot berth around him in an instant in the midst of such a packed crowd amazed him. And spoke volumes about the fear this king instilled in his people.

No one had stood up to this man by daring to compete in the Battle for the Throne in centuries. With the Dark King's gaze fixed on Javan, Javan began to understand why. An obnoxious form of power-hungry evil emanated from the Dark King, and Javan was tempted to join the quivering crowd behind him. A glance at his mother, however, encouraged him to stand his ground.

Javan adjusted his hat, cleared his throat and said, "I did."

Think I'll eat him, too, just for disturbing my meal, Vasilis said.

I would, Serenity said. *As lean as he is, he won't be very filling, though.*

Doesn't matter. He's young. He'll have a nice crunch to him.

Hearing the telepathic dragon conversation unnerved Javan further. They were, after all, discussing his demise. But he didn't want to clue them in to the fact that he could understand them. As long as he was able to eavesdrop, he might be able to pick up some interesting information about dragons or the Dark King that could provide an advantage for him in the competition.

Nevertheless, he couldn't resist looking up into the angry eyes of the half-golden dragon as he floated above the heads of those standing on the stage. The view into the two large black pools of hatred sent shivers down Javan's spine. He didn't detect one ounce of kindness in the dragon's heart, but maybe that was because they were meeting at the height of its feeding time and it wanted to make a meal out of him.

Vasilis snorted a puff of smoke in Javan's direction, then began making slow circles above the people in Stalker Square while awaiting his master's command to commence his meal.

"You?" The outrage in Omri's voice disappeared, and he resumed his relaxed demeanor. "Why, you are too young to know the significance of what happens when you touch that column." He stretched his hand and waved it over the crowd. "Many people are here today. One of them must have bumped you into the column. You may apologize to the people for your unfortunate accident and for stalling the justice that awaits Esmeralda."

The commanding tone of Omri's voice was unmistakable. Javan wanted to back down and follow the king's admonition to apologize. That sure was easier than standing his ground and risking becoming part of the Noon Stalker's next meal. But if he caved, his mother would die.

"I cannot apologize because it was not an accident." Javan stepped forward and took his hat off. "I am Javan from the Collector Bloodline. I came here today to enter the Battle for the Throne."

As one, the people sucked in a breath of shock and held it as they awaited Omri's response. Even the dragons joined the breathless silence.

Omri crossed his arms and narrowed his eyes. "No one has dared challenge me in 400 years."

"I am not challenging you, sir." Javan felt his voice begin to falter and had to work to make it sound strong and steady. He took a deep breath and made himself say his well-rehearsed words. "I am simply acting in willing obedience to the Laws of the Land. Your justice demands I be allowed to compete in the Battle for the Throne."

"Wait," Micah said, walking over to stand beside Omri, "you look familiar."

"That's because we have met before," Javan said. Apparently Micah beat up so many people he didn't remember them all.

"We have?"

"You have?" Omri asked.

"Yes." Javan nodded toward Esmeralda. "On the day she opened the portal. I was with her when you captured her. If you had given her a chance to explain, you would have learned she was trying to send me to Earth so I would not enter the Battle for the Throne. She was acting in King Omri's best interest and should be released."

"Micah, explain." Omri turned his wrath on Micah. "Why was this rebel not arrested?"

"Esmeralda was the known rebel. He, umm, didn't seem important."

"Well, clearly he is a problem that needs to be dealt with." Omri slapped Micah's face. "You are no longer my son. Now, *soldier*, arrest him."

Javan almost felt sorry for Micah as he bowed his head, rubbed his cheek and headed for the stairs. All pity washed away, however, when Javan remembered Micah was on his way to arrest him.

"You cannot arrest me," Javan said. Even though Omri was reacting as Ravier had predicted, Javan still didn't like the prospect of being arrested. He took a deep breath and made himself say the words he had rehearsed that would set Ravier up for his speech. "I am a competitor in the Battle for the Throne. The law which you so nobly uphold allows me the freedom to compete without fear of infringement from the current ruler."

"He is right, King Omri." Ravier's bold declaration drew all attention in his direction. He zipped up the staircase to the stage, blocking Micah's descent. With all eyes on him, he began reading from the parchment he had smuggled in under his hat. "According to the Law of the Land, 'A Battle for the Throne shall determine who rules Zandador. The Battle shall take place in the final year of a ruler's 100-year-reign. A person from any one of the four Bloodlines—except for the reigning king or queen—may enter the competition at any point during a Battle year without fear of infringement from the current ruler.

"'To officially enter the Battle for the Throne, a person must touch a Bloodline Column in Stalker Square in front of no less than twelve witnesses. If his or her Bloodline is pure, handprints will remain in the column and four scale slots will appear. The first person to fill the scale slots from the stalkers he has collected, protected, hunted or destroyed will become the new king or queen.

"'If no one fills the slots by sundown of the final day of the Battle Year, the reigning ruler will retain the throne for 100 more years.'"

Once the echo of Ravier's words faded away, he continued. "King Omri, you have praised your people for obeying the law. Shouldn't you do the same and allow the Battle to commence? After all, disobedience is not tolerated in your kingdom."

Javan watched Omri fume at hearing his own words repeated back to him. He had been backed in to a corner, and Javan could tell the man wasn't sure how to respond.

Meanwhile, more and more of Vasilis's scales were turning golden as he floated above the crowd. Javan could feel the dragon's mood darken with each changing scale. If Vasilis wasn't allowed to eat soon, his appetite would become insatiable. Then no one in the Square would be safe.

"Of course my father will allow the Battle to commence." Micah's words turned the infuriated look on Omri's face to one of stone cold anger.

◊　　◊　　◊

Micah shot his father a sideways glance and knew he was standing on shaky ground. Nevertheless, he continued to address the crowd. He didn't want to spend any more time in the dungeon and knew that's where he was headed if he didn't talk fast.

"King Omri is an honorable man who upholds the Law and only wants what is best for the people of Zandador. It is a Battle for the Throne year, and you deserve to experience the thrill and excitement of such a battle. But there is no battle without an opponent."

He paused and smiled. He was about to make history. "On behalf of King Omri and the Hunter Bloodline, I present myself as a proxy competitor in the Battle for the Throne!"

The crowd cheered Micah's announcement. They liked his idea. But would his father? He held his breath and waited for Omri's reaction.

CHAPTER 41

A Dragon or Death

"My son is right," Omri said, quieting the crowd. "Many of you have never witnessed a Battle for the Throne. It is a time of adventure, anticipation and exhilaration as the bravest among you put their lives on the line to conquer dragons. Micah will compete for me as my proxy, so every dragon he hunts he hunts for me. When the battle is over and Micah is the victor, I will retain my throne and be the first Hunter King to control eight Dragon Stalkers."

If all eight survive once you put us together, Serenity said. She shifted her feet on the stage behind Omri and spoke to her stalker companions. *I can barely tolerate the three of you.*

We don't much like you, either, Dahlia said. *But I can't have another Dawn Stalker to compete with. I am the most beautiful of us all and want to keep it that way.*

Get over yourself, Vasilis said, coasting over the stage. *You can't even fly.*

You can't teleport.

Javan was rather amused by the insults the stalkers were shooting at one another, but Ravier's sharp response reminded him of the seriousness of the human conversation underway.

"I object," Ravier said. "The law explicitly prohibits the reigning king from competing, and there is no law stating a proxy competitor is allowed."

"There is now," said Omri. "I hereby declare that anyone can enter the Battle for the Throne as a proxy for the current ruler. Any Dragon Stalkers won by the proxy belong to the ruler and qualify as his stalkers. Anyone here opposed to such a law?"

Javan wanted to oppose him, but Ravier shook his head indicating not to make such a move. No one else risked opposing him either.

"Good," Omri said. "Then it is set. Micah, enter the Battle."

"Gladly." Micah pushed past Ravier, descended the stairs and pranced to the column on the opposite corner from Javan.

Just like what happened with Javan, the column lit up and vibrated when Micah touched it. He stepped back, and Javan could tell by the oohs and ahhs of the crowd that his handprints remained and the vertical line of four triangles were appearing above his handprints.

The people around Micah began slapping his back and wishing him good luck in the Battle. Javan, on the other hand, still stood alone.

"Now," Omri said, regaining control of the crowd, "it is time to finish what we gathered here for today. But because we have made Vasilis wait so patiently, he will get to feast on Esmeralda as well as a man who used to be my trusted commander. He betrayed me fifteen years ago and has been in hiding ever since. Today it is my pleasure to finally deliver justice to Ravier."

"I thought you might recognize me," Ravier said.

"You were foolish to come here."

"Perhaps. But for the first time in 400 years, we have two competitors in a Battle for the Throne. Javan will collect his dragons, and you will be out of power. My sacrifice is worth it."

His sacrifice? Now his mother and grandfather were going to die? This wasn't right! They were supposed to prevent the execution, not add to it. Javan turned to Astor. "Astor, what's happening?"

"Ravier knew this was a possibility." Several soldiers led Ravier to the place on the stage beside Esmeralda. "He is sacrificing his life so you can compete."

"That's not the plan! I already told Omri that Esmeralda was acting in his best interest by activating the portal. He was supposed to let her go." Javan watched Vasilis soar over the castle walls and begin to circle back toward the stage. "We have to save her. And Ravier. How do we do that now?"

"We don't. The goal was to present you as a competitor and get Omri to accept your entry. We did that."

"You mean you never thought we could save my mom?"

"No."

Javan began to hyperventilate while Omri snapped his fingers. "Vasilis, your feast!"

It's about time, Vasilis said, zeroing in on the stage.

Tears filled Javan's eyes as he looked helplessly at his mother. Still strong and confident, Esmeralda mouthed the words *I love you* to Javan. He mouthed the same words back and looked at Ravier. His face turned to stone as he returned Javan's look and simply said, "Win."

The dragon was fifty feet away and gaining quickly when Javan yelled, "Stop! Me for them!" he yelled, running to the stairs. "Me for them! Me for them!"

"Vasilis, wait." Omri held up his hand to stop his dragon from feasting for a second time and began walking toward the staircase. "What did you say?"

Vasilis screamed a stream of fire into the air, dusting the crowd with ashes. *That's twice now boy. You mess with my meal again, and I'm coming for you.* Vasilis skirted the stage and resumed his holding pattern above the crowd.

Despite the threat of the dragon, Javan rushed up the stairs. "Me for them," he said, breathless. "If I don't collect my first dragon within a month, you kill me instead of them. Then the Battle is over and the throne remains yours."

"And if you do?" Omri asked.

"You let them go and see how the Battle plays out."

"Interesting." Omri crossed his arms and studied Javan.

"Javan," Ravier said, "that's suicidal. Let us go. You don't need the added pressure of a month's timetable to collect your first dragon."

"I can't stand here and watch you die, not when I can do something about it." Javan turned to Omri. "Well?"

"Agreed," Omri said, "but with one exception. You have a week."

"A week? That's not enough time."

"It's all the time I will allow. Return here in one week. If you return with a dragon, I will release these prisoners. If you return without a dragon, I will have my dragons kill you instead of them. If you fail to return at all, my dragons will kill these prisoners and then come for you."

"Don't do it, Javan," Esmeralda pleaded. "Your life is more important than the both of ours."

Javan heard her desperate words but dared not look at her. He wouldn't be able to do what needed to be done otherwise. "I have your word that you'll let them go if I return here in one week with a dragon?"

"You have my word."

"You can't trust him, Javan," Ravier said. "We're dead either way."

"The people are my witnesses," Omri said. He turned to address the crowd. "Good people of Zandador, the execution scheduled for today will have to wait. Vasilis, off to your hunting grounds to eat your meal!"

I had a craving for humans, but anything will do at this point, Vasilis said and flew away as swiftly as he had arrived.

"Now," Omri continued, "I order you to all return in one week's time. You will either witness an execution of these rebels or meet this young Collector's first dragon." He climbed on the back of his Midnight Stalker. "Now get back to your homes and back to work!"

Serenity spread her wings and took off, carrying the Dark King with her.

With the dragon gone, the soldiers immediately surrounded Esmeralda and Ravier. "Take them to the dungeon," Micah ordered, having returned to the stage from the back staircase.

"I believe in you, Javan," Esmeralda said as the soldiers led her away. "Good luck."

Ravier, on the other hand, said nothing. Judging by the incensed look on his face, he wasn't as confident in Javan's collecting skills as his mother.

Once the stage cleared, Micah walked up to Javan and whispered in his ear. "I will meet you on the battlefield. Don't expect to survive the encounter." With that, Micah sprinted across the stage, jumped on Eli's back and ran the dragon back through the castle gates.

Javan watched them disappear, then closed his eyes and took a deep breath. One week. He had one week to collect his first dragon. Or die.

CHAPTER 42

Parting Ways

"You are a fool!"

Javan lifted his head and looked around to find a man at the bottom of the stairs pointing in his direction. Not one person in the crowd seemed to have left the stadium, and all eyes were on him as he stood alone on the stage. "Excuse me?"

"Only a fool would enter the Battle for the Throne with just four months to go, then give himself a mere week to collect his first dragon."

"Now Micah will be hunting dragons, too," said another man further back in the crowd. "How much more will we have to suffer if he succeeds?"

"It doesn't matter if Micah succeeds or not." A woman in the crowd behind Javan spoke this time. "You have angered King Omri. Who do you think he's going to take his anger out on?"

"Us!" someone else answered. At that one word, pandemonium erupted in the form of screams, curses and insults in Javan's direction. If they had rotten tomatoes available to them, Javan was certain he'd be covered in smelly, slimy red juice.

He stood dumbstruck on stage as he looked at the faces of the sea of people below him. He felt the fury in their cries and saw the hate in their eyes. This wasn't the warm reception he had expected from the people he was here to help. Where were the cheers? Where was the support? Where was the encouragement?

"Come, Javan," Hamilton said. He had joined Javan on stage and was tugging on his arm. "We have to get out of here. Now."

"They hate me," Javan said. "They're not supposed to hate me."

"They're scared. You disrupted the status quo. All they see is what they fear, which is a more powerful King Omri. In time, they'll come around."

"Maybe if I show them my eyes," he said, reaching for his sunglasses, "they'll calm down and get excited about me being the answer to the prophecy."

"No." Hamilton stopped him from taking his glasses off. "Word will get back to Omri, and we can't play that hand yet."

"How else am I supposed to get them to like me?"

"You don't. Being liked isn't necessary; being respected is. You earn their respect by collecting dragons. But right now they want your head. We have to go before they decide to take it."

"Right." Javan snapped out of his stupor and descended the stairs with Hamilton on his heels. Astor was waiting at the bottom for them, and the three of them walked as one through the spitting, shouting, slapping crowd.

◊   ◊   ◊

Fortunately the bitter, furious people didn't feel the need to escort Javan, Hamilton and Astor out of the city. But their cries of woe and desperation stuck with Javan as he half walked/half jogged back through the inner and outer city with his silent companions under the watchful eyes of the king's soldiers stationed along the route.

He was also a little worried about Micah's threat to kill him. The man was an intimidating, brutal soldier with real fighting experience. The only experience Javan had was in a simulated fighting environment. Would he be able to compete with Micah? Or would he freeze when the time came to test his fighting skills?

When he added all that to the fact that the lives of his mother and grandfather— not to mention his own life—depended on him to overcome the overwhelming odds, he wished he could close his eyes, pretend it was all a dream and wake up in the safety of his dragon-free home in Montana.

Reaching the okties waiting for them outside the city confirmed that this wasn't a dream. This was real. And he was in real trouble.

Javan took a deep breath as he climbed onto the back of his okty. "Where to now? Back to Gri?"

"No," Hamilton said, settling on his own okty, "Gri is only safe as long as we don't return."

"What? Why? It's protected by an invisibility shield."

"The Dark King will be watching you now." Hamilton nodded toward the soldiers observing them from the wall. "If he sees you disappear beyond the shield, he'll know where to attack."

"He can break through the shield?"

"It's not easy, but yes. He has that capability."

"So what do we do now?"

"We don't know." Hamilton lifted his okty, allowing it to hover about ten feet from the ground. "You kind of ruined the plan we had."

Javan nudged his okty up so that he was eye to eye with the floating Hamilton. "I only deviated from the plan cause you guys didn't tell me what the real plan was. I went there today to save my mom, not watch her die like you wanted to. Besides, I still think that keeping Ravier and my mom alive for another week is a better idea than letting that dragon eat them today."

"That dragon is going to be eating you in a week."

"Not if I show up riding a dragon of my own."

"Dragon collecting takes time, something you didn't give yourself enough of."

"Trust me, I get that. But I had to do something."

"If you are done arguing about what is done," Astor said, looking up at them from the ground, "I will tell you what we are going to do."

Javan and Hamilton glared at each other, then turned their attention to Astor. "What's the plan?" Hamilton asked.

"Hamilton, you take Javan to Dusk Stalker territory and track down Mertzer."

"Mertzer?" Javan shook his head. "No. That's a bad plan. Mertzer won't let me ride him unless I prove myself by collecting another dragon first."

"You bonded with Mertzer," Astor said. "He's your best bet."

"No. I'd be wasting my time. My best bet is to collect another dragon first. Then Mertzer will be an easy second dragon to add to my collection, and I'll be halfway to my goal."

"Kid's got a point," Hamilton said.

"He does indeed." Astor adjusted his glasses and pursed his lips. "Go to Dawn Stalker territory. Set up camp under the Whistling Waterfall. I'll send supplies. You two focus on doing whatever it takes to collect a Dawn Stalker."

"Yes, sir." Hamilton followed up his salute to Astor with an order to Javan. "Let's go, kid."

"Wait," Javan said. "Astor, aren't you coming with us?"

"No. I must stay here and keep an eye on Micah. I'll send word if he does anything you need to know about."

"You'll send word?" They had no phones, email or old-fashioned telegraph lines. From what Javan had observed, they didn't even have any kind of postal delivery system. How could they possibly stay in touch? Javan scratched his head. "How?"

"There are ways. Now go."

Javan didn't feel right about leaving such an old man to fend for himself in this hostile environment. "Are you sure you want to stay here?"

Astor pointed south. "Go."

"Yes, sir." Against his better judgment, he flew away with Hamilton in the direction of Dawn Stalker territory.

CHAPTER 43

A Sticky Situation

B acon? Was he really smelling bacon? Javan sat up and rubbed his eyes in the cave he and Hamilton had claimed as a camping spot the night before. The "door" to the cave was a sheet of water that sounded like it was whistling as it cascaded down from a cliff a hundred feet above them and dropped into a pool of clear water two hundred feet below them.

The soothing sound of the cascading water had lulled him to sleep last night in spite of the underlying whistling notes the water played. Now the smell of bacon sparked his senses and woke him up.

A small campfire was burning about thirty feet away from him near the entrance. Holding a black pan above the fire was a young woman with striking blue eyes and light brown hair that spilled past her tiny waist. She looked somewhat familiar, but Javan couldn't place where they might have met before. As for Hamilton, he was nowhere to be seen.

"Umm...hello?" He latched his hand around the handle of one of his stalker swords just in case he needed it. "Who are you? And where is Hamilton?"

"You're awake." A smile stretched across her face, and Javan felt his heart do a strange sort of somersault. This girl was pretty.

"Yeah." Javan coughed to clear his throat. He wasn't used to speaking to pretty girls. "You...umm...didn't...umm...answer my...umm...questions." Why couldn't he talk without using the word "umm" three million times?

"Sorry." This time she laughed. Now she was even more attractive. If she kept this up, he wasn't going to be able to utter any comprehensible words. "Hamilton's out scouting for dragons. He'll be back soon."

"Oh. Okay." Javan rolled his eyes. He was such a brilliant conversationalist.

"We've met before." She pulled the pan away from the fire and placed it on the ground. As she divvied up the meat she had been cooking onto three separate plates already filled with berries and bread, she said, "We met in Gri. I brought you your lunch."

"That's where I know you from! My grandmother called you..." Javan snapped his fingers several times while trying to recall her name. The snapping didn't help.

"Gesha."

"Right. Gesha. I'm Javan."

"I know."

"Right. So...umm...how did you know I was here?"

"The UCN."

"The what?"

"The Underground Communication Network. Astor sent a message. He told us where you were and what you needed. I volunteered to bring the supplies." She shrugged. "And me. You needed someone to hunt and cook for you while you do your dragon collecting thing."

"Right." Goodness! Did he really say 'right' again? He mentally slapped himself for his verbal ineptitude. "Well, umm, thanks for coming."

"Sure." Keeping her eyes averted, she delivered a plate to Javan and returned to her spot by the fire. "I hope you like cicko meat. It was the best I could do on such short notice."

"It...umm...smells good." Cicko meat? What kind of animal was a cicko? He would sound like an idiot if he asked. So he didn't ask. Instead, he took a bite. Much to his relief, it did taste similar to bacon. Only a touch tougher. "Tasty."

"Glad you like it." She blushed and popped a handful of berries in her mouth.

He was mesmerized by the way she chewed. She tilted her head slightly to the side, closed her eyes and barely moved her jaw. She might have noticed him staring, too, if Hamilton hadn't burst into the cave the second she opened her eyes to reach for another bite.

"Morning!" Hamilton scooted in from the narrow ledge that separated the waterfall from the rock wall. "Gesha, something smells delicious. You got a plate for me?"

"Yes, sir."

She handed him a plate, and he walked over to sit beside Javan. He stuffed his mouth full of both meat and berries, but didn't let that stop him from talking. "Eat quick, kid. I found the perfect place for you to hang out and wait for a dragon to stroll by, jump on and ride."

"That's the plan? I just wait for a dragon to come to me?"

"Yup."

"What if no dragons happen to stroll by?"

"One will if I do my job right." Hamilton stuffed another round of food in his mouth as though he were a starved barbarian. "Just trust me."

Javan took a civilized bite of his own food and swallowed it before asking, "Trust you to do what?"

"Herd a dragon to you."

"Herd me a dragon? How are you going to do that?"

"Easy. Dawn Stalkers are scared of insects. I've been out catching those annoying little creatures. I'll use them to get the dragon to go where I want him to go—straight to where you're hiding."

"Really? That's going to work?"

"You have a better idea, kid?"

Javan shook his head. "Nope."

"Then finish your food and strap on your stalker swords." Hamilton slapped Javan on the back. "It's time to collect you a Dawn Stalker!"

◊   ◊   ◊

Javan wiped the sweat from his eyes for the umpteenth time. The ritual sweat-wiping was the only action he had taken all day as he sat perched high above the ground in the tree Hamilton had picked out for him.

It was a cool tree to climb and sit in. It looked like a weeping willow except the leaves were ten times as big, the branches were five times as thick and the trunk grew two times as tall as any weeping willow he had ever seen.

The large, drooping leaves camouflaged him perfectly while the sturdy branches made sitting comfortable and safe. The only problem was that he was stuck in one spot and had been for a good eight hours or so. His legs had fallen asleep, his back was getting sore and he had long ago finished the nuts, fruit and beef jerky Gesha had given him to snack on.

He did have a fantastic view of the Whistling Waterfall to his right. He couldn't hear the whistling from where he was, but he could certainly enjoy the sight of the sheet of water as wide as an eight-lane highway spilling over the edge of the cliff, rushing past the labyrinth of caves and dropping into the peaceful lake below. Waist high shrubs and knee high grass filled the distance between him and the water. Trees like the one Javan sat in covered the land as far as he could see when he looked to his left.

The terrain on the other side of the waterfall was completely different. It was marked by a series of rocky, moss-covered hills, streams and mini waterfalls. As he drank the last of his water, he found himself wondering if any of those waterfalls hid caves as well.

How do they keep finding me? The high-pitched, fear-filled thoughts of the snow white dragon startled Javan. It appeared out of nowhere and was just past jumping range for Javan. The dragon shivered and looked around. *I think I finally escaped those vicious little creatures.*

Javan wasn't sure how Hamilton had managed to get the dragon to teleport to this exact spot, but he was sure he would take advantage of the situation. As quietly as he could, he retrieved a stun ball from his belt and moved himself into a squatting position on the branch he had been sitting on.

The dragon began strutting toward the water. He couldn't allow her to walk out of throwing range, so he moved some leaves from a branch above him out of his way with his left arm, cocked his right arm and sent the stun ball spiraling toward the unsuspecting Dawn Stalker.

The claws of the stun ball lodged into the base of the dragon's long neck, rendering the dragon immobile. "Yes!" Javan shouted. "Gotcha!"

He worked his way down the tree, marveling at how easy collecting his first dragon was going to be. He didn't need a week or a month; all he needed was a day. He couldn't wait to see the look on King Omri's face when Javan rode into town on this beautiful dragon.

Did she already have a name? Should he re-name her even if she did? Was that proper collection etiquette? If so, what should he call her? Was there a book of dragon names he could rent from some library somewhere in Zandador? Did they have libraries in Zandador?

Growing impatient with his tedious climb down, Javan decided the puffy green bushes at the base of the tree would be soft enough to break his fall. So from about twenty feet up, he let go and launched himself butt first into the bushes below.

They were soft.

They did absorb his fall.

But Javan didn't realize until it was too late that he had willingly thrown himself into a patch of sticky bushes Astor had warned him about just last week.

The leaves on these particular bushes secreted some sort of tacky substance that was so strong the people used it in place of nails when building things like furniture. Or houses.

Now he was stuck, glued in place from his neck to his heels.

While he fought to free himself, he heard the stun ball on the dragon's neck drop to the ground. That clunk was followed by the sound of the dragon galloping away.

He let out a defeated, frustrated sigh and tried not to consider the possibility that he might have just ruined his one and only opportunity to collect a dragon.

CHAPTER 44

Gesha to the Rescue

Javan could feel the sticky substance the bushes secreted cementing itself to his skin and clothes. The longer he stayed put, the more entrenched he became.

"Not good. This is so not good." He dropped his head back in despair. The sticky leaves immediately latched onto his hair, rendering him completely immobile. "Great. Now what am I supposed to do?"

He watched the sky change from blue to a collage of pink, red, orange and purple as the sun began its farewell tour. In the hue of the setting sun, Javan finally heard Hamilton's voice.

"Kid, what have you gotten yourself into?"

"I'm stuck," Javan said, as though his predicament wasn't obvious. "I'm hot. I'm hungry. And I really need to pee. Please just cut me loose."

"Ooohh." Hamilton leaned over Javan and shook his head. "No can do, kid."

"Yes can do." He tried to nod, but his head wouldn't move. "Unsheathe one of my swords and chop away at these bushes."

"These here are sticky bushes." Hamilton slowly walked around the bushes. "If I try to cut you out, the sword will get stuck along with the rest of you."

"Come on, dude." Javan really should have paid more attention to Astor when he was telling him about these bushes. He was sure the old man mentioned the trick to getting out of one if he ever got stuck. "There has to be a way to get me out of here."

"Well...there is."

"Good." He knew a way out existed. "What is it?"

"I've seen people make some kind of creamy mixture that forces the leaves to unstick from what they're stuck to."

"Okay. Fantastic. Make the cream."

"I would, but..."

"But what?"

Hamilton stopped his pacing and bent over so Javan could see his face. "I have no idea how to make it."

"What?" Javan started to panic. "You mean I'm going to be stuck here for forever?"

"Calm down. Maybe Gesha knows." Hamilton patted Javan's forehead and chuckled. "Stay here. I'll be right back."

◇　◇　◇

Hamilton's idea of right back turned in to a gap of several hours, enough time for the sun to set and allow the moon to take over the sky. In that time, Javan's muscles started cramping, and his stomach wouldn't stop growling. That uncomfortableness was nothing, however, compared to the overwhelming need to empty his bladder, something he almost did when he heard Hamilton's booming voice interrupt the quiet of the night.

"Good news, kid!" Hamilton approached Javan carrying a torch. "Gesha knew exactly what to do."

"Sorry we took so long," Gesha said. She spoke softly out of Javan's line of sight, making deciphering her words difficult. "Finding some of the leaves and bugs I needed in the dark was a little challenging."

"Leaves and bugs, huh?" The thought of having bug guts spread all over him was not appealing. "That's the only way to get me out of here?"

"Yes," Gesha said. "My brother's leg got stuck once, and my mom taught me how to make this cream to get him out."

"I'll have to thank your mom, then. Does she live in Gri, too?"

"No." Her words became almost inaudible. "She's loyal to the Dark King and cooks for his army. I haven't spoken to her in over a year, not since I ran away from my post as a soldier in the army."

"I didn't know you were in the army." Javan had a hard time picturing the quiet, frail Gesha in the role of a soldier. "Why did you run away?"

"Everyone has to join the army, but not everyone is cut out for it. I wasn't. They weed out the weaker people like me by working them to death. The only chance I had to survive was to run away."

"I found her sick and shivering and starving in the woods near Gri about six months ago." Hamilton's voice sounded louder than normal compared to Gesha's soft tone. "The ladies of our village took her in, and she's been a part of our little community ever since."

"Enough about me," Gesha said, her voice faint but growing stronger as she changed subjects. "Javan, this cream is going to feel cold to the touch. You ready?"

"Yes!" He tried to lift his head up so he could see her, but that only strained his neck and added to the agony of his cramping muscles.

Even though he couldn't see her, he could feel Gesha start to apply the cream with shaky strokes under his right arm. The cool, mushy, gooey substance she spread on him obscured the tingle of her touch. So did her question. "How did you get yourself stuck here?"

He figured he would have to explain his predicament to Hamilton. He just wished he didn't have to explain it to Gesha; it wouldn't exactly paint him as a hero in her eyes. Sighing, he began telling his tale. "A dragon teleported here to get away from some insects."

"Ha!" Hamilton said. "I knew my plan would work."

"Anyway," Javan continued, "I stunned it with a stun ball from my perch in the tree. Climbing down was taking too long, so I jumped, thinking these bushes would break my fall."

"Hold up." Hamilton lowered the torch so close to Javan's head that it nearly singed his hair. "You jumped into sticky bushes on purpose?"

"I didn't realize they were sticky bushes."

"How could you not know they were sticky bushes? Everybody knows about sticky bushes."

"Hamilton, let him finish the story." Gesha adjusted the torch so that it was a safe distance away from Javan's face and moved over to his left arm. "What happened to the dragon?"

"The stun ball wore off, dropped to the ground and the dragon got away." Javan raised his right arm and wiggled it. "Hey! Your cream is working!"

"Good." She finished with his left arm, freed his hair from its sticky prison and drew one of his swords from his belt. "Now all we have to do is cut you out of your clothes."

"Excuse me?" Javan held his head up in alarm. "Why do you want to cut me out of my clothes?"

"Sorry," she said, shrugging, "but I'm almost out of cream. Now hold on to Hamilton's arm while I cut you loose, and don't let any part of your skin touch these leaves again."

"That sword is sharp. What if you cut me?"

"I'll be careful."

"Be *very* careful." This was much more humiliating than telling her about leaping into sticky bushes on purpose. He just wanted to get back to the cave, curl under his blanket and never look at her again. "Let's get this over with."

Gesha and Hamilton both moved to stand in front of Javan, Gesha by his left foot and Hamilton by his right. Hamilton held his left arm out so Javan could grab it. Once Javan latched his hands on to Hamilton's forearm, Gesha began cutting away at Javan's shirt.

Javan held his breath as the sharp blades on the sword easily sliced the brown fabric while narrowly missing his skin. In less than a minute, Javan pulled himself into a sitting position. The front of his shirt fell into his lap while the back of his shirt still stuck to the bushes.

"Okay. Progress," Gesha said. "I'm going to use what cream I have left to unstick your belt and swords. Then I'll cut your pants off."

"Whoa!" Javan bent over into protective mode and covered his pants with his hands. "How about I cut my own pants off?"

Gesha let out a sigh of relief. "No problem. I'll just get your belt unstuck for you."

"Okay." Javan sat up and felt her breath on his bare skin as she carefully reached around his waist to apply the cream to his belt. After what seemed like forever, the bushes released their hold on his belt. He carefully took it off and gave it to Gesha. She handed him his sword in return. He waited for her to turn around, but she kept staring at him.

"Come on, kid," Hamilton said. "Cut, cut, cut."

"Not while she's watching," Javan said under his breath through gritted teeth.

Hamilton rolled his eyes. "Gesha, the kid's shy. You mind not looking?"

She giggled and turned around. That didn't stop Javan's cheeks from flaming with embarrassment as he carved his pants to shreds and let Hamilton lift his mostly naked self out of the stupid sticky bushes.

His legs wobbled a bit when they first hit the ground, and he had to use Hamilton as a prop to keep from falling. "You all right, kid?" Hamilton asked.

"I just need to get the blood flowing again. And I need to pee." Javan let go of Hamilton and leaned against the tree he had fallen from. "You two go ahead. I'll catch up."

"Understood, kid," Hamilton said. "We'll walk slow."

Javan watched them leave, went around to the other side of the tree and took care of his business. Then bowing his head in shame, he walked back to the cave behind Gesha and Hamilton while dressed only in his underwear, certain that life could not possibly get any more humiliating.

The next few days, however, would prove that theory horribly wrong.

CHAPTER 45

Elusive Dragons
and Wailing Wawrahs

ressing in his one spare outfit upon returning to the cave helped restore Javan's confidence, but he still didn't feel sure enough of himself to talk to Gesha. Although he wanted to learn more about her and how she survived on her own as an enemy of the Dark King before Hamilton found her, regret over the day's events consumed him too much to allow him to engage her in conversation over dinner. He let her and Hamilton talk by the fire while he sulked in the corner with his plate of freshly cooked fish.

That dragon had been so close.

He had seen it but didn't attempt to jump on its back. He had heard its thoughts but didn't try to chat with it. He had stunned it but lost his focus and sabotaged his chance to ride it.

Some Collector he was turning out to be.

"Well, kid," Hamilton said, walking over and sitting beside Javan, "I say today was a great day."

Javan choked his last bite of food down and looked at Hamilton. "Are you delusional?"

"Think about it. You stunned the first dragon you saw with the first stun ball you threw. You proved you're as good with those things in real life as you are in practice. That makes today a great day."

"Big deal. I let the dragon get away."

"You're new to this, kid. Making mistakes is part of the process. What you can't do is let your mistakes take you out of the game. Focus on what you did right; learn from what you did wrong. We've still got five whole days left, but we're going to need a new strategy."

"Agreed."

"So what's the plan?"

"I thought you had a plan."

"We already tried my plan."

"That's the only plan you had?"

"Yup." Hamilton shrugged. "I'm not much of an idea guy. Ravier and Astor usually handle that stuff."

"They're not here!"

"No, they're not. You are. You're smart. You're creative. You'll figure something out." Hamilton patted Javan on the back. "Sleep on it, and tell me your plan in the morning. Good night."

Sleep? How was he supposed to sleep with that kind of pressure thrown on him just before bed? He was used to following plans, not coming up with them on his own. That's what adults were for!

He watched Hamilton settle under his covers while Gesha snuffed out the fire and settled under her own covers along the wall opposite Hamilton. His bed stretched across the back wall of the cave so that when he lay down, his head was near Hamilton's head and his feet were near Gesha's head.

Lying down didn't help him think or sleep. He simply stared at the rock ceiling for hours listening to the whistling of the waterfall and praying for help as the deadline of his death moved closer and closer with each passing minute.

◊ ◊ ◊

Painful memories were the only things Javan collected over the next three sleepless days and nights.

Although he made countless attempts to jump from the back of his okty to unsuspecting dragons, he missed every time. His landings on the ground, on rocks, in thorns, in trees and even into water left him scratched, bruised and beaten by the end of Tuesday.

He nearly died of an acid bath when he snuck up on a sleeping dragon on Wednesday, and the one dragon he lured on Thursday morning with a small mountain of nuts Dawn Stalkers had a taste for teleported in and out of the trap so fast that Javan didn't have time to aim his stun ball, much less throw it.

The rest of Thursday was filled with bad stun ball aim and more in-flight jumping misses. He called it a day after falling into a mound of dragon poop while trying to escape a swarm of angry bumblebees, six of which stung him.

The tension around the dinner fire that night was more pronounced than the welts developing on Javan's face, neck and arms from the bee stings. Everyone knew he was running out of time, but no one wanted to be the one to say it.

The pain from the welts and the nightmares of being eaten by the king's dragons kept sleep away until exhaustion finally took over late that night. But Javan didn't awaken on Friday morning to the smell of breakfast cooking or the sound of Hamilton humming to the tune of the whistling water.

The job of waking him up fell to a slimy, slug-like companion a few feet longer and wider than Javan that crawled under his covers and delivered a deafening shriek inches away from his left ear.

"Don't move," Hamilton said. He was lying motionless on his stomach, his head ten feet from both Javan's head and the head of the slug. "Sudden moves make them angry."

"Wailing in my ear makes me angry." Javan looked into the big bulging black eyes of the bluish green blob snuggled beside him. "What is this thing?"

"It's a wailing wawrah."

"It's ugly. It's loud. And it stinks. But is it dangerous?"

"Only if you make it mad."

"Then I guess I won't make it mad." Javan tried to check on Gesha without moving his head, but the wawrah was blocking his view of her bed. "Gesha, you okay over there?"

When she didn't respond, he lifted himself onto his elbows to get a better view. That small movement sent the blob into a tizzy. It wailed louder than before as its nostrils flared, its ears popped up and its fins spread out, framing its hideous face. "What's it doing?"

"It's going to attack!"

"Why?" Javan had trouble yelling over the noise of the high-pitched howl. "I didn't do anything!"

"You moved! Now grab your sword! Chop its head off before it bites your neck!"

"My neck? Is this thing like some kind of slimy vampire?" Javan said as he rolled over, snagged both his swords from his belt beside him and turned back to the wawrah just in time to see it open its mouth. It wailed again and spewed a stream of thick, rancid, gunky puke all over Javan's face.

"Ahhh! How disgusting!" Javan choked down puke of his own as he wiped his eyes with the back of his hands. "Die, you stinking wawrah!"

He slashed at the blob, but it slithered out of the way and moved itself onto Javan's legs. From there, it lifted itself up like an attacking cobra, bared its fangs and lunged for Javan's neck. Javan caught a whiff of its rancid breath as he slid the sword under its mouth and sliced upward.

The wawrah's body collapsed. It's head, however, bounced off Javan's chest and rolled across the floor, landing at Gesha's feet. She stood there stunned, her face flushed of all color.

"Don't worry, Gesha," he said, working to catch his breath, "I killed it." He was proud of himself for protecting her; she was, after all, too scared to even respond to his inquiry about her well-being just moments ago.

"Good," she said, "but that's not what I'm worried about." She held up a piece of paper. "As I was out hunting for breakfast, I retrieved a message from Astor. Micah is on his way to Dusk Stalker territory with a countless number of soldiers. He's going after Mertzer."

CHAPTER 46

Outnumbered

"**N**o!" Javan shoved the body of the dead wawrah off his legs and stood. "He can't have Mertzer. Mertzer is *my* dragon. We've got to get to Dusk Stalker territory now. Isn't there a portal around here somewhere?"

"Micah has soldiers guarding the Dusk Territory portal." Gesha attempted to hand the paper she held to Javan, but his hands still dripped with wawrah slime. Hamilton took it from her instead.

"You'll have to travel by okty while avoiding populated areas," she continued. "Astor has checkpoints set up along the way where you'll have food and fresh okties waiting for you. The roundabout journey will take all day, but you should be able to get there by sundown."

"You mean 'we' should be able to get there by sundown," Javan said. "You're coming with us. Right?"

Gesha shook her head. "You don't need me traveling with you. I would only slow you down."

"You won't slow us down. And you have to come. I can't cook; I certainly don't want to eat anything Hamilton cooks."

"I wouldn't either, but I'm sure you'll be fine." Gesha smiled. "Just beat Micah to Mertzer, and I'll make you a big celebration dinner when you return to Gri. When it's safe for all of us to return to Gri, anyway."

"Okay," Javan said, returning Gesha's smile. "I like that idea."

"Me, too," Hamilton said, "but I'm not traveling anywhere with you until you take a bath. Go jump in the water and clean yourself off. I'll get the okties ready. Gesha, you work on getting everything packed." He clapped his hands. "Be quick about it, you two. We've got to get Javan to his dragon." Without another word, the three of them split up and carried out their assigned tasks.

Less than twenty minutes later with his hair and clothes still dripping wet, Javan met his companions by the water's edge.

"Guess this is goodbye," Gesha said, handing Javan his bag.

"Guess so."

"Ah, we'll see each other again soon," Hamilton said. He buried Gesha in a hug. "Thanks for your help. You have somewhere safe to hide until this is all over?"

"I know of a place just outside of Torix. I should be safe there."

"Good, good." Hamilton released her and climbed onto his okty. "Kid, your turn. Give the girl a hug and mount up."

Javan blushed, looked at his feet, then up at Gesha. They stared at each other in awkward silence until both moved in to hug each other at the same time. Instead of embracing, they bumped heads. "Sorry," Javan said.

"No, I'm sorry." She rubbed her head, gave Javan a quick squeeze and an even quicker kiss on the cheek. "Good luck, Dragon Collector."

"Thanks." Dragon Collector. He liked the sound of that. Especially the way she said it. "See you back in Gri. Eventually." He climbed onto his okty, waved and flew away.

◊   ◊   ◊

He spent the first part of the flight imagining how impressed Gesha was going to be when she saw him riding into Gri on the back of Mertzer. But as the day wore on, Javan grew more and more concerned that they wouldn't get to Mertzer in time.

After all, Micah wasn't running a solo dragon hunting expedition. He had an entire army with him to help him trap and capture Mertzer. Plus he had the help of his dragon-hunting dad. Maybe he even had all of his dad's dragons helping him. How was Javan supposed to compete with two Hunters, four dragons and an army of soldiers?

Javan's resources included one Hamilton, two stalker swords and seven stun balls. Not exactly an even match. The lopsided nature of the battle he was flying into became increasingly evident as he and Hamilton entered the heart of Dusk Stalker territory just before sunset.

The clanging of the armor reached their ears first. It sounded like a massive one-instrument marching band that played the same note as loud as possible over and over again.

The sound only made the sight more chilling. Thousands of soldiers miles wide and half a mile deep stretched across the meadows and woods near where Javan had previously encountered Mertzer. From Javan's vantage point in the sky, their helmets, swords and shields made them look like a wall of impenetrable robots striding to a steady beat in a uniform direction toward the coast.

What were they doing? Trying to flush Mertzer out by marching over every inch of Dusk Stalker territory?

Javan steered his fourth okty of the day beside Hamilton and yelled across the wings of their rides. "Do you see him?" Javan asked. "Do you see Mertzer?"

"No." Hamilton shook his head. "All I see are Micah's minions."

"Let's fly ahead of them, see where they're marching to."

"Lead the way."

Javan nodded and proceeded forward. Even if they did find Mertzer first, Javan wasn't sure it would do much good. Without wings, Mertzer couldn't fly over the army. And with the numbers against him, he wouldn't be able to run his way through them without being pierced, jabbed and stabbed with the swords and spears of the soldiers.

"One problem at a time," Javan mumbled to himself. "Find Mertzer. Ride him. Then figure out how to escape."

Javan urged his okty to quicken her pace. As they flew eastward, the sounds of the clanging army faded away and were soon replaced with the sound of crashing waves. When the shoreline came into view, Javan caught a glimpse of more soldiers. This group, however, stood in a single file line along the water with their backs to the purple ocean and facing the woods in front of them.

The only soldier who moved paced back and forth at the edge of the trees. He wore no armor but had dreadlocks and carried a shield and sword.

Micah.

"I know what they're doing," Javan said. He turned his okty around so that he could face Hamilton. "Mertzer is terrified of water, so they're herding him toward the shore."

"So he's somewhere between the shore and the army."

"Yes. I doubt Micah will attack until Mertzer is close to the water."

"All we have to do is find the dragon and keep him from getting to the ocean."

"Yup. We're gonna to have to fly closer to the trees to make it easier to spot him."

"That will make it easier for the soldiers to spot us."

"I know. But it's a risk we have to take."

"You're the boss, kid." Hamilton tightened the shoulder strap of the long sword sheath he wore across his back and pointed to the ground. "Let's find that dragon before any of those soldiers armed with arrows shoot us out of the sky."

CHAPTER 47

Hunter vs. Collector

avan took a deep breath and plummeted toward the trees. He pulled up in time to avoid a collision, and with Hamilton at his heels, he began flying in a zig zag pattern between the shore and the marching soldiers.

The zigs and zags became shorter and shorter the closer the soldiers trudged to the ocean. Fortunately they seemed too focused on the terrain in front of them to notice anything or anyone flying above them.

Then, in a patch of bushes up ahead, Javan spotted a half-white, half-rainbow colored dragon feasting on whatever kind of fruit or berries the bushes produced. "I see him!"

"And the soldiers see us!"

Javan glanced back at Hamilton. "Are you sure?"

An arrow pierced the front left wings of Hamilton's okty. It screeched, flapped its injured wings and began spiraling toward the ground. "Pretty sure, kid," Hamilton yelled as he descended.

Another arrow zipped past Javan. It impaled the bill of his hat and knocked it clean off his head. "Whoa! That was close!" More arrows flew past him, forcing Javan to maneuver his way through the onslaught and land further from Mertzer than he intended.

Hamilton had survived his crash landing in a clearing just behind Javan and pulled Javan off his okty as soon as he touched the ground. "We've got to get to that dragon," Hamilton said. "It's only a matter of minutes before those soldiers catch up to us."

Utilizing the cover of woods on either side of them, they sprinted the fifty yards across the clearing to Mertzer. He stood in the middle of a wide patch of gooey globe shrubs chomping away on the large blackberries. He seemed oblivious to the deafening beat of the clinking soldiers on their left and the rumbling of the crashing of the waves on their right.

Hamilton stopped a good thirty feet away while Javan approached the feeding dragon. "Hey, um, Mertzer? Sorry to interrupt your dinner, but it's me, Javan. You have to let me ride you. Now."

I have to do no such thing. Mertzer chomped another mouthful of berries and the last of his scales turned to white. *Unless you already collected another dragon.* He looked up at Javan, gooey goodness dripping from his snout. *You collected the Dawn Stalker Ratha, didn't you? I always knew she had a soft spot for Collectors.*

"I wish I had known that," Javan said, "but no. A Hunter is after you with what looks like the entire army. You have to let me ride you before he has a chance to enslave you."

I am aware of the approaching army; they have made an endless amount of noise all day. But I have escaped many Hunters before. I shall escape this one as well.

"This time is different." Javan wondered if Mertzer had any idea how close he was to the ocean. "Trust me on this. You need me."

"I can only hear one side of the conversation here, kid," Hamilton said. "I can hear those soldiers, though, and they are getting close. What's going on?"

Tell your friend this dragon isn't ready to be hunted or collected. Mertzer stepped out of the shrubs, shook off any berry goo still stuck on him and pranced forward. Away from the soldiers. Toward the ocean.

"Wait!" Javan ran after Mertzer. "Don't go that way!"

But he was too late. Mertzer stepped through the trees. Onto the sandy shore. And froze at the sight of the ocean.

◊   ◊   ◊

"Dragon!"

"The dragon's here!"

"Quick! Get Micah!"

The shrieks of the startled soldiers rang out as twilight settled in, and they scrambled south in a hurry. Apparently none of them wanted to stand their ground and keep an eye on the immobile dragon.

Javan saw his opportunity and took it. He sprinted to the white beast, climbed up scale by scale and perched himself at the base of Mertzer's neck. "Run, Mertzer! Run!"

The dragon didn't think a thought or move a muscle.

"Go!" Javan prodded him again, this time kicking his heels into Mertzer's scales. "Move! Now!"

Can't. The water. It's so...

"It's just water. No big deal. I'm here for you. Let me take you away from it."

"Get that dragon to move!" Hamilton shouted from the ground below. "Micah's almost here. I'll try to hold him off, but you have to get out of here now!"

"What are you going to do?"

"Whatever it takes." He drew his sword and charged toward the oncoming enemy.

Javan leaned against Mertzer's neck, closed his eyes and tried to ignore the sounds of the skirmish behind him. "Come on, buddy," he whispered. "You can do this. Start with one little step forward."

Steel clashed with steel behind him.

Mertzer remained silent.

Then Hamilton's voice rose above the fight. "Javan! Watch out! He got by me!"

Javan jerked up and looked back. While Hamilton engaged a dozen soldiers in a sword fight, Micah rushed forward, sword drawn, eyes focused on Mertzer's long tail.

"You are not cutting my dragon's tail off." Javan turned himself around, snatched a stun ball from his belt and hurled it toward Micah.

◊　　◊　　◊

Micah dodged whatever it was the Collector threw at him and grabbed Mertzer's tail. "I win," he said, pulling his sword back.

"Not yet you don't." Javan drew his swords, slid down Mertzer's tail and kicked Micah in the chest before he could complete his dramatic victory. The two of them crashed onto the ground, scrambled to their feet and found themselves in a standoff with each other.

Micah noted that Javan's two swords were half the size and not even close to the width of his own sword, the tip of which was pointed at Javan. "I told you I would meet you on the battlefield," Micah said, "and here we are. Do you remember what else I told you?"

"You mentioned something about me not surviving the encounter."

"Good memory." Micah lashed at Javan. Javan used both swords to block the blow. "Those tiny swords won't hold up much longer."

"We'll see." Javan lunged forward but couldn't get close enough to do any damage.

The two traded strikes, each parrying the other's attacks.

Until Micah broke through Javan's defenses.

CHAPTER 48

Beaten

Javan raised his swords to block a blow to his head, but that left his core unprotected. Micah took advantage of the opportunity and stabbed at Javan's stomach.

"Got you now, Collector boy," Micah said as the tip of his sword punctured Javan's abdomen.

"Not quite." Javan crossed his swords in an X pattern below Micah's sword and forced the sword up before Micah had a chance to shove it in. But the tip of the sharp sword was still too close to Javan. As he pushed it up, it slashed his skin from his belly button to his clavicle.

He clutched his bleeding chest and staggered backwards, breathless from the intense pain.

"I should finish you," Micah said, "but I want you to see this." He turned and headed for Mertzer's tail, which lay as still as ever a mere ten steps from Micah.

Javan's pain vanished at the thought of losing Mertzer. "Back away from my dragon!" He charged at Micah, but Micah was ready for the attack. He met Javan with a kick to his wounded chest and sent him sprawling into the sand.

"He's my dragon now." Micah picked up Mertzer's tail and sliced through the scales with his sword.

Javan watched through tears as Mertzer jumped, flopped his shortened, bloodied tail and screamed the most agonizing scream Javan had ever heard.

"Shut up, you stupid dragon." Micah tied his belt near the end of the newly created stump to minimize the loss of blood, then draped the lifeless five feet of Mertzer's tail around his neck and climbed on to Mertzer's back. Looking down at Javan, he said, "I'll see you in Japheth in less than two days' time. I'll have my dragon ready. Good luck finding one of your own between now and then." He slapped Mertzer with the side of his sword. "Move!"

The last thing Javan heard before he lost consciousness was the sound of Mertzer   screaming   as   he   sped   away   into   the   woods.

CHAPTER 49

Surrender

"It's not deep."

Javan didn't recognize the calm voice of the man inspecting his wound, nor did he bother opening his eyes to look at him. He was content to finally lay on a flat, soft surface after spending a restless, painful night being jostled around in Hamilton's arms. Unlike their okties, the oversized man had survived his skirmish with the soldiers and had carried Javan to whatever place they were in now.

"So the kid's going to be okay?" Hamilton sounded exhausted. And concerned.

"He's lost a lot of blood," the stranger said, "but once we patch him up, he should recover without any problem."

"Hamilton, you've done well. Now get some rest."

This time Javan forced his heavy eyes open. "Astor?"

"Yes, Javan, I'm here." Sure enough, Astor was sitting on the right hand side of the bed Javan was lying in. "Here" was a one-room hut with a dirt floor. The only other furniture in the place was a table and chairs by the fireplace across from Javan and a second bed in the opposite corner.

"Kid, you're awake!" Hamilton towered over Astor. Dried blood caked his face from a cut above his left eye, but that was nothing compared to his blood-stained shirt. That seemed odd since his shirt wasn't cut and he didn't appear to have any major wounds. Then Javan realized that was his own blood on Hamilton's shirt. "You had me worried."

"Where are we?" Javan asked.

"Bacquie's farm," Astor said. He nodded to the balding man on the other side of Javan's bed who appeared to be in his sixties. Or six hundreds by Zandadorian age standards. "It's a secluded place outside of Dusk Stalker territory. Hamilton had to walk all night to get you here since the soldiers stole your okties."

"Didn't go anywhere without gathering all the stun balls you threw." Hamilton looked and sounded exhausted. "I put them back on your belt for you."

"Thanks," Javan said. "For everything."

"You're welcome, kid. Now that I know you're okay, I'm going to sleep." Hamilton nodded, strode across the room and belly-flopped onto the bed. The bottom half of his legs hung off the end of the bed, but that didn't keep him from immediately zonking out.

Javan also closed his eyes while Bacquie worked on washing his wound. He was too tired and too haunted by Mertzer's screams to care about the pain. Until something wet and cold touched his skin. Javan shuddered and looked up. "What is that?"

"Sealing mud," Bacquie said. "Once it dries, it will keep your skin together until the wound heals." He finished spreading the mud along the slashed skin and stood. "I have some things to attend to outside. I'll let you two talk."

Javan waited for Bacquie to leave, then turned to Astor. "I'm sorry, Astor. I failed. Micah beat me. He got Mertzer."

"I know. Hamilton told me what happened."

"And no matter what I tried, I just couldn't find a way to ride one of those Dawn Stalkers. I'm no Collector." Javan looked up at the ceiling and signed, resigning himself to the way his life would end. "But at least I'll be able to save my mom and Ravier when I trade my life for theirs tomorrow."

"Young one, you still have--"

"A time trap!" Bacquie burst through the door before Astor could finish his sentence. A breathless young girl with blonde pigtails who looked to be about seven or eight entered behind him. "Merilyn's been scouting the Noon Territory, and she says a Noon Stalker is caught in a time trap!"

"It's true! It's true!" The girl ran to Javan and enclosed his hand in hers. Her big brown eyes bulged with excitement. "The time trap stretches from the jungle to the meadows, and one of the dragons never leaves the jungle. If you go now, you can catch it and ride it. Imagine the look on the Dark King's face when you show up in Stalker Square tomorrow riding a Noon Stalker!"

The girl made the news sound so hopeful. Javan wasn't convinced. He remembered Ravier mentioning time traps before but never did get around to inquiring about it. Guess he should now. He looked at Astor, sighed and asked, "What's a time trap?"

CHAPTER 50

Time Trap

"So it's a storm that slows down time?" Javan, dressed in one of Bacquie's brown shirts that was two sizes too big for him, stood in a meadow with Astor under the heat of the blazing late-morning sun. They had ridden together across the river and into Noon Stalker territory on the back of Bacquie's only okty. Javan's chest hurt and his head pounded, but thanks to the meal Merilyn fed them before they left, hunger wasn't a problem.

The air ahead of them looked wrinkled and warped, but that was the only difference Javan could discern.

"Yes," Astor said. "You can be stuck inside one of these storms for days or weeks, but it only feels like a few hours have passed."

"How is that going to help me catch a dragon? I only have one day left."

"You eat these." Astor handed Javan the leather pouch he had been wearing across his chest. Javan opened the pouch to find it full of cherries.

"Cherries. Cherries are the secret to beating a time trap?"

"They're called energy balls. They have green beans inside them. Bite one and see."

"Okay." Javan bit one of the cherries in half. Sure enough, the outer fruit protected the inner bean.

"The beans give you a burst of energy that allows you to move faster than everything in the time trap, including dragons."

"Hey," Javan said, studying the bean more closely, "I know what these are. They're coffee cherries!"

"Coffee cherries?"

"Yeah. On Earth, we take the fruit off these cherries, dry the beans out, roast them, crush them up and use them to make a drink we call coffee."

"Interesting."

"We drink coffee to give us energy. I used to go to Starbucks on the way to school every day to get coffee to help wake me up. I thought that caffeine was a lifesaver. Now it will be. Literally."

"Just don't eat too many before you find a dragon. You'll need to feed a good chunk to the dragon you ride so it will be able to fly out of the time trap."

"Gotcha."

"Find it and ride it before all of its scales turn golden. Otherwise it will want to eat you rather than the cherries."

"Gotcha."

"And remember to use your strengths. Don't try to surprise him or overpower him. Connect with his mind. Talk to him. Reason with him. Convince him to let you ride him. Let the dragon choose you to be his Collector."

"Gotcha." Javan wasn't sure that was the best strategy, but agreeing with Astor seemed like the wise thing to do at the moment. "You're going to come with me and help me, right?"

"No, my son. I'll be putting together a feast for the dragon. It will want to eat once its free from the trap. I also need to be able to come and rescue you if you're stuck for too long."

"Hold up." Javan didn't like this news one little bit. How was he supposed to make his way through a time trap and collect his first dragon by himself? "You mean I have to do this on my own?"

"Yes. You're ready. I believe in you. Now go."

"Do I at least get to take the okty?"

"It would require too many energy balls; you need to save them for you and the dragon." Astor put his hands on Javan's shoulders. "The jungle is only a few miles away. You can easily run that distance."

"Yay." Javan rolled his eyes. "Running. My favorite thing."

"What is necessary is not always enjoyable."

"I so wish running wasn't necessary." Nevertheless, Javan gulped, ate a handful of cherries and stepped into the warped air of the time trap.

◊   ◊   ◊

Despite the raw caffeine in his system, Javan felt everything slow down. His steps. His breaths. Even the blinking of his eyes.

A hummingbird inched along in the sky. A cricket let out a long, leisurely chirp. A breeze drifted through his hair strand by strand.

"Javan!" The intensity of Astor's voice startled Javan. "Noon is approaching. Eat another handful of cherries and find that dragon!"

Javan turned, gave Astor a thumbs up and chomped on some more cherries. His heart rate quickened and with it the pace of his steps. Next stop: the back of a Noon Stalker.

CHAPTER 51

Striking a Deal

As Javan sprinted across the land, the meadows changed to flowery fields. The flowery fields soon gave way to a vibrant jungle full of giant green plants and tall trees with green leaves of every shape and size. The mountains lay beyond the jungle, but Javan wouldn't need to go that far.

The dragon he was after made his home in the jungle.

Only the jungle was the size of Hawaii, and Javan was on foot in a time trap with no help of any sort. The long, drawn-out songs and chirps and slithers of the animals around him didn't exactly put his mind at ease. He slowed to a walk but ate a few more energy balls just in case. If any of those noise-making animals were dangerous and tried to attack him, he liked knowing he had the ability to outrun them.

"Okay, Noon Stalker, where are you?" Javan crossed over a creek, dipped under an ivy canopy and walked through a cluster of pointy ferns. No matter which way he twisted and turned, though, he couldn't avoid their prickly tips. "Ouch, ouch, ouch, ouch, ouch!" He finally spun his way out of the cluster and collapsed onto a bed of clovers.

Which he shared with a black panther.

The jolt of pain from his fresh wound colliding with the ground was nothing compared to the fear coursing through his system as he stared from his hands and knees into the panther's yellow eyes. It hissed, snarled and bared its fangs.

Fortunately it did so in slow motion, allowing Javan time to stand and begin backing away. He inspected his wound in the process and was happy to note that the sealing mud had done its job and kept his cut sealed.

A human? Where did he come from? If he causes my meal to run away...

Forgetting about his cut, Javan reached for his stalker swords and surveyed the narrow clearing in which he stood. Vines draped across the palm trees that surrounded him and dangled to the green, puffy-leafed plants and barbed ferns all around him. He could hear the dragon's thoughts but couldn't see him anywhere.

How could he not see a gigantic golden dragon in the middle of all this green?

Hmm...he looks like he's looking for me. But that's not possible. I'm cloaked. He can't know I'm here.

"You're cloaked? Ha! That's why I can't see you."

You can hear me?

"Yes." Javan sighed. "I can hear your thoughts." He hated having to explain this thought-reading thing to every new dragon he met. He needed a shirt that said "I am a Collector and can read Stalker's minds. Get over it."

I have never met such a human before. You intrigue me. What else can you do?

"Well..." Javan continued to look for the dragon while he steadily backed away from the angry panther deliberately plodding toward him. "I'm pretty good with stun balls. I would throw one now at this charming cat that wants to eat me, but this time trap would slow it down too much to make it work."

The time trap should be slowing you down, too. Why isn't it?

Javan patted his leather pouch. "Energy balls." Where was that dragon? He had to be close. "You have to be getting hungry. I'll share—if you let me ride you."

The panther let out a loud, long roar, obscuring whatever response the dragon might have made. Javan jumped, calmed himself down, then said, "So is it a deal? I save you from the time trap, and you save me from the panther?"

The dragon laughed. *I've outlasted time traps before. I'll outlast this one. I may be unbearably hungry when it passes, but I'll still be free.*

"Not for long. A Hunter just captured Mertzer with the help of the entire Zandadorian army. He'll soon set his sights on the Noon Stalkers. With only three of you left, your odds of escaping him are not good."

Considering you have yet to find me even though you can speak with me, I'm not worried about this Hunter you speak of.

The dragon had a good point. How was Javan supposed to counter that argument? "Well, you may be able to elude the Hunter, but his father is the king and not someone you'll be able to ignore much longer. If he is able to reign for another hundred years, he will see to it that all dragons outside his captivity are eliminated."

Aren't you the dramatic one.

"Just warning you." Javan, careful to avoid the angry panther, began to make his way around the clover-covered clearing. He waved at the air as he walked, hoping to connect with the dragon. "The Dark King is the reason Silverspike and Skylark are hiding on earth."

Skylark? Did you say Skylark? You've seen her? She's still alive?

"Yes, I've seen her," Javan said. He recognized that sense of desperate interest behind those words. This dragon had a little dragon crush.

That's how Javan used to talk about his crush, Julianne. Wow. Julianne. The girl who once dominated his thoughts now seemed so far away. And insignificant.

Skylark is well?

"Yes." Javan shook his head to clear that chapter of his life away. If he wanted to survive this chapter he was currently living, Javan had to convince this dragon to let him ride him. "Her Collector is taking good care of her. He'll bring her back to Zandador once my own collection is complete and the Dark King is no longer a threat."

How close are you to completing your collection?

Javan winced. "Well, once I add you, I'll only need three more dragons."

So you've got nothing right now.

Javan made his way to the tail end of the panther and paused his air-striking endeavor. "True."

And you expect me to let you hop on and be the first dragon you ever ride?

"Yes and no. You should let me hop on so we can become partners in the fight against the Dark King. Otherwise your choices are captivity or death." Javan swiped the air behind him. Nothing. "But you won't be the first dragon I've ever ridden. Skylark let me ride her."

She did?

"Yes." How else could he use this Skylark thing to his advantage? "She even defended me when Silverspike wanted to zap me with one of his lightning bolts."

Hmm. Then perhaps you are worthy to be my Collector.

"Does that mean you'll let me ride you?" Javan held his breath as he awaited the response.

You're sure that Skylark will return to Zandador once you complete your collection?

"Yes. I'm certain."

It took the dragon a few minutes, but he finally replied. *Then yes, you may ride me.*

"Fantastic!" Javan jumped with excitement and clapped his hands. Astor was right. Connecting with the dragon and reasoning with him worked. "You won't regret this. I promise."

Just get on before I change my mind.

"Right. Of course. Sorry for the emotional outburst. It's just that you're saving my life. Because if I don't have a dragon by tomorrow--"

You're still talking when you should be riding. I'm hungry and want out of this time trap.

"Oh. Sorry. My bad. Getting on...wait." Javan spun around and still couldn't spot the dragon. "Where are you?"

Where I've been this whole time. Look up.

CHAPTER 52

Trust?

ook up? The dragon was above him?

Javan obeyed the dragon's command but saw nothing except patches of blue sky between the leaves of the towering trees. "Yeah. I still don't see you."

I'm here. I'm trying to uncloak myself, but the time trap is making that difficult.

"If I can't see you, how am I supposed to ride you?"

You're going to have scramble up one of these trees and leap.

"Leap into thin air and hope I choose the right direction? That sounds insane."

I'll guide you.

The panther was working on turning itself around. Javan decided climbing a tree wasn't such a bad idea. The further away from that oversized cat he got, the safer he would feel, even if the panther was perfectly capable of climbing trees.

"Okay," Javan said. "Which tree?"

The one behind you. Climb up. I'll tell you when to jump.

Javan turned and rolled his eyes. "Fantastic." The towering tree had no low-growing branches, but it did have several vines hanging down from the branches above. He grabbed one of the vines and pulled himself up hand over hand as though he were climbing a rope in gym class.

Sweat dripped from his forehead and every muscle in his arms, chest and back screamed in agony by the time he reached the first branch a good thirty feet above the ground. "Made it," Javan said. "Now where are you? Which way should I jump?"

You're not high enough. Keep going.

"All right." Javan took a deep breath and scurried branch by branch another twenty feet into the air. "Now?"

Almost. You need to get to the top.

"I'm not sure I can." Fifteen or so feet spanned the remaining distance to the top, but climbing any higher made Javan nervous. "The branches are getting thinner and might not hold me."

Trust me. They'll hold. Climb.

Trust him? Javan didn't even know the dragon's name. For all Javan knew, the dragon he had yet to lay eyes on was nowhere near him and liked convincing humans to climb trees and plummet to their deaths. Trust was risky, but the risk was necessary. So Javan climbed.

The branches creaked under his weight but held.

When he could climb no higher, he said, "Now?"

Now. Aim for the panther, and you'll crash into me on the way down.

Javan closed his eyes, said a quick prayer and looked down. The view terrified him. He could see nothing but clear air in the sixty-five feet between him and the panther that looked like nothing more than a black dot on the ground below. "You sure you're right above that panther? I can't miss you if I jump from here?"

I'm sure. You can't miss me. Now jump. Before those branches break.

"You said they would hold me!"

Not if you stay up there. Jump!

Javan could feel the branches breaking beneath his feet. It was either jump or fall. "Ready or not, here I come!"

Hoping the dragon and not the panther would break his fall, Javan leapt feet first into the air.

CHAPTER 53

The First Ride

Down, down, down Javan dropped. His feet flailed. His stomach flip-flopped. His heart stopped.

Where was that dragon?

Had Javan overshot the jump?

Had he leapt in the wrong direction?

This isn't how he wanted to die!

As he sailed past the first branch of the tree he had encountered on the way up, Javan curled himself into a ball and braced for impact with the ground.

Impact came seconds later, but it wasn't the ground he collided with. The soft, round wing of a dragon broke his fall instead.

He slid down the smooth wing, across the dragon's wide, scaly back and halfway up the other wing before slipping back down and settling on the golden scales.

Welcome.

Just like with Skylark on earth, direct contact with the cloaked dragon allowed Javan to see the dragon's entire body. Its long tail and even longer body hung in the air with its wings spread. It looked like it was suspended in the canvas of a painting, and Javan was the only moving part in the picture.

His ability to move allowed him to display his frustration. Postponing his awe of the magnificent creature, he crawled up to the base of the dragon's neck and beat both sides of it like a punching bag. "You didn't need to make me climb that high!"

Probably not. The dragon chuckled. *I wanted to see if you trusted me enough to do it.*

"Glad I passed your test." Javan sat back and shook his sore hands. Perhaps punching the dragon's tough scales wasn't the smartest way to retaliate. "By the way, my name's Javan. What's yours?"

Varjiek.

"Good to meet you, Varjiek. Now fly us out of here."

Can't. Time trap, remember?

"Right. You need the energy balls." Javan scrambled up Varjiek's neck, over his head and onto his snout. "Sorry if this is uncomfortable, but I can't think of a better way to get these energy balls into your mouth."

Just be quick about it.

Javan slithered between Varjiek's eyes and sprawled out over his cold, wet nose. "Wow. This hurts."

You're on my nose and are making me want to sneeze. How does this hurt you?

"I got a little scraped up in a sword fight yesterday. The cut on my chest is still raw."

Oh. Sorry. But I am going to sneeze if you don't hurry.

"Hurrying up." Javan reached over the edge of Varjiek's nose and emptied the bag of energy balls into the dragon's slightly open mouth. "Done. Chew up, and let's get out of here."

Javan scurried back to his riding position at the bottom of Varjiek's neck and watched another of Varjiek's scales turn golden. Only a handful remained grey. "Why aren't we moving?"

"We" need time to chew these energy balls.

Two more scales turned to gold before Varjiek flapped his right wing. *Haha! I feel the energy balls working!*

"Finally."

Hold on, Javan, Varjiek said as he flitted up and back down. *If you fall off, I'm not coming back for you.*

Javan gripped two scales. "Ready."

Excellent.

They shot straight up into the sky, spun around in some clouds and sped across the land Javan had traversed on his way to the jungle. "This is awesome! I'm never gonna want to ride another okty again!"

Okties are boring!

Varjiek flipped and turned, dove and climbed. But right in the middle of the exhilarating ride toward the sun, Varjiek stopped. Spread his wings. Drifted through the sky.

"Varjiek? You okay?" Javan leaned in, placed his head on Varjiek's neck and listened. He could hear the rhythm of Varjiek's heartbeat change as it began to beat in tune with Javan.

The change brought with it a new sense of responsibility that exceeded anything he had ever felt for his horse, Storm.

Strange things are happening to me.

"Me, too," Javan said. He felt older. Wiser. More mature. He now had someone to take care of and think about besides himself, and he knew his life would never be the same from that moment on.

I feel connected to you, as though it is my duty to protect you, fight for you and serve you. I thought I liked my independence, but I think I like this feeling of purpose serving you as my Collector brings me.

Javan wasn't sure how to respond to those humbling words, so he switched subjects. "Thanks, but enough sappiness. We need to get you fed before you decide I'd make a better meal than a leader."

I am hungry. Where to?

"The meadows in the southwest tip of your territory. My friends should have your meal waiting for us there."

Yes, sir. To the meadows we go. Varjiek made a sharp left and raced across the sky.

◇   ◇   ◇

"There they are!" Javan spotted Hamilton and Astor pacing in front of piles and piles of hay as well as several goats. He steered Varjiek to a landing behind the hay and slid off his front leg. "Eat up, big guy."

Gladly.

While Varjiek feasted on the hay and goats, Javan ran over to his mentors. "I did it! I found the dragon, rode him, and now he's mine. I'm a Dragon Collector who actually has a dragon in his collection!"

"Javan, what has taken you so long?" Astor's question was riddled with irritation.

"We're almost out of time," Hamilton said. He also sounded upset.

"What's the problem?" This was not the excited response Javan expected. "It's not even noon yet. We still have 24 hours to get to Japheth, and it won't take nearly that long on the back of this fast flying dragon. That I collected. That you haven't congratulated me for yet."

"Javan," Hamilton said, sounding a little more calm, "you've been gone for almost 24 hours. This is Sunday morning."

"What? How is that possible?"

"The time trap warps your perception of time, even with energy balls," Astor said. "It's nearly 11:00. You have just over an hour to get to Stalker Square or your mother and Ravier are dead."

CHAPTER 54

Back to Stalker Square

"**F**aster! Faster! Faster!" Javan urged the grey-scaled dragon onward.

Thanks to Varjiek's ability to cloak himself, they flew undetected over the land. The westward flight seemed to be taking forever even though they were flying so fast that the land below them was nothing more than a blur, and Javan's cheeks were pressed back to his ears from the force of the wind as they flew. He kept his sunglasses hooked to the front of his shirt to make sure they wouldn't fly off his face.

If I could teleport there, I would, but this dragon has wings and must fly.

"Just get me there in time. Please." If he was so much as a minute late, he would regret it for the rest of his life. How could he live with himself knowing his mother and grandfather died because he couldn't get to Stalker Square on time? Would Omri even let him live and allow the Battle for the Throne to continue if Javan showed up late?

Would Javan want to live and continue to compete?

I will get you there, Varjiek said. *Vasilis often made a habit of sabotaging my meals before he was captured by the Hunter. I look forward to thwarting one of his. He won't be eating your family today.*

Thankful for the bad blood between the Noon Stalkers, Javan leaned in a little closer and held on a little tighter as Varjiek pushed the pace. Then, before Javan even realized where they were, Varjiek cut sharply to the left.

We're here, he said, carving a circle in the sky. He slowed his speed from the long, fast flight as he spiraled his way down toward Stalker Square. *Let me know when you want me to uncloak myself.*

Quiet, submissive, defeated people dressed all in brown once again filled the Square, the stands and the road that led to the stadium. Spots of red and black indicated soldiers strategically placed around and throughout the crowd. And Omri's four dragons dominated the center of the Square.

The two white Dawn and Dusk Stalkers stood among the crowd at either end of the stage while the grey Midnight Stalker claimed the area behind the stage. The mostly golden Noon Stalker shared the stage with three people: Omri, Esmeralda and Ravier.

Micah and Mertzer were nowhere to be seen.

Javan found that odd. He thought Omri would be proudly parading his son and newest dragon in front of the people to display his increasing dominance over them.

"A week ago," Omri was saying, "one of your own dared interrupt the execution of these rebels by initiating the Battle for the Throne. Out of respect for the law, I allowed him to compete. I even had my son join as a proxy competitor because you, my people, deserve to witness a fair fight between a Hunter and a Collector."

Javan put his sunglasses on to hide his eyes and guided Varjiek to the front of the stage. They hovered just high enough above the crowd to keep the people from sensing the dragon's presence.

Now? Varjiek asked.

"Not yet," Javan whispered. He wanted to hear more of Omri's pompous speech.

"But why drag out a battle if your competitors are weak and incompetent? So I gave them a week." Omri stepped forward and spoke louder. "My son Micah proved his worth. He successfully hunted and captured the Dusk Stalker Mertzer on my behalf. I wanted to introduce you to my newest dragon today, but a more important mission arose. I felt it was critical to immerse Mertzer in his new role as my dragon slave and entrusted him and Micah with the mission which they are carrying out as we speak."

Javan tensed at the mention of Mertzer and cringed as he recalled the agonizing screams of the dragon the night Micah cut off his tail.

"Your Collector, however," Omri continued, "has proven himself to be nothing more than a coward. Not only did he fail to collect a dragon, he didn't even have the courage to return here today and face the fate he agreed to: his life for those of these rebel prisoners." Omri turned to the dragon standing behind him. "Vasilis, enjoy your meal."

Finally, Vasilis said. He turned his head toward Esmeralda and Ravier and opened his mouth.

Javan nudged Varjiek and shouted, "Stop! I'm here!" The collective gasp Javan heard from the crowd let him know that Varjiek had taken the cue and uncloaked himself.

Varjiek! Vasilis roared and spewed a stream of fire into the air. The people below screamed and scurried out of the way of the falling ashes. *How dare you interrupt my meal.*

As if you haven't done the same to me many times. Get over it and go find you something a little less human to eat.

"Think you could have cut that any closer, Javan?" Ravier said, interrupting the dragon taunting and shaking his head in obvious relief.

Javan just smiled and addressed Omri. "King Omri, I would like to introduce you and Zandador to my dragon." The people below Varjiek moved out of the way, allowing the dragon to land. "This is Varjiek, the first dragon in my collection."

Despite the hatred in Omri's eyes, he clapped and said, "Well done. We didn't think you were going to make it."

"I said I would return and I did. Now it's your turn to honor your word. You agreed to let these prisoners go if I returned here with a dragon."

"I am a man of my word." Omri forced a smile and nodded toward the captives. "You are free to go."

While Ravier grabbed Esmeralda's arm and led her down the stairs, Omri lowered his voice and spoke directly to Javan. "I think I shall find it amusing to watch you and my son compete against one another in the Battle for the Throne. But know this. The fight is already over.

"Micah has claimed the one and only Dusk Stalker. I am allowing the Battle to continue because I want to give him a chance to hunt the other three as well. Having eight dragons under my control will magnify my power and ensure my place on the throne for centuries to come."

Omri climbed on Vasilis and turned his attention to the crowd. "People of Zandador, be sure to thank your Collector for making your King more powerful than ever!" Laughing, Omri looked back at Javan. "And Collector, be sure to thank Gesha. She has been a most cooperative citizen and very helpful in determining Mertzer's first mission."

With that, he flew away.

CHAPTER 55

Mertzer's Mission

Gesha? A cooperative citizen? What did that mean? And what did she have to do with determining Mertzer's mission?

He began scanning the crowd for her from his seat atop Varjiek, but it was hard to spot her familiar face in the commotion that ensued during the departure of the Dark King's other dragons. Ravier finally interrupted his search.

"Javan," Ravier said from the ground below, "take one of the scales from under your dragon's right leg and place it in the slot on the column."

"You want me to do what?" Jerking a scale off a dragon he barely knew in front of a large group of hostile people didn't seem like a smart idea.

"When you touched the column and entered the Battle for the Throne, four scale slots appeared. Your job is to fill each of those slots with a scale from each dragon you collect. You have your first dragon, so you need to fill your first slot."

"You hear that Varjiek? I apparently need to separate you from one of your scales."

Go ahead, Collector. It is necessary.

"Okay." Javan slid off the dragon, walked over to Varjiek's right leg and placed his hands on a grey scale. "Here goes." It took both his hands and a forceful pull, but he managed to yank the scale off cleanly. Varjiek shrieked and stomped his leg, shaking the entire square.

"Sorry," Javan said. "I shouldn't ever need to do that again."

I won't ever let you.

The shaking of the ground redirected the people's focus to Javan and Varjiek. Their murmurings ceased as Javan walked slowly through the parting people to the column.

With all eyes on him, he placed the scale in the top slot. It faded to a dull grey, let out a series of loud pops, then beamed with an intense, golden glow.

One by one, the crowd began clapping. Soon the entire place roared with cheers for Javan as he walked back toward Varjiek. They pat him on the back, congratulated him and made him feel like a conquering hero.

Esmeralda met him halfway and smothered him with a hug. "Well done, my son," she whispered in his ear. "I knew you could do it."

"Thanks." He smiled, content to be in his mother's arms. Then he saw Gesha. "Excuse me, mom. I need to talk to someone."

He walked over to her. But she wasn't smiling. Or crying. She just looked...guilty. "I'm sorry, Javan," she said. "I'm so sorry."

"Sorry for what? What's wrong?"

"Some of the king's men. They found me."

"What did they do to you?" Javan reached for his swords, ready to fight anyone who dared hurt her.

"Nothing. Except give me what I wanted."

"What did they have that you wanted?"

"An offer from the King. To come out of hiding. And work with my mother."

Javan's stomach churned. He didn't like where this was going. "What did the Dark King want in exchange?"

"He wanted to know the location of Gri." No remorse dripped from her words. "The King sent Micah and his dragon to destroy it."

CHAPTER 56

The Vow

Javan and Varjiek raced across the land for the second time that day. This flight, however, included two additional passengers: Ravier and Esmeralda. Javan had left Gesha alone in Japheth. He wasn't sure he ever wanted to see her again.

Worry consumed him as they traversed the miles through the late afternoon air. What had Micah done to Hannah and the town? Had she survived the attack? Had anyone survived?

"There's Gri," Ravier said, pointing straight ahead. "I don't like that we can see it. That means the invisibility shield is down."

Javan urged Varjiek to slow down, and they coasted over the village. All they saw were crumpled houses and destroyed buildings. No people were anywhere to be seen.

When they reached the farm, the barns were flattened; all the okties were gone.

"Land," Ravier said. "Now."

Javan guided Varjiek to the ground in front of the house. Half the roof was caved in, but the rest of the structure was still intact. With Ravier leading the way, the three of them ran inside.

"Hannah," Ravier yelled. He rushed through the house in a panic. "Hannah, are you here?"

Javan and Esmeralda just stood by the fireplace listening to the silence that greeted Ravier's desperate questions.

"She's gone," Ravier said, ending his search and leaning against the table. "She's gone."

"Maybe she cleared out before Micah arrived," Esmeralda said. "She's resourceful. She and the rest of the town are probably hiding somewhere in the mountains."

"Then we have to go find her," Javan said.

"Not you," Ravier said. He walked over and put his hands on Javan's shoulders. He looked like he hadn't eaten or slept the entire week he had been in the dungeon. But despite his sunken cheeks and hollowed eyes, his voice remained strong. "With Micah on the hunt, time is critical. You must focus on collecting your next dragon."

"Okay, grandfather," Javan said, "I'll do as you wish." Right after I find Micah, he added to himself. He wasn't about to let anyone enslave his dragon, destroy his home and chase his family away without answering for it.

Before Javan collected another dragon, he would hunt down and defeat the Dragon Hunter.

END OF BOOK ONE

The beginning of book two is a page away.
Keep reading to follow the adventure!

THE
DRAGON
HUNTER

Book Two of The Dragon Stalker Bloodlines Saga

D.K. Drake

Dream Doers Publishing LLC
North Carolina

PROLOGUE

(Sixty-four Years Ago)

At age thirteen, Micah hated his life.

Ever since he got his father's approval and moved into the castle three years ago, all he did was train, eat, and sleep. He never got to see his mother, his father, his half-siblings, or any other kids his age. His life consisted only of sword training, exercising, and reading about sword training, Dragon Hunting, or the laws of Zandador.

He wanted more adventure. More excitement. And more attention from his father. But Omri was an elusive, powerful man. Micah was only able to catch glimpses of him now and then. When he did see him, Micah noted how he walked, how he talked, and how the people around him catered to his every demand. Someday he was going to be just like his Dad.

Today, though, he wanted to escape the confines of the castle. He was supposed to return to the training room after dinner. Instead, he walked right past the room, down the stairs, and snuck out one of the back doors of the castle.

He breathed in the evening air, took a stroll through the woods, climbed a few trees, and tossed some rocks into the lake. He really should come outside more often. This was much more fun than spending his life in that damp, dark, windowless training room.

The sound of a twig snapping behind him caused him to turn around. A dragon stood ten feet away, and his colorful scales indicated he was a hungry Dusk Stalker in search of food.

Micah gulped. This was why he wasn't supposed to exit the castle through the back. He had walked right into the feeding grounds of his father's four dragons.

"You must be Eli," Micah said, trying to sound calm and confident. He found himself fascinated by the ten-foot high, wingless, beautiful creature. The dragon stood his ground while Micah took a step closer. "My father is your master, so you aren't allowed to eat me."

The dragon nodded as though he understood, and Micah walked even closer. He was only an arms-length away now and noticed the dragon had a collar with spikes protruding into his scales wrapped around the base of his neck.

"Why do you have this on? That must make eating painful. Bend down, and I'll take it off for you."

Eli complied with Micah's instructions. Micah unlatched the heavy collar and freed it from the dragon's neck. As soon as he took it off, Eli nudged Micah's shoulder as if to say thanks and sprinted away.

"What do you think you are doing?" Omri's booming voice startled Micah, and he dropped the collar, cutting his leg with one of the spikes in the process.

"I was helping the dragon. He looked sad and hurt."

"You are never to help the dragons, especially that one. They deserve no mercy and are to be treated like the slaves they are. If you cannot understand that, you will never be a Dragon Hunter."

"No mercy. I understand now, sir."

"I don't think you do, but you will."

Omri was right. After spending the next six months in the dungeon wearing a collar like the one he took off of Eli, Micah understood the meaning of no mercy. And he vowed to never again treat any dragon as anything other than a mindless slave.

CHAPTER 1

Unexpected Reactions

(Present Day)

"You...you can't go in there." A shaky, scrawny soldier holding a spear stepped in front of the double wooden doors. Like that was going to stop Micah from entering the throne room.

"Of course I can, you twit." Micah purposefully let his black dreadlocks fall in the man's pale face as his 6'3" muscular frame towered above the runt. How did this guy earn guard duty for the King?

"I am King Omri's son," Micah said. "His favorite son. The son who just won him another dragon. I go where I please, when I please. Now move." Micah shoved the wimp out of the way and burst through the doors.

A handful of the king's advisors huddled in the corner chatting amongst themselves. King Omri paced alone on the stage in front of his throne at the far end of the room.

Moonlight shone through the wall of windows behind him, casting long shadows on the red carpet from his tall height and wide shoulders. His white shirt popped against his black skin, and his short, tight braids looked more regal than Micah's long dreadlocks. Maybe Micah would change his hairstyle once he became King.

"Father!" The word bounced off the marble floors and stone walls of the spacious room. "You can congratulate me. Your newest dragon and I have destroyed the rebel city of Gri."

"Congratulate you?" Omri stopped pacing and began walking towards Micah.

Micah smiled and waited for his father to approach. Omri had to be pleased with him. So pleased he was bound to lavish him with gifts.

It would probably start with a feast. Perhaps followed by awarding him a wing of the castle. Along with a wife.

Sure, he was still underage, but he had earned that kind of privilege. The laws of marriage everyone else had to abide by didn't really apply to him. After all, he was Micah, the thirteenth son of the King. A fierce captain in the elite Justice Unit of the army. And now Dragon Hunter.

But as Omri reached Micah, Micah's smile vanished. Instead of pride, he recognized rage in his father's harsh brown eyes. He had seen that rage before and braced himself for the beating he knew was coming.

"After the way you humiliated me," Omri said, punching Micah in the gut, "I ought to kill you."

◊　　◊　　◊

Javan let himself drift off to sleep on the back of Varjiek as darkness settled in. He trusted his dragon to carry him back to the capital city to face Micah and didn't need to be awake to navigate the flight.

Only he didn't feel rested at all when they landed a short time later. "Why are we stopping?" Javan asked.

I thought landing was a better option than crashing. Listening to you snore makes me want to sleep.

Javan cringed. He should have known better than to ask Varjiek to keep flying after already making one intense cross-country flight that day. After covering thousands of miles, the dragon had to be beyond exhausted. "Sorry, buddy. I forgot you're not a robot."

What's a robot?

"And I forgot you're not from Earth." Javan sighed. How to explain this? "A robot is a like a person, but it's mechanical. You tell it what to do and it does it. It never gets tired or hungry or talks back."

No, I am not a robot. Varjiek yawned. *Get some sleep, young Collector. We will fly again in the morning.*

Javan slid off Varjiek's back and stretched his sore, stiff body. Carefully. He wanted to reach his arms to the sky and clasp his hands behind his back and pull, but either exaggerated stretch would bust the sealing mud and cause his chest wound to split open. Right now, sealing mud was working like stitches to keep the sword cut that spanned from his belly button to his clavicle together.

At least he had gained some muscles beneath his tan skin during his month or so here in Zandador. Otherwise that cut would have sliced right down to his ribs. Nevertheless, he had lost a great deal of blood thanks to that cut inflicted by Micah and was feeling the fatiguing effects. Getting a solid night of sleep on the ground was probably a better idea than dozing fitfully on the dragon's back.

Javan did like the looks of his room for the night. The dragon had found a nice little grassy spot by the river where the moonlight danced off the water.

The water.

They shouldn't be near the water at all. And they certainly shouldn't be on the south side of the river. What was this dragon doing?

"Varjiek," Javan said between gritted teeth as he walked around to face the dragon. His grey scales made the dragon easy to see in the dark. His massive size helped. The dragon stood twelve feet tall from his legs to his back, and his long neck added another six feet to the distance from the ground to his head. At only five foot nine inches tall, Javan felt like a dwarf next to the dragon. That didn't mean he couldn't still be mad at the creature whose thoughts he could read. "Why are we on the southern shore of the river? We're supposed to be heading east, toward Japheth."

Ah. I was wondering how long it would take you to notice we weren't going in the direction you wanted.

"That doesn't answer my question."

We're heading south because you need to collect a Dawn Stalker. We won't find any Dawn Stalkers in Japheth.

"I don't want a Dawn Stalker right now. I want Micah."

You need to collect dragons, not humans. Collecting a Dragon Hunter is not going to help you win the throne.

Javan rolled his eyes. "I know that. But I can't focus on dragon collecting until I make Micah pay for what he has done."

I agreed to let you ride me because you promised me Skylark. The sooner I help you collect your other three dragons, the sooner I get to see Skylark. So we're going after a dragon, not a Dragon Hunter.

"Hold up there, buddy! I may only be fifteen in earth years, but I look like I'm 150 here in Zandador."

I have seen many humans in my time, and you don't look a day over a hundred.

"Not according to my mother, thank you very much. She told me I looked older than her, and she's 147."

You don't. She was just trying to instill confidence in your young soul.

Javan had grown accustomed to the idea that he looked like he was a good 150 years old. It did help his confidence and made him feel like he was old enough to be a king.

If this dragon was right, and he only looked like he was a hundred, would the people still be willing to follow him if he were to collect all four Dragon Stalkers and win the Battle for the Throne?

Then again, in a world where people lived to be 700-1000 years old, did fifty years really make that big of a difference?

"No matter how old I look, I still look like an adult who can make his own decisions. Besides, you let me ride you. I am your leader now. You are part of my dragon collection. You have to obey me. Your job is to do what I tell you to do."

Is that so? Varjiek stood and towered over Javan. *I don't just look like I'm 623 here in Zandador; I have actually been alive for 623 years. That makes me much older and wiser. You gained my lifelong loyalty the moment you first rode me, but I remain able think for myself and make decisions that are best for both of us.*

He bent his head so his large black eyes were even with Javan's bright green ones. *If you wanted a robot, you should have become a Hunter and cut off my tail.*

The dragon covered Javan with a puff of smoke and walked away.

CHAPTER 2

Dragon Round-Up

"I don't understand. How did I humiliate you?" Micah lifted himself up on his hands and knees while swallowing a mouthful of blood. His father would kick him again if he dared get a drop of blood on the floor. "I sliced that Collector's chest open and left him for dead the night I won Mertzer."

"You should have made sure he was dead." Omri stomped on Micah's back, sending him crumpling to the floor. "Not only did that Collector survive, but he collected a Noon Stalker. He forced me to release the prisoners and made me look like a fool in front of my people. Now Javan has a flying dragon with the power of invisibility. All you have is a wingless dragon who can't even teleport."

Micah eased himself into a sitting position and looked up at Omri. "Mertzer is the last of the Dusk Stalkers. Javan has no hope of winning the competition since I already claimed that dragon."

"Now you are the fool!" Omri pulled Micah to his feet by his hair. "All the Collector has to do is kill you, and the dragon becomes his. I'm tempted to go ahead and kill you myself just to prevent that from happening."

"Father, please." Micah had to find a way to keep himself alive; he knew his father didn't issue idle threats. "Keep me alive, and I'll hunt you more dragons. Imagine how powerful you'll be with eight dragons under your control."

Omri released Micah's hair. "I'm only letting you live, because I want more dragons. Clean yourself up. Gather soldiers. Go to midnight territory. I want a Midnight Stalker next."

Micah's blood-soaked mouth went dry. "A Midnight Stalker? Shouldn't I get a little more practice hunting the other dragons first?"

"Those are my orders. It's the only way to show the people that I am more powerful than that Collector." Omri glared into Micah's eyes. "If you return here without a Midnight Stalker, I'll feed you to my dragons. I've seen the way you treat them. They'll be happy to tear you limb from limb. Now go."

"Yes, sir." Micah nodded and left the room.

As he made his way down the long spiral staircase to the Dragon Quarters, rage and confusion masked the pain of the beating he had just endured. How could his father hurt him after Micah brought home a dragon for him? That was a feat no one else had ever done or even thought of doing. So why did his father hurt him? He had done nothing wrong.

That's what the boy Micah whipped a little over a week ago told him. Micah had whipped him anyway. Had he been wrong to punish that boy?

No. The boy had violated curfew. He should have returned from hunting before dark. So what if his family was hungry and wanted the food? He broke the law by ignoring the curfew. It was Micah's job to make sure people respected the King and the King's laws.

Maybe that's why Omri had beaten Micah. To instill respect.

He would let his bruised ribs serve as a reminder to be more respectful. He hoped he had a chance to demonstrate his increased respect for his father. This trip to hunt a Midnight Stalker could easily turn into a suicide mission. Did his father expect him to succeed in capturing a Midnight Stalker or die in the process?

After being humiliated by the Collector, Micah didn't think Omri cared one way or the other about Micah's life.

"So I'll make him care," he muttered to himself. He would hunt a Midnight Stalker. Then a Noon Stalker. Then a Dawn Stalker.

Once he had all four dragons and was able to keep his father in power, Omri would have to care. Then Micah would finally know what it felt like to be loved by his father.

His entire life had been dedicated to pleasing his father, making him the favored successor. The fact that he grew taller and stronger faster than others his age didn't hurt. Most weren't strong enough to join the army until they reached 100; he became a soldier at age fifty. Now at seventy-seven, he had already accomplished more than most men twice his age.

He knew he would have to wait several hundred more years, but he was still young. By the time his father retired in another two or three hundred years, Micah would be plenty young enough to rule for a good seven hundred or so years.

At least that was the plan until Javan came along. That Collector had to pay for the damage he was causing. He needed to die. And he would. After Micah captured himself a Midnight Stalker.

◊   ◊   ◊

Micah stormed his way through the double doors at the bottom of the stairs. He hated coming to the Dragon Quarters. The packed dirt floor made everything about this wing of the castle feel dirty. The wide hallway and thirty-foot high ceiling made it spacious enough to house the dragons, but no windows and poor lighting created a depressing atmosphere. The stone walls and ceiling left a constant chill in the air.

It didn't help that Omri wouldn't allow the dragon keepers to clean the stalls more than once a month. Micah understood the need to not pamper the dragons, but he wondered if the dragons would be less temperamental and easier to control if they didn't have to live in their own excrement.

The filthy stalls made the stench unbearable for any humans that entered the area; it had to have been worse for the dragons with their heightened sense of smell. How the dragons lived with the smell or how the dragon keepers stayed down here for eight hours at a time without puking their guts out baffled Micah.

The current keepers on duty were closing the massive stone door at the end of the hall. It was too big and heavy for one man to close alone. The two of them thus had to work together to pull the door closed using a thick, rough rope connected to a pulley on the ceiling. The system had been devised centuries ago to open and close the door for the dragons when they needed to leave the castle to hunt.

The dragons didn't have to go far to hunt. A wooded area behind the castle was constantly stocked with animals and vegetation the dragons enjoyed eating. Years ago, the keepers brought the dragons their food. The dragons didn't appreciate being caged up at all times and being given their food without having to work for it.

They took to feasting on the keepers just for sport. Omri tired of having to replace his help every other day and re-established the dragon hunting grounds.

Now Micah had added one more dragon to the mix. Once he finished his job and captured three more, they were going to have to increase the size of the grounds and the food supply. Otherwise the dragons would start fighting each other, and that would defeat the purpose of Micah working to hunt more dragons.

He would let Omri deal with the feeding problem. Right now, he had to do whatever was necessary to acquire a Midnight Stalker.

"Harness the dragons," Micah said. The keeper looked familiar, but he had never cared enough about the help to bother learning names. "I need them ready to ride in ten minutes. Don't bother with Eli, though. I've got Mertzer." Besides, Eli was unpredictable and never cooperative.

"Sir, that's impossible. I just sent Serenity out to feed. She won't be back for at least an hour."

"Fine. Get her ready when she returns, but get the other three ready now. While you're at it, gather the captains of the Justice Units. I need all of them and their units prepared to leave with me."

231

"It's getting late, sir. They're all settling into their quarters. There's no way they'll be ready to leave--"

"I don't care what time it is," Micah said, interrupting the man. "Just do as you're told. I am on a mission for the king. It is your job to assist me, and it is their job to follow orders. Got it?"

"Got it."

"I'll be back in an hour. I expect to see all of the dragons and Justice Units prepared to leave."

Micah turned and left. Next stop: the kitchen. He needed food now and for the journey. He just might have to hurt someone if any of the cooks tried to talk back to him.

He kind of hoped one of them would. He was itching to fight. Beating someone to a bloody pulp would improve his darkening mood.

CHAPTER 3

The Dragon's Secret

Nestled on the soft grass fifteen feet from the shore of the river, sleep easily overtook Javan. He kept his stalker swords within reach just in case he had to fend off wild animals or enemy soldiers who were sure to be tracking him. First, however, the offending party would have to get past Varjiek. Knowing he had a dragon to protect him allowed him to sleep without worry.

He didn't think about waking up until he felt something sharp poking his back. Figuring it was just a rock he rolled onto, he adjusted his position.

A few minutes later, a warm breeze shot over his face. Annoying. He hadn't slept long enough. He covered his face with his left arm and kept sleeping.

Until the shaking ground startled him enough to open his eyes. It reminded him of the tree tremors he experienced in Dusk Stalker territory. But that shouldn't be happening here. Not by the river.

Earthquake. It had to be an earthquake.

Javan sat up only to discover Varjiek running toward the river, causing the earthquake.

The dragon ran forward, sailed through the air, ducked his head and curled his wings and legs into his body. When he was about to the middle of the wide river, his balled-up body splashed into the water. It was the coolest cannonball Javan had ever seen, but he was so entranced by the sight that he didn't bother getting out of the way of the resulting wave.

The water splashed up and over Javan, drenching him from head to toe. The entire shore was soaked as well.

Varjiek popped his head up from near the middle of the river. *Ha! I finally got you to wake up.* Some of the scales on his neck were gold, indicating that noon was less than three hours away.

Javan stood and pushed his wet black hair out of his eyes. "You couldn't have tried a gentle nudge on the shoulder?"

I tried all sorts of things. I yelled at you, but you apparently can't hear my screaming thoughts when you are asleep. So I poked you with my tail. I snorted smoke over your face. I almost blew a stream of fire over your head but was afraid the fire might get too close and burn you. Then I came up with the jumping in the water idea. Glad I did. That was fun.

"Are you always this perky in the morning?"

This is the time of day I feel most alive. I'm just starting to get hungry, and hunting for food is the most excitement I have all day. He dove into the water and came up chomping on a fish. *Tasty!*

Javan's stomach started to rumble, but he didn't want a fish for breakfast. He'd make a meal out of some of the food his mother had packed for him. That food would only last a few days. Soon he'd have to hunt right alongside Varjiek. "Hurry up and find you enough food. We need to get going."

We do have a long trip ahead of us. I'll probably have to hunt several more times before we get there.

"What are you talking about? Dawn territory is just to the south of us. I was able to get there in several hours riding an okty not too long ago."

Javan had thought himself to have achieved the epitome of coolness the day he first rode that overgrown dragonfly with its fuzzy body, six legs and pink wings—all eight of them, four on each side with one shorter pair stacked atop a longer, thicker pair. Now he rode a dragon. Definitely cooler.

We're not going to Dawn territory.

"Where else am I going to track down a Dawn Stalker?"

In Keckrick.

"Keckrick? You want to leave Zandador?"

Indeed. All of the Stalker territories are going to be patrolled by soldiers. They are unsafe for us. So we're going to Keckrick.

"But I need to collect another dragon."

You will. In Keckrick.

"You're not making any sense. Dragons live in Zandador, not Keckrick."

Correction. Most dragons live in Zandador. I have heard rumors of a Dawn Stalker born not too long ago who is hiding out in Keckrick.

"That can't be true. Dragon eggs can't hatch in this dimension. They can only hatch on earth. The Dark King hasn't allowed anyone through that portal with a dragon egg or a dragon in centuries."

These rumors began about fifteen years ago, right around the same time there were rumors that a baby had been smuggled to earth. How old did you say you were, boy born in Zandador but raised on earth?

"Fifteen." The possibility that a dragon as old as him weakened Javan's knees. He plopped to the muddy ground. "How can you be sure the rumors are true?"

I can't. Not until we get to Keckrick.

NOVELS BY D.K. DRAKE

The Dragon Stalker Bloodlines Saga

BOOK 1: **The Dragon Collector**
BOOK 2: **The Dragon Hunter**
BOOK 3: **The Dragon Protector**
BOOK 4: **The Dragon Destroyer** *(coming soon)*

ABOUT THE AUTHOR

D.K. Drake brings you entertaining, engaging, wholesome adventures too packed with action to leave room for eye-rolling sappiness or mind-numbing fluff.

She is a Christian, a foster parent, and an avid runner. One of her goals is to run some sort of race in every state and (almost) every continent (no thanks, ice-covered Antarctica!).

She lives with two of her sisters in the great state of North Carolina and encourages you to trust God, believe in yourself, and fight for your dreams.

Get Exclusive Access to More {FREE} Stories Today!

Want to know a secret? Then come a little closer. That's it. Now lean in. Listen closely with your eyes because I'm typing these words with a whisper...

D.K. Drake doesn't exist.

I made her up. Just like I make up the characters in my books. In other words, D.K. Drake is my pen name. Why did I choose to write under this pen name? What do the "D" and "K" stand for? What is my true identity?

I answer all those questions and more for those who want to be email buddies.

When you become one of my email buddies, you get FREE access to the D.K. Drake starter library that includes the short story "Cops, Robbers...and Dragons?" (This is the story that sparked the idea for the entire Saga!)

You'll also get notified about new books and deals, have a chance to join the Advanced Reader Team, and keep up with my real-life adventures as an author, a runner, and a foster parent. All you have to do is visit www.AuthorDKDrake.com and sign up to the Insiders mailing list for FREE today.

A PERSONAL STORY
FROM THE AUTHOR

I love making up stories and living in the world of my imagination. But the story I most enjoy sharing is the true story of the day I accepted Jesus Christ as my Savior. So I want to share that story with you now...

As I listened to my mother read the Bible to me and my three older sisters before bed that night, I realized something important: I was a sinner.

I may have only been four years old, but I knew right from wrong. I knew it was a lot easier to choose to do the wrong thing than to do the right thing. I knew when I did something wrong, I got in trouble.

I knew my natural tendency was to tell lies to cover my mistakes. I knew my natural tendency was to be impolite to those in authority over me. I knew my natural tendency was to be selfish rather than look out for others.

So when I heard that "all have sinned and fall short of the glory of God (Romans 3:23)," I knew that verse was talking about me. I had sinned. That meant I had fallen short of God's glory.

When I heard that "the wages of sin is death, but the gift of God is eternal life in Christ Jesus our Lord (Romans 6:23)," I knew I was deserving of death but wanted God's gift of eternal life.

When I heard that Jesus said, "I am the way, the truth and the life. No one comes to the Father except through Me (John 14:6)," I understood that believing in Jesus was the only way to experience that eternal life and see the kingdom of God.

So when my mother finished reading the Bible that night, I asked her what I needed to do to be saved.

She sent my sisters to bed and sat down with me with her Bible open. She made sure I understood I was a sinner in need of God's forgiving grace. She made sure I understood that salvation comes by grace through faith, not by anything I do.

I told her I understood and wanted to ask God to save me. We thus knelt side by side along the couch, and she prayed with me as I asked God to forgive me and save me.

Then something wonderful happened: God saved me! The instant I asked for salvation, I felt His presence wash over me. I felt different. Renewed. Alive. I didn't quite understand it at the time, but now I realize that presence I felt was the Holy Spirit. He came to reside in my soul at that moment, and He has never and will never leave.

I was still a sinner, but now I was a sinner saved by grace. My sin nature still lived in me, but now so did God in the person of the Holy Spirit. Now I was equipped to fight my sin nature, and the battle between my fleshly desires and my Godly desires is a battle that will rage within me until the day I die.

As I fight that battle, I have learned to structure my life in such a way that allows me to stand strong in Christ. I do that by making seeking Him, serving Him, and sharing Him my number one priority in life.

I find great comfort, joy, and delight in living for God and obeying His commandments. I am far from perfect and still get derailed from time to time. I have made more mistakes in my life than I care to admit and have disappointed my God in ways that break my heart to recall.

But I serve a gracious, forgiving, loving God. He made me. He saved me. And he gave me gifts to use, dreams to pursue, and people to love along the way.

That's what makes life fun. Seeking God. Serving God. Sharing God. And loving others.

If you haven't experienced the kind of fun, peace, and joy that comes from knowing God, I encourage you to open your Bible and seek Him today.

Don't have a Bible or aren't sure how to seek God? Then contact me by sending an email to dk@authordkdrake.com. I would love to hear from you!

AUTHORDKDRAKE.COM

www.ingramcontent.com/pod-product-compliance
Lightning Source LLC
Chambersburg PA
CBHW022006170626
46808CB00001B/312